PSYCHO: SANITARIUM

PSYCHO:
SANITARIUM

CHET
WILLIAMSON

THOMAS DUNNE BOOKS ☒ ST. MARTIN'S PRESS NEW YORK

THOMAS DUNNE BOOKS.
An imprint of St. Martin's Press.

PSYCHO: SANITARIUM. Copyright © 2016 by Sally A. Francy. All rights reserved. Printed in the United States of America. For information, address St. Martin's Press, 175 Fifth Avenue, New York, N.Y. 10010.

www.thomasdunnebooks.com
www.stmartins.com

Designed by Steven Seighman

The Library of Congress Cataloging-in-Publication Data
is available upon request.

ISBN 978-1-250-06105-8 (hardcover)
ISBN 978-1-4668-6677-5 (e-book)

Our books may be purchased in bulk for promotional, educational, or business use. Please contact your local bookseller or the Macmillan Corporate and Premium Sales Department at 1-800-221-7945, extension 5442, or by e-mail at MacmillanSpecialMarkets@macmillan.com.

First Edition: April 2016

10   9   8   7   6   5   4   3   2   1

To Robert Bloch, Ray Bradbury, and Richard Matheson,
whose stories grabbed my imagination and never let go

We're all not quite as sane as we pretend to be.
—Robert Bloch, *Psycho* (1959)

Hieronimo is mad againe.
—subtitle of Thomas Kyd's *The Spanish Tragedie* (1587)

PROLOGUE

In a small town in the Midwestern part of the country, a boy closed the magazine he was reading and looked for the hundredth time at the garish, brightly colored cover. On it was the face of a man in a half mask. His hair seemed a mass of brown flames leaping from behind the mask's top edge, and his mouth and jaw were fissured with scars. There were several words in the magazine's title, but the most prominent was MONSTERS, the letters appearing to be carved on a tombstone.

It was the boy's favorite magazine. He'd found the fifth issue on the newsstand several months before, and this was now the tenth. He thought he'd like to send away for the back issues when he had some extra money. The magazine was filled with stories about and photographs of the famous monsters of the movies, and the man who wrote most of the stories was like a kid himself, the boy could tell. He just *loved* those movies the way the boy did, at least the few he'd seen.

"Dad," he said to the man sitting in the easy chair and reading a copy of *The Saturday Evening Post* with John Kennedy on the cover. "Could I maybe stay up tonight to watch the movie?"

"What movie?" his father said, his eyes still on the *Post*. "*Horror Theater?*"

"They've got *The Phantom of the Opera* tonight," the boy said. "It's the *silent* one."

"You're a little young to stay up that late," his father said.

"I'm twelve—"

"Eleven."

"In a few months, I was gonna say."

His father put the *Post* in his lap. "Tell you what. The week you turn twelve, you can stay up Friday night to watch the movie. *If* it's okay with your mother, and if you promise to sleep in the next morning."

"*Deal!*" the boy cried, and ran into the kitchen, magazine in hand, to persuade his mother. He hoped that there would be a really scary movie on *Horror Theater* the Friday night after his birthday. Something with a monster like *Dracula* or *The Phantom of the Opera* or *The Wolfman* or *The Mummy*.

Or, if he was lucky, something even worse. Something he'd never known about before, never dreamed of. The scariest creature he could imagine.

A monster that would haunt his dreams.

1

"How's that? . . . How's *that,* you godforsaken *monster?*"

Myron Gunn, the head attendant, shoved the doughy man down onto the bed with all his prodigious strength. The man's head hit the padding on the wall, and his face twitched, but that was the only reaction he made. His stubby-fingered hands fell to his side, his head drooped on his thick neck, and his gaze locked once again on the floor.

"Whatsamatter, *Nor-*man?" Myron said. "Did you bump your little head? Maybe Mama can help, huh? Mama kiss it and make it better? You wanna let Mama out, huh? Yeah, I'd like to meet her—like to put a little fear of God into her." A small cushioned chair sat under a table with rounded corners, and Myron pulled it out and perched on it, leaning toward the man, who sat silently and still.

"I know what you are, you miserable little faker," Myron said softly. "You and your double-identity crap. You're a killer. Satan got into you, boy, not your dead mama. Satan made you what you are. He made you a murdering *monster.*"

Myron leaned still closer, lowering his head to try and see the man's eyes, to actually *see* the monster in them. Maybe, he thought, he could even see the Devil.

That October of 1960, the State Hospital for the Criminally Insane housed a collection of monsters. Murderers and rapists and men guilty of torture and mutilation all lived within its thick stone walls. Every patient there posed a danger to society, and every patient there would probably leave only in a casket, if he wasn't quietly buried in the small cemetery on the hospital grounds.

Although they were called patients, the residents were really all inmates, prisoners. This wasn't the kind of facility to which one committed oneself, or was committed by one's family or loved ones. It hadn't served that purpose since it had been known as the Ollinger Sanitarium, which had closed its doors over forty years earlier. The courts committed these present patients, with the understanding that while they were too sick to execute or place in a regular prison, they were also too sick to ever walk free again.

The courts made such a decision in the case of Norman Bates, who had the deaths of four people on his hands, or at least four of which the state was aware. The swamp near the Bates Motel hadn't been thoroughly dredged after the discovery of the car that had belonged to Mary Crane, Norman's third victim, and rumors spread that there were other cars and other victims sunk deep below. Still, there were no unaccounted-for disappearances in the area, and the four murders Norman had indeed committed were enough to lock him away for the rest of his life.

The first two victims, Norma Bates and Joe Considine, had died twenty years earlier. Norman had poisoned his mother and her lover when he learned that his mother was planning to sell their motel and run away with Considine. Norman didn't like that. He loved his mother. He loved her so much that he couldn't bear her absence, loved her so much that, after the law accepted his staged scenario that Norma and Joe had died together in a suicide pact, he couldn't let her go. So Norman, who counted taxidermy among his hobbies, had disinterred Norma's corpse and preserved it, keeping it in the old house next to the motel, treating his mother as though she were alive, allowing her to dominate him in death as she had in life.

Mother was the one who killed Mary Crane when she came to the motel. She killed her because she knew that Norman was attracted to her, that Norman *wanted* her, and Mother couldn't allow that to happen, couldn't allow that filthy bitch to seduce her boy.

What Mother hadn't counted on, however, was that Mary Crane had stolen money from her employer, so much money that they sent a detective on her trail, a man named Arbogast, who snooped around and learned that Mary Crane had come to the motel. He almost found Mother, but Mother found him first and killed him too.

Then more people came, too many—Mary Crane's sister and the man Mary was going to marry, and Mother tried to kill them, but the man was too strong, and he caught her, and then the police took her away, took them *both* away, her and Norman.

And it was she and Norman now, together, sitting in this little room, listening to this man say terrible things about her and her boy, taunting them, trying to make Norman talk to him. But she wouldn't let him.

She was in charge now, not Norman. Not that bad boy who had read those filthy books and peeked through a hole in the wall at those bitches, and told them, actually told that prying, nosy doctor before she had been able to take over, that *she* had killed those people.

Still, he was her son, and she loved him, and she would do what she had to do to keep him safe, even if he lied about her. And if the only way to keep him from lying was not to let him talk at all, well then, that's what she would do. She would talk if she absolutely had to, but there was no point in talking to this big, stupid man who kept telling her and Norman about God and the Devil. She knew his kind. He talked about God, but he had the Devil inside him. He liked hurting people, and he liked hurting Norman. And she would do nothing to make him hurt Norman more. She would be as quiet as a mouse.

"Cat got your tongue, *Nor*-man?" Myron Gunn turned his head sideways and leaned in closer until his face and that of Norman Bates were only inches away. "Mama don't want Norman to come out and play? Huh?"

Myron bumped his forehead against Norman's nose, and Norman winced. A small whimper escaped him.

"I believe that'll be enough, Mr. Gunn," came a voice from the door. Myron Gunn looked up and saw Dr. Reed standing in the doorway, a clipboard in his hands.

"Oh, hi, Doc," Myron said, slowly getting to his feet. "Just making sure Norman was settled in okay. He doesn't seem to like his weekly physical very much."

"Thank you for accompanying him back," Reed said, "but bringing him to his room is all that's necessary, as you well know."

"Absolutely, Doc," Myron said, still as assured as he had been with Norman. Dr. Reed didn't scare him. He'd been at the hospital too long and was too sure of his place to back down to a relative newcomer like Reed, and a pretty boy to boot. Reed was a good name for this guy, since he was built like one. Myron would just like to see Reed try and manhandle some of the bigger patients the way Myron did. Those sick sons of Satan would have him on the ground before he could blink. No, Reed could complain about Myron's little love taps to the patients as much as he liked, but Myron was here to stay.

Myron stood up and patted Norman Bates gently on the arm, relishing the man's second wince. Then he sauntered past Reed, brushing the thin doctor's shoulder with his own just enough to put him off balance. "Sorry, Doc. Tight quarters," he said as he continued down the hall.

Myron Gunn, Felix Reed thought, was just the kind of man who gave the state hospital, and state hospitals everywhere, the reputation for brutality and callousness that it bore. There were too many people like Gunn in the mental illness profession. If it was Reed's decision, he'd have dismissed the hulking fool immediately.

But it wasn't, so he just sighed and pushed back his annoyance. He didn't want Norman Bates to read any hostility in him. He stepped farther into the cell and looked at the patient sitting on the single bed. "Hello, Norman," he said. "How are you today?"

None of that chirpy "How are we today?"—not for Norman Bates. Norman's whole problem was that he was a we already, a multiple personality. Dr. Goldberg, the hospital superintendent, had sent Dr. Steiner to deal with Norman shortly after he had been captured, and Steiner had determined that three different people inhabited the man.

There was the adult Norman Bates (whom Steiner, not too

cleverly, Reed thought, called Normal), the man who ran the motel and lived in the real world. There was the child Norman, the
little boy who couldn't bear to be parted from his mother. And
finally and most disturbingly, there was *Norma,* the mother herself, whose death the child Norman would not accept. Norma
Bates, the one personality of the three that dominated the host
body in times of crisis. Steiner had called Norman's multiple personalities "an unholy trinity."

Reed hated the term. *Unholy* was as judgmental a word as
could be imagined. In truth, there was no holy and unholy, no
good and evil. There was only sickness and health. Norman Bates
had been very, very sick. And it was the job of this institution,
this *hospital,* to make the sick well again, to make the wounded
whole, like the fabled balm in Gilead "to heal the sin-sick soul," if
Reed had believed in the concept of sin, which he didn't. Still, the
words of the old hymn resonated in light of what he had to do.

Norman was Reed's patient now. He'd had to beg Goldberg to
allow him to treat Norman. Goldberg had discussed it with Steiner,
who was Reed's superior only in terms of seniority, and Steiner
had agreed. Nicholas Steiner was a good man, more temperate
and kindly than Dr. Goldberg. In a way, Steiner seemed relieved
to have Reed on the case, and Reed suspected that he'd seen
something in Norman Bates that he didn't like. Something deep
and dreadful, or else why would he have used the word *unholy*?

As shorthanded as the hospital was, it was unusual for a single
patient, and probably one who would never be released, to receive
individualized psychotherapy on a near daily basis. But Norman
Bates was an unusual case, the most pronounced example of multiple personalities any of the doctors, including Dr. Goldberg,
had ever seen. It was this aspect of the case that had helped Reed
to convince Goldberg to allow him to take on Norman as a pet
project. He had stressed repeatedly to Goldberg that this was not

mere schizophrenia but a far more uncommon case of multiple personalities, and at last Goldberg had grudgingly acquiesced, as long as Reed continued to perform his other duties.

Felix Reed's treatment had barely started, and as yet had brought about no response from the patient. After his initial interviews with Steiner, Norman had gradually grown quieter, responding at first only in monosyllables, then saying nothing at all. It was almost, Steiner had suggested, as if he realized he had said too much already, and Norma, the dominant aspect of the three, had shut down all communication. Now Norman was almost beyond amnesic fugue, approaching catatonia, in which the patient ignores external stimuli until strongly pressured to respond.

Reed sat on the chair. "Norman?" he said, putting a hand on the man's shoulder. Norman said nothing. Gently, Reed took Norman's face in both hands and lifted his head until Norman's eyes, staring undeviatingly straight ahead, looked into his own.

There was intelligence there. Reed could see it. Norman saw Reed's face, he heard his words, Reed was certain. But he didn't respond.

"I'm here, Norman," Reed said softly. "And I'm going to *be* here for you. Whenever you're ready to talk to me, Norman. Whenever you're ready to share your thoughts. Because I know that you *want* to do that. You want to come back. You've been away for a while, and I understand that. You *had* to go away, to get things in order inside yourself. But you can't do that alone. I want to help you. And so does Nurse Marie, and Ben, and Dick. We all do. We want you to come back, Norman. We're not going to hurt you, understand that. We want to help. We want to help you feel better, about yourself, about where you are and what you might have done.

"But we're in no hurry, Norman. We can take our time. As much time as you need."

Reed heard a footstep and the slight clearing of a throat. He turned his head and saw Marie Radcliffe, the ward nurse, standing in the doorway with a tray of food in her hands.

"I can come back," she said quietly.

"No, that's fine. I imagine Norman must be hungry." Slowly Reed let the weight of Norman's head down on the thick stalk of his neck until the man was once more looking at the floor. Reed stood up and saw, in the hall just behind Marie, Ben Blake and Dick O'Brien.

Usually the attendants, all of them male, brought meals and fed patients in Norman's condition, but when Norman hadn't responded well to the attendants, Reed had thought a gentler presence might be more effective. With Goldberg's reluctant approval, Reed had asked Marie to feed Norman, and the results had been good.

Just the same, two attendants were always present when Marie fed him. He seemed docile, but patients could be unpredictable, as they'd found out just a week before when Elvin Bailey, a predictably placid man who had murdered his wife and two young children ten years earlier, erupted and took a student nurse to the floor. The attendants had pulled him off and subdued him, and the girl had only a few bruises as a result. Reed had to give the girl credit, since she was back at work the next day.

"Come on in," he told Marie, picked up his clipboard, and edged past her out the door, stopping next to the attendants to watch Marie's procedure.

"Hello, Norman," Marie said as she set the tray on the table. The dishes were all plastic, as were the utensils and the tray itself. The drinking glass was tin. "We have meat loaf tonight. With mashed potatoes and gravy, and carrots with butter. And chocolate cake for dessert."

As she talked, she put a hand under Norman's arm and lifted

the big man from the bed. It didn't take force, just direction, and Norman obeyed. Reed found himself wishing he could do the same thing with Norman mentally as Marie did physically, but it wasn't so easy.

Marie guided Norman until his bulk was seated on the cushioned chair, the tray in front of him. "Would you like to feed yourself today for a change?" Marie asked, holding out a plastic spoon. There were no forks. Anything sharp wasn't permitted.

Norman didn't respond, didn't look up.

"All right then," Marie said. "I'll be happy to help you. Here we go. Shall we start with meat loaf?"

Reed couldn't help but smile, just a little, at the way Marie wheedled Norman into opening his mouth by delicately tugging on his lower lip, the way mothers often did when their children were reluctant to try something new. "Have a nice dinner, Norman," he said, nodded to Marie and the attendants, and headed toward his office, wishing that tugging on a man's lip could make him speak as easily as it could make him eat.

Norman liked the taste of the meat loaf. He liked the taste of nearly everything when Nurse Marie fed him. The meat loaf wasn't as good as Mother had made, but it wasn't bad. It was softer. It fell apart in his mouth more easily. The mashed potatoes weren't nearly as good as Mother's. Hers were fresh, and had some lumps in them. There weren't any lumps in these, and Norman thought it was because they were made from some kind of powder. The gravy made them passable, though, and the carrots were fresh and not overcooked. They crunched a little when Norman chewed them, just the way he liked carrots.

Nurse Marie was talking to him, but he tried not to listen to her. If he listened too closely or, even worse, if he tried to respond to her, to thank her for feeding him, or to tell her that the meat loaf was good or he liked the cake, Mother would get mad and yell at him. He hated it when she did that. It was too quiet in here, and there wasn't anywhere else he could go to get away from her.

Nurse Marie put down the plastic spoon and picked up the paper napkin. She touched it to Norman's mouth, dabbed either side of it, then wiped it. It felt good when she did that, when he felt her fingers through the thin paper trace across his lips as though he were kissing them, and when they were just under his nose he inhaled, trying to get the smell of her flesh into his nostrils. He did it again now, and there was an audible sniff, which he hoped Nurse Marie hadn't noticed, and then . . .

Bitch.

Norman froze. He stopped chewing and listened, fearing the worst.

"Norman?" he heard Nurse Marie say. "Is anything wrong?"

In spite of himself, he was about to answer, to open his mouth full of carrots and tell her, even though he knew that would be a big mistake. But it was already too late.

Yes, Norman . . . is anything wrong?

Mother. She was angry. She knew that Nurse Marie's wiping of his lips had made him have bad thoughts. She knew. Mother knew everything.

Is anything wrong, Norman? Why don't you tell the bitch? Tell her how much you like having her touch you! Maybe you could dribble in your lap and see if she would wipe it up! You'd like that, wouldn't you, you dirty boy!

Stop it, Mother. Please.

Then you stop thinking that way, Norman. It was those kinds of thoughts that made you kill that other girl, wasn't it? You couldn't have her in your dirty way, so you had to kill her, isn't that right?

No, Mother! You killed her, not me!

You wouldn't have done it if you hadn't wanted to, Norman. Don't you blame me.

"Norman?" he heard Nurse Marie ask again. "Aren't you hungry anymore? Have you had enough to eat?"

Norman didn't answer, but he started to chew again. He chewed the carrots, and the crunching sound was loud inside his head, loud enough to drown out Mother, and he swallowed.

Crunch away, but I know what you're thinking, boy. I always know.

It was only a whisper in his head, but he heard it clearly. He was finished eating now. He thought Nurse Marie had said something about chocolate cake, and he liked chocolate cake, but he didn't want Mother to get mad again.

Mad.

That was it, wasn't it? Mother had gone mad and killed the girl, and Norman had let her. He tried not to think about it, because his thoughts were never his own. So instead he thought about books he had read when he lived at home with Mother. He let the eyes of memory roam over the spines on the bookshelves in his little bedroom, and there were Von Hagen's *Realm of the Incas,* Murray's *The Witch-Cult in Western Europe,* Ouspensky's *A New Model of the Universe.*

They were books that had expanded his horizons beyond the house and the motel, books that made him think there were things beyond his knowing, that magic could exist in the world, and that people who seemed unimportant and powerless could be stronger than anyone could imagine. Curses could be cast, spells woven, the dead brought back to life.

And that last he had done, hadn't he? *Mother . . .*

In brief seconds, Norman had a nightmare vision of an open grave, an open casket illuminated by the glint of a flashlight and the full moon, a face, once loved and dreaded, now sunken in, hollowed out, with pits for eyes, lips curled back, yellow teeth grinning.

He had been mad too, hadn't he? He must have been to have done what he did.

He forced his mind back to the bookshelves, and there were the books on taxidermy, but better not to think of them. No, there on the bottom shelves, beneath Huysmans's *Là-bas* and de Sade's *Justine* . . . those few books without names on the spines, the ones he would page through when Mother was sleeping, those with the pictures that made him feel . . .

But no. Better not look at those either. Mother was never sleeping here.

Norman . . .

Was that her again?

Norman, do you want . . .

Mother? Or . . .

". . . some cake?"

Nurse Marie. Oh, God, yes, Nurse Marie. And he *did* want some cake, in spite of Mother. He opened his mouth, hoping that Mother wouldn't speak aloud out of it.

Marie Radcliffe finished putting the last bite of chocolate cake into Norman's mouth, then efficiently wiped his lips and chin one final time. "There now," she said as she stood and picked up the tray, "that was good, wasn't it?"

"He liked that cake," said Ben Blake from where he was standing against the padded wall, his arms folded. He smiled as he watched Norman, and the smile got wider when he looked at Marie.

"There's extra back in the kitchen," Marie said, "if you boys are hungry later." Giving them both a nod, she left the cell with the tray.

Ben and Dick O'Brien got on either side of Norman Bates and lifted him so that he stood, then positioned him over the bed and let him sit. "There you go, Norman," Ben said. "We'll turn the lights off, and you can go to sleep whenever you like."

They left the cell, making sure the door was locked behind them, then Dick pressed a switch that turned off the lights inside. Ben slid back a several-inch-wide slot in the door so that the light from the hall would provide Norman with the equivalent of a night-light should he need it, and together the two attendants walked down the hall toward their next charge.

"Got ten minutes," Dick said. "Grab a smoke?"

"Sure," Ben replied. "Maybe a coffee too."

There was no one else in the break room. They got two coffees from the machine, lit their cigarettes, sat, and looked through the wide windows. It was already dark outside. The time change had occurred a week earlier, stealing another hour's worth of sunlight, and the moon shone upon the fenced-in stretch of lawn that was used as an exercise yard for the patients. On the other side of the chain-link fence that was topped by concertina wire, pine trees grew so thickly that they smothered the moonlight as soon as the beams touched them.

"Halloween's coming," Ben said. "Your kids excited?"

"Hell, yeah," Dick said with a chuckle and a plume of smoke. "Gettin' their costumes ready for trick-or-treat. I told Marge they just oughta wear the outfits the patients wear here—hard to think of anything scarier than some of these freaks."

"That's the truth," Ben said. "Tough to believe, looking at some of these guys, that they did what they did. Bates, for example."

"Yeah. Seems gentle as a kitten when Marie feeds him. But

when you think about what he did—not just killing those people, but digging up his mother and . . . Jesus."

"Pretty sick," Ben said. He took another puff. "I know *I'd* behave if Marie fed *me*."

"Aha. I *thought* your mind wasn't just on your work when she's around. You should ask her out."

"I did. We have a date next weekend."

"Well, good for you, Benny boy. She's a good-looking woman. And nice too. Sometimes I think she's *too* nice for this place. You never know when these characters are gonna explode." He inhaled deeply and let the smoke come out, watching it as it burst against the window. "I always think they go a little funny this time of year. Maybe it's Halloween, or the weather, I don't know." He paused, then said softly, "Maybe it's the ghosts."

"Sure."

"Seriously. You've heard the stories."

"Ah, Dick, you get those stories around any old building, especially one that's got a history like this."

"Yeah, but there were ghost stories way back when it was the Ollinger Sanitarium," Dick said. "The patients saw ghosts *all* the time."

"Maybe that's why they were in a sanitarium. Look, *our* patients see things, don't they? But did *you* ever see any of the things they do?"

"Okay, you got a point. Still, where there's smoke—"

"There's less than a minute *left* of smoke before we get going." Ben laughed, then sucked down the last half inch of his Lucky and butted it out in the metal ashtray. "Finish that smoke and down that coffee."

Dick emptied the contents of the cardboard cup down his throat and extinguished his Camel. "Yeah, time to feed the *next* nut . . ."

2

Myron Gunn had the Devil in him again. He had wanted so badly to give that evil bastard Norman Bates more than a piddling head bump. Truth be told, what Myron really wanted to do to Norman wasn't very Christian, and it wasn't something that he could tell Jesus in the quietness of his heart or even tell Pastor Oley Crowe of the First Baptist Holiness Church. Neither one of them would appreciate the details.

The problem was that now Myron Gunn had a meanness in him. His daddy, rest his soul, had said he had the *Devil* in him when he got this way, but Myron knew that wasn't true. It was a meanness due to seeing injustice and not being able to do anything about it. If Jesus hadn't been able to drive the moneychangers from the temple, even *he* would've had that kind of meanness in him and would've had to do *something* about it.

It just made Myron so mad sometimes to see these monsters treated like they were staying at the Ritz. Take Norman Bates. That bastard didn't need special treatment, all that sweet talk and chocolate cake—he needed bread and water and daily whippings to drive Satan out of him once and for all. At the very least he needed a smack upside his head like Myron had tried to give him before Reed walked in on them.

And now Myron was left with the meanness inside and no patients to work it out on. Fine, he'd just do what he often did when he had some meanness to get out of him. And he straightened his collar, smoothed back his blond hair streaked with gray, and headed for the nurses' station.

Head Nurse Eleanor Lindstrom was sitting in her small office, going over the daily nurses' reports that chronicled anything out of the ordinary. It was seven thirty, there were blessedly few incidents, all the nighttime meds had been doled out, and she was looking forward to getting home, having vodka with some lime juice, and watching *The Real McCoys, My Three Sons,* and *The Tennessee Ernie Ford Show.* That Tennessee Ernie was a good-looking man, and by that time she'd have enough vodka inside her that she could imagine snuggling on the couch with old Ern' while he sang to her.

She had just slapped the thin report folder shut when there was a knock on her office door. "Shit," she muttered, wondering what-the-hell problem was going to keep her from her drink and shows. "Yes?" she said, and the door opened to reveal Myron Gunn standing there, a thin smile on his face.

"Had a question for you," Myron asked in his deep bass voice that sounded sandpapered by whiskey and cigarettes, though Myron neither drank nor smoked, to Eleanor's knowledge, since she'd never smelled booze or tobacco on his breath.

"Yes?" Eleanor said again, hoping, but trying not to smile, trying to remain *professional.*

"Think there might've been some inappropriate activity in

the laundry," Myron said. There was a little flame in his eyes, and Eleanor felt a flame lick up in her as well. "I'd like to show you, see what you think. If you have a minute."

"Of course," she said, and stood up, following Myron out past the nurses' station into the hall. Two nurses on the evening shift were talking to each other, barely looking up as Myron and Eleanor walked by.

Myron led Eleanor to a stairwell, and they went down two flights to the basement, where the laundry was located. Laundry workers finished at five, so no one was there now. The laundry was all clean, and the carts would be wheeled up to the wards in the morning, where the nurses would change the bedding and give the patients clean uniforms. Now, all those clean, soft sheets were lying on pallets, ready to be loaded into the carts.

Myron stopped walking next to a pallet, turned, and faced Eleanor. He looked angry. "What is it?" she said.

"Reed. He saw me . . . disciplining Norman Bates."

Eleanor felt the anger seep from Myron Gunn like a hot wave. It excited her, because she knew what his anger would lead to if she stoked the fires correctly.

"Skinny little bastard," she said, moving closer to Myron. "What does *he* know? He doesn't realize what you have to deal with every single day, the strength you have to show to tame these monsters." She put her hands on his upper arms, and could feel the corded biceps beneath the fabric of his shirt. "He could *never* do that. All he does is talk, just talk . . ."

"That's right," Myron said. "He couldn't do a thing, one of these guys tried to mess with him. Little sissy boy, he'd just cry and curl up like a ball. You gotta be *mean* to deal with them."

"And strong," Eleanor said, moving her body against his. "God, Myron, you're *so* strong . . ."

And then his hands were cupping her face, forcing her head to his, crushing his mouth on hers, and she let herself be pulled down, down onto the clean white sheets . . .

Several minutes later, he was still lying on top of her, the meanness gone out of him. Her womanly body, firm yet soft where it mattered, supported him the way that his bony wife's never had, and she seemed to have no trouble breathing, even with his weight on her chest. She was as strong as he was, and that was saying something.

He propped himself on his elbows and kissed her, as much from affection as from duty. Eleanor understood him in ways his wife never could, and he appreciated her, the way she allowed him to take out his meanness on her, the way she listened when he talked, told him what he needed to hear, gave him what he wanted when he wanted it.

But now was the dangerous time, when he felt as vulnerable as he ever did, when she would suggest how good it would be if they were together all the time, when she would hint, and hint only, God bless her, that it was easier in these modern times to end a loveless marriage.

What she didn't understand, and what he'd tried to explain to her, was that once a man took a woman in the sight of God, he couldn't put her away from him. The Bible said not to do that, and Myron didn't have any intention of disobeying God's laws. Sure, there was that commandment about adultery, but Myron thought that God surely knew what his marriage was like, how he and Marybelle hadn't had relations in nine years, and that a man *needed* certain things.

Myron had never been with a whore, but when, seven years

earlier, he'd sensed that Eleanor Lindstrom's needs were just as great as his own, he'd made an arrangement with Jesus. If he honored his marriage by staying with Marybelle, then Jesus would look the other way when he found ease with Eleanor. And he would honor that arrangement by working even harder to bring whatever justice he could to these *truly* evil men around whom he worked. Thank God that Eleanor, his secret lover, felt the same way about these satanic creatures that he did.

But now that he *had* found ease and gotten that meanness out, it was time to part, before he said something to Eleanor that he'd regret and that might haunt him later. Just as he pushed himself off of her, there was a loud *clunk* from a dark corner, and Eleanor stiffened under him.

"What was that?" she whispered. "Somebody there?"

"Relax," Myron said, getting to his feet. "Just a heat pipe—no door over there. Nobody's here."

Eleanor sat up and readjusted her clothing. "Sometimes this place . . . at night, y'know?"

"What?" Myron said, zipping up.

"Oh, the stories. As long as you've been here, you must have heard them."

"Sure, I've heard them all, and I don't believe a one. I've been all over this hospital, all hours of the day and night, and never saw or heard a thing that I couldn't explain. No ghosts here."

Eleanor stood, smoothed down her dress, and ran a hand through Myron's hair. "I wouldn't even be afraid of ghosts, as long as you were around."

"Who needs ghosts when you've got a building full of devils," Myron said. Eleanor started to laugh, and Myron looked at her. It was a hard look that told her he wasn't joking, and her laughter stopped.

Three floors above, in the office of Dr. Isaac Goldberg, superintendent of the state hospital, an opera recording was playing on the console, and Dr. Felix Reed was sitting otherwise alone in the room. Reed thought it might be Verdi, but he wasn't sure. He hadn't heard anything he recognized since he entered.

Judy Pearson, Dr. Goldberg's personal secretary, had told Reed to make himself comfortable, and that Dr. Goldberg would be there soon. He had apparently gone to the staff dining room, as he occasionally did, to eat and mingle with the evening shift. Judy, a girl in her early twenties without any personality that Reed could detect, offered him coffee, which he accepted.

As he sipped it and listened to (maybe) Verdi, he checked the clock on Goldberg's desk against his own watch. It was five minutes past eight on each instrument, and Goldberg had asked Reed to be there at eight. The tardiness was typical of Goldberg, and Reed expected it. Still, it would never do to be late himself. Goldberg demanded punctiliousness from all his underlings.

So Reed sat and listened to opera and looked around the office. Goldberg had several symbols of his faith displayed. A brass, seven-branched menorah sat on one of the many bookcases that covered the walls, and a framed Star of David made of intricately inlaid polished stones hung between the windows behind the desk.

Reed stood and browsed the floor-to-ceiling bookcases, as he usually did when he had to wait for Goldberg. Nothing had changed. It was still the same combination of essential texts in the field mixed with classical literature and philosophy, much of it in German.

Reed then surveyed the framed diplomas that are part of the decor of every medical man's office. In Goldberg's case they were few, only a couple advanced degrees from American psychiatric schools in the late 1940s. There was nothing from Goldberg's early years in Vienna before the war. The Nazis hadn't allowed doctors to take their diplomas into the death camps.

The door to the office opened and Goldberg entered, holding a cup of coffee. Even at the end of the day, his shirtfront and suit still seemed crisp and freshly pressed, his full beard neatly trimmed and bristling. "Felix!" His voice was loud and heavy with the accent of Mitteleuropa. "Sit! Please. Do you need more coffee?"

"No thanks, Dr. Goldberg, I'm fine."

Goldberg sat behind his wide desk as Reed perched on the edge of the chair opposite. "Perhaps a cookie?" The older man opened a desk drawer and brought up a package of Oreos. "I love them, eh?"

"Not for me, thank you, but you go ahead."

"I will. A tiny dessert." As Reed watched, Goldberg took an Oreo, separated the two halves, dunked the dry one in his coffee, popped it in his mouth, chewed and swallowed, and then ate the other half with the sweet filling without dunking it first.

"Now," he said, touching a white handkerchief to his lips, "I trust you have closely observed my method of eating an Oreo cookie, and that you have come to some conclusion about my psyche as a result."

Reed stared at Goldberg for a moment, then saw the corners of the man's mouth twitch upward and realized he was joking. Reed laughed. "I do the same thing, only I lick the icing off before I eat the second cookie. If I could somehow keep the icing separate, I'd eat it last."

"Ah! So we are both practitioners of delayed gratification, but in slightly different ways. I compromise by eating both final cookie and icing simultaneously, while you are willing to have the

relative bitterness of the second cookie replace the pure and undi-
luted sweetness of the icing alone." Goldberg raised an eyebrow.
"Perhaps we should collaborate on a paper, *ja*?" Reed chuckled politely, and Goldberg went on. "Well, now. I really asked you here
to chat about your patients. One in particular. Bates."

Reed nodded, fearing what might be coming. "Norman
Bates."

"*Ja*. Have you had any breakthrough, anything at all?"

"He is . . . responsive in that he reacts to physical stimuli
more than he did before." Reed described how the nurse and attendants could move Norman around with just touches. "I also
know that he's hearing me when I speak to him, and when the
nurse does too. There are physical responses."

"But speech?"

"Not . . . yet. I feel certain it will come."

Goldberg sat back in his chair, placed his elbows on the arms,
and steepled his fingers. "I wish I shared your optimism, Felix. As
you know, I suggested quite a different treatment for Bates."

"I know, Doctor. I just feel that I can reach Bates without . . .
those methods."

"They are not dirty words," Goldberg said, frowning. "Electroshock therapy, even the now-discarded insulin shock . . . these
are treatments that have been used for many years to great
effect. I have seen the efficacy of them, in Vienna and here in the
United States. Oh, I know that among the *younger* crowd," he
said, waving his hand dismissively, "these methods are considered
cruel, but temporary discomfort in the service of a long-term
improvement—"

"It's more than discomfort, Doctor. It can be traumatic.
There's the risk of seizure complications, and other things can
happen as well." Reed leaned toward Goldberg. "Once, in the
state facility where I trained, a patient received succinylcholine,

but they forgot to administer the sedative. The patient couldn't breathe or move, but she knew everything that was happening, and she felt *all* the pain. It was devastating."

Goldberg sighed and nodded his head. "*Ja,* I am aware of what happens when sedation is not used in the presence of a paralyzing agent, Doctor. I am not a student. It is like being buried alive. Unpleasant, I grant you. But that has *never* happened here during my tenure." A thin smile creased his face. "Often a shock to the system is what is needed, what is *required,* for certain patients to improve, Felix."

"I understand that, sir. I just don't think it's necessary in the case of Norman Bates. He's essentially a very *gentle* person. I truly think I can reach him, and can do so without traumatic shock."

Goldberg nodded slowly and pursed his lips. After what seemed an eternity, he inhaled sharply enough to startle Reed, and said, "Since it seems that Bates poses no threat of violence in the near-catatonic state in which he now resides, *and* his case is such an intriguing one, I can see no harm in allowing you to continue to treat him as you like. *But* . . . my patience is not infinite. We cannot afford to keep *pets* in our cages. The patients here are criminals who in many cases have committed terrible crimes for which they are not truly responsible. *Illness* is responsible, and it is our task to cure it and banish it from their minds. And if, instead of easing it out, we must *cut* it out, then so be it." The older man leaned over his desk toward Reed. "You may ease and cajole, but if you are not successful, stronger measures must and will be used. Do you understand, Felix?"

"I do. Thank you for allowing me to continue. I promise I won't disappoint you."

"It's not me you'd be disappointing. It's Norman Bates."

———

He slept.

The sound was deafening. It roared inside his head like a hundred waterfalls. The room was cloudy, and he felt as though he was walking through a dream. He tried to look down at himself, to see what he was wearing.

What he was holding.

But he couldn't. He could only look straight ahead. Straight toward the curtain.

On the other side of it, he thought he saw movement. Someone was in there, and when he realized that, he knew that he had to turn around and leave the room. It wasn't right for him to invade someone's privacy in that way, to be in the same room when someone was naked on the other side of the thin curtain. That wasn't good at all. If Mother knew that he was there, she would be very mad.

But when he tried to turn around and leave, he couldn't, not any more than he could stop walking, or look down at himself to see what he was wearing.

Or what he was holding.

He thought he could see something on either side of his head, but dimly, as though he might be wearing a hood or a helmet of some kind that encroached upon his peripheral vision. Through the mist, he could smell something odd, sickly sweet and dry. Was it powder? The kind his mother wore?

The curtain was getting nearer, and now he was sure that whoever was behind it was moving, turning as if in a dance, and through the fabric's translucency he could make out the line of her body.

For it was *a woman, no doubt. The breasts, the swell of the hips, the way the arms lifted as she turned, the way the head bowed. It was true. A naked young woman was behind the curtain, and he was growing excited. He wanted to touch her, caress the soft wet skin, but at the same time he wanted to turn and leave. Leaving was the only thing that could keep him out of trouble.*

He tried to turn, but he couldn't make himself do it. He could only move closer to the curtain, and he felt the pressure, and he knew that he was helpless. He knew that he would do what he had always wanted to do to a woman but never had before. He would take her, grip her in his hands, and make her love him.

His left hand rose in front of his eyes and grasped the edge of the curtain, and as it did he noticed that his arm was clad, not in a shirt, but in a cloth printed with a pattern of flowers, with white lace trim at the cuff. The surprising sight made him want to stop and examine more closely what he was wearing, but he couldn't. He could only push back the curtain.

But in the split second before he did, the girl's scream began, piercing through the roar. And then the curtain no longer separated them, and he clearly saw the wet, naked girl revealed, standing in the watery stream, her face twisted toward him, her startled eyes wide in shock, her screaming mouth open wider than her eyes.

Her nudity, her vulnerability, her fear, all inflamed him, and it was when he reached out his right hand to touch her bare flesh that he finally saw it was not empty.

He saw what he was holding.

He saw his right arm, festooned with flowers and lace, draw the butcher knife across his field of vision until his right wrist touched his left shoulder, then sweep forward in a backhand slash that sliced across the woman's neck, severing flesh, windpipe, and arteries. The blow was so powerful that it shattered the bones of her neck, and her head tipped back and dangled from what little tissue remained intact, while blood both poured and jetted from her.

He looked on in horror as his arm raised the knife again and stabbed the body even as it sank toward white porcelain, piercing white flesh, all growing red. The blood continued to pump, and there was a whooshing sound of displaced air as the lungs battled to keep alive an organism whose heart had already surrendered.

He wanted to stop but could not, and he raised the knife and brought it down over and over and over again, until he was blinded by blood and steam, blinded by the water still pouring from the shower.

Blinded by his own tears.

Oh, Mother, he said deep inside himself, as the arm slowed and finally stopped its up-and-down, up-and-down motion. Oh, Mother, why?

Because you had to see, Mother answered. You kept telling them that I did it, when it was you. You were drunk before, but now you see, don't you? You see through your own eyes what your own hands did.

No . . . no . . .

Well, if you don't believe me, boy, then I'll have to show you again. I'll show you every night until you finally accept it. And all the doctors in all the hospitals in the world won't be able to make my truth a lie.

Mother . . . please . . .

He awoke.

"I think Dr. Reed will reach him somehow. I'll be very surprised if he doesn't."

It was Saturday night, and Marie Radcliffe and Ben Blake were sitting across from each other at a table in the Stockyard Steakhouse, the best and most expensive of the several dining establishments in Fairvale, the county seat, about twenty miles from the state hospital.

Even though they had worked together for months, this was their first actual date, so their conversation was tentative, centering around the hospital and their jobs there. It hadn't taken long to get to Norman Bates.

"I've got to confess, I'm surprised at the kid-gloves treatment he's been getting," Ben said.

"Dr. Reed doesn't want anything to traumatize Norman,"

Marie said. "I've noticed how carefully he has you and Dick shower and shave him." She gave a lopsided smile. "A whole lot different than the way other patients are treated."

"Hey, don't lump me in with Myron Gunn and that bunch. I don't like the way they treat patients any better than Doc Reed does." Ben took a drink from his beer glass.

"I didn't mean to," Marie replied. "You're good with Norman, I know."

"Well, you can't help but feel sorry for the guy. He seems like an oversized kid." Ben's smile faded and he shook his head. "But when you think about what it was he really did . . ."

"What *Mother* did," Marie said.

"Yeah, I know. But Mother's still rattling around in there somewhere. Crazy as a loon and violent as a shark. And even if she was gone for good, after what Norman did, he's never going to get out of the hospital."

"I know. But at least his life can be a little better." Marie sipped from her glass of Chablis and Ben watched her. She was sure easy on the eyes, as his dad always said about his mother, and she was as nice a person as he'd ever run into, in the state hospital or outside of it.

"I never asked you," he said, "how you got into this line of work."

"After I got my nursing degree, I worked in Montrose Hospital for a few years. It was handy, because my home was there in Montrose. My mother died when I was fifteen, of cancer—that was partly why I wanted to be a nurse—and I kept living at home with my daddy. No rent to pay, you know? Well, Daddy started changing the second year I was at the hospital. Forgetting things, at first. Then it got worse. One time he turned on the gas for the stove and then just walked away from it and sat on the porch. I found him there when I got home, the house full of gas. Another time he started filling the tub with water and, again, just walked away. Ruined the floor, the water came down all over his books . . ." She waved a hand.

"Dementia?" Ben asked.

"Oh, yeah. And it just got worse. I knew I either had to stop working and take care of him full-time or . . . have him put somewhere."

"So what did you do?" Ben saw tears glimmering in Marie's eyes, though none had fallen down her cheek.

"I didn't have to decide," she said. "He had some moments— not often, just sometimes—when he was lucid, when he knew what was happening to him, and those were the worst. His face . . . it was like he was horrified to find himself the way he was. He'd ask, 'What's happening to me, honey?' And I couldn't tell him. We went to doctors, and they put him on some medication, but it didn't really help.

"I'd pretty much made up my mind to stay with him at home for a while, but he'd already made the decision. I got home one day and found him dead." She stopped talking.

"Gas?" Ben asked quietly.

Marie shook her head. "I turned off the gas outside every day when I left. He went upstairs and got a . . . a 22 pistol we used to plunk tin cans with. Then he went down to the basement and shot himself in the head."

"My God . . ."

"I think—I *know*—it was during one of his lucid moments. He went to the basement because it . . . it would be easier . . ."

The words choked in her throat, and Ben nodded to tell her he understood. *It would be easier to clean up.*

Her voice sounded thin and pinched. He saw the tears on her cheeks now. "I should've . . . remembered that gun. Hidden it away somewhere."

"It left him a choice," Ben said. "You can't blame yourself for it. He did what he thought was best for himself. And for you."

She nodded and took a long sip of wine. "I've told myself that. And I think it's true." She sniffed then and shook herself, like shaking off a bad dream. "But that, in less than a nutshell, is what made me want to get into the field of mental health. To help people like my daddy. So I took the extra courses and got certified. There were no openings at private institutions, but there *was* one at the state hospital, and I got it."

"But a hospital for the criminally insane—wasn't that a little scary?"

"Oh yeah," Marie said with a little laugh. "It still is. But as frightening as it is, it's also fulfilling. These people are sick in a different way, but they're still sick."

"And mean and violent—some of them anyway. Like Ronald Miller. I wouldn't turn my back on that guy. Mean as a snake."

Marie nodded. "Multiple rape. Horrible man. He's one of the few that I think belongs in a regular prison. He may be sick, but I don't know if it's the kind of sick that can be cured."

"Well, I've overheard some scuttlebutt that he may not be here much longer. The docs are starting to believe that he's faking the whole mentally ill thing, and I think they're right. He manipulates people. Just don't ever get yourself alone with him."

"Believe me, I don't want to find myself alone with *any* of them, not even Norman."

Their steaks came at last, and they both dug in. Talk was minimal as they ate, only an occasional muttered *terrific* or *delicious* passing across the table.

When steaks, baked potatoes, and salads were nothing but a satisfying memory, they both sat back and smiled in appreciation of each other's appetite. "Dessert?" Ben asked.

"Not for a month, at least," Marie replied, and Ben laughed.

"Okay, coffee then," he said, and ordered two when the waiter took away the plates. "So . . . you looking for another job, or are you planning to stay among our particular crazies for a while?"

"I like the work," Marie said. "It's not ideal, but . . ."

"How do you like working under Santa?"

"Santa?" She looked confused.

"Our Head Nurse Lindstrom."

"I've never heard her called Santa before."

"The patients call her that. Because she's knows if you've been sleeping, and she knows if you're awake. You can't pull the wool over Santa's eyes. Many have tried, to their peril."

"Peril is right."

"What, you've seen an example?"

"A lot of them," Marie said. "She's more Torquemada than Florence Nightingale."

"The Spanish Inquisition guy?"

"That's the one. She has these little . . . punishments she doles out, regardless of treatment protocols. For example, you know Warren Russell?"

"The fat klepto, yeah. Steals anything that isn't nailed down."

"He's on behavioral modification and meds, nothing else. So one day last week the patients were lined up for their pills, and Warren gets his from Nurse Lindstrom, swallows them, and grabs a sweater that she's put over the back of a chair and stuffs it under his shirt. He's so big that nobody notices another few inches around his middle, and he goes back to the social hall."

Marie paused as the waiter brought the coffee, then continued.

"Lindstrom finishes giving out the meds and notices her sweater is missing and figures it out fast. She and Myron Gunn find Warren, make him pull up his shirt, and there's her sweater . . . predictably loaded with Warren Russell *sweat*."

"Ouch," Ben said.

"Ouch is right. So I've been helping hand out meds, and I've seen all this play out. I figure they'll take away his social hall privileges or something, but instead of taking him back to his cell, they go the other way, toward the old hydrotherapy room. I follow them, staying far behind, and they go in and close the door. I can't see what's happening, but I can hear just fine. Warren's squealing, and I hear Myron telling him to strip, and Nurse Lindstrom is saying something I can't make out, and laughing."

"Jeez."

"A little later I hear a big splash, and I know they've put Warren in one of the old hydro tubs, and then he stops squealing for a little while, and then I hear him gasping, a big intake of breath, and he starts crying, and then he's quiet again."

Ben nodded. "Myron's holding him underwater."

"That's what I figured too," Marie said. "This happens a few times, until Warren is crying when he's not gasping for air. Then I hear water splashing, and I know they're taking him out of the tub, so I leave before they come out."

"Unbelievable. That's 'behavior modification' with a vengeance. Did you say anything to anyone?"

"You," she said, and laughed. "I don't know what good it would do. Both of them are wedged in there for good, I think. Maybe if they *killed* a patient, but even then I suspect they'd only get a reprimand."

"I can't help but think Dr. Reed would do something about it," Ben said.

"What could he do? It's Dr. Goldberg's decision, and he's a results guy. Myron Gunn and Nurse Lindstrom get the job done. Would Dr. Steiner have more of an impact than Reed? You've been here much longer than I have."

Ben frowned. "I think Steiner has more influence, but he's

pretty much a yes man. Doesn't want to rock the boat. After all, he's next in line when Goldberg retires. The state board decides, but Goldberg's recommendation would carry a lot of weight."

"So Myron and Lindstrom can pretty much dunk patients at will," Marie said.

"That's the extent of it. Unless somebody dunks *them*."

Marie took a sip of coffee and looked at Ben over the rim of her cup. "Sometimes I think that psychiatry hasn't advanced all that much in the past fifty years . . ."

3

August 17, 1909

It is with great delight that I put pen to paper to chronicle that the funds have been fully raised to proceed with my life's dream. I have nothing but the deepest gratitude for those gentlemen of means who have come together into a consortium that will, by this time next year (should all go as planned), permit the doors of the Adolph Ollinger Sanitarium to open to patients near and far.

The praise that I have for these selfless donors is tempered only by what I detect is their own familial self-interest. It seems to be a sad reality that the children of the wealthy are not always blessed with the original diligence, morality, and work habits that have allowed their parents to achieve such success. On the contrary, oftentimes these descendants are corrupted by the easy flow of riches to which they have become all too easily accustomed.

This corruption can lead, unfortunately, to vices such as alcoholism, addiction to certain baleful drugs, venereal diseases that can affect both body and mind, and states of distemper which reveal themselves through such external behavior as sadism, cruelty, and even extreme violence toward those not on the same social level. Idle hands are the Devil's playground all too often, and I predict that in time these same gentlemen who have proven so generous with their donations and investments may call upon me to succor their own offspring from the hands of legal authorities who have found their actions objectionable, if not also criminal. Indeed, I have had some inform me privately that they wish to house their own relatives here, removing them from the cold and uncomfortable clinics in which they now reside. To that purpose, it has been suggested that the furnishings and appurtenances of my sanitarium should be of a standard far higher than those in institutions already in existence. It shall be so.

When the time comes, I will have no hesitation in admitting these unfortunates. I truly believe that nearly all criminal acts, be they destructive to others or to oneself, are the result of illnesses of the mind, and can in time be cured. The children of these wealthy families will not go to prison, but will come here. They will come and be cured.

Though I have not as yet revealed to my erstwhile investors the techniques I hope to utilize to bring about these cures, in my own mind, and in this most private journal, I shall refer to it as Spiritual Repulsion Therapy. It stems from the concept that if malefactors and perpetrators are exposed to the spiritual results of their transgressions, the core morality that lies within the heart and mind of every man and woman will be touched and transformed. It is a psychological exploration of Christ's Golden Rule and the more homespun notion of walking a mile in the other fellow's shoes.

The technique is dependent upon the structural plant of the building as well as the dedication and skills of those who work within it, and now that funding for the construction is completed, it is time to discuss with the builders—and with them alone—the final physical plans that will allow me to bring Spiritual Repulsion Therapy to vibrant and healing life at the Ollinger Sanitarium.

In psychotherapy, the dramatic breakthrough moments are few and far between. In most cases, progress is achieved an inch at a time, with a slow and constant breaking down of a patient's defenses. For every instance of a patient suddenly shouting out, *I remember everything now!* there are a thousand cases like that of Norman Bates, in which steady attrition wears away the psychological guards the patient has erected, like rain wearing away a mountain.

At times the process felt that slow to Felix Reed, but he persisted, spending as much time out of every day as he could with Norman, speaking slowly and softly, reasoning with the patience of Socrates, though there were no questions from Norman for him to answer.

And ever so slowly and softly there were responses, slight and physical. There were twitches of a hand, the tiny jerk of a head, an occasional shift in the gaze, things that told Reed that Norman was performing the mental task of listening as well as the merely physiological response of hearing.

And when these responses occurred, Reed persisted, trying to widen the mental crack that Norman had allowed in his otherwise impregnable psyche. He tried subtly to disabuse Norman of the notion that his late mother had any control over him, to command or to punish.

In this strategy, Reed used Nurse Marie Radcliffe as his chief ally. Every time she fed Norman, she spoke continually to him, but softly and slowly, as slowly as Norman ate. In a woman's voice, the yin to Reed's yang, she reinforced Reed's comforting, nonjudgmental words with her own, nurtured further by food and drink.

And they watched, and they waited.

Norman.

. . . Yes, Mother.

He's lying to you. And so is she.

All right, Mother.

Don't you "All right, Mother" me. They don't care about you, boy. They don't love you, not the way a mother does. Oh, that bitch feeds you and wipes your little mouth, and I'm sure you'd like her to touch more than that. And she talks to you so pretty, just the way she's talking now, but—

Mother?

What, Norman?

Be quiet, please. Nurse Marie is talking to me. I want to listen.

Be . . . quiet?

Yes, Mother. I'm eating. And Nurse Marie is talking.

Norman, I—

Thank you, Mother.

Norman would look at Reed for a moment, then look away again. His head wouldn't turn, but his eyes moved, and when Reed saw Norman's glance fall on him then flick away, he was encouraged, and his next words were more intent, though never invasive. This had to be a treaty between their two countries, not an attack of one upon the other.

Eventually the gaze held longer, lowered thoughtfully as if in contemplation of Reed's words, then returned again. Reed smiled. It seemed to him that he was always smiling, but it was important.

Norman had to feel as though Reed and everyone who worked at the hospital truly cared about him and wanted to see him come back into the world, into reality.

The gaze began to hold on Reed now, and then on Marie. Marie was making further progress with Norman's eating, getting him to feed himself, guiding his hands with a light touch of her own on his wrist, his forearm, placing the single utensil between his fingers that at first seemed to have trouble retaining it, then held it in a death grip, and finally, after a period of weeks, grasped it lightly but firmly. Marie smiled just as much as Reed did, confident in the presence of attendants Ben Blake and Dick O'Brien just behind her.

And then audible responses began to be heard. At first they were no more than whispered exhalations of breath, but soon they acquired resonance, became an *mmm,* an actual humming in the throat of Norman Bates, as though he were considering what Reed and Marie told him, as though it made sense to him and he was speaking inside himself.

You're not here, are you, Mother? You're really not here at all.

I'm here, boy.

No. No, you're not. You were just part of me. I wanted you to be here, and I made you stay. And you made me do terrible things. Things I wouldn't have done on my own.

You did them yourself, Norman. You were a naughty boy. A dirty boy.

No. I don't believe that. You made me sick, Mother. But I want to get better.

You need me, Norman. A boy needs his mother.

I want to get better, *Mother. And I know now there's only one way that can happen.*

A boy needs his mother to take care of him.

I need you to leave, Mother. I need you to go away and leave me alone.

Norman, I'm your Mother . . .

Go away, Mother.

Norman . . .

Go away. I don't need you anymore. I don't want you anymore. Go away.

And then those sounds became words, spoken so softly that Reed couldn't understand them. It took several days for Norman's words to grow loud enough for Reed to comprehend the sibilants and fricatives, consonants and vowels that made up the syllables that built the words.

At first they were simple. *Yes* and *no,* expanding to several words, such as *I know, I see, I understand.* For Marie, the guttural sounds gradually evolved into *please* and *thank you.* Sentences continued to lengthen, facial expressions answered by similar ones, and Norman Bates was smiling. The smiles were infrequent, and never lasted long. They were directed primarily at Marie, occasionally at Reed.

But when Ben and Dick took Norman to get washed and shaved, the communication ceased. Since they were not the ones who had chipped away Norman's facade of uncommunicativeness, Reed surmised, they would not reap the results.

And neither, it seemed, would anyone other than the two people closest to him. But for the time being, that was enough. A typical session between Reed and Norman now consisted of a greeting, and then Reed would sit in the chair, and Norman would lie back comfortably on his bed, a pillow under his head, and the two of them would talk. Many times Norman would close his eyes, trying to re-create the memories that were required to answer Reed's questions. At times it almost seemed as though he were sleeping, and that was good for Reed, since Norman was more open then, answering Reed's questions and responding to him slowly but, Reed felt, honestly.

At such times, Norman's defenses were at their lowest, and Reed guided him gently, almost hypnotically, along the paths of memory down which Reed wanted him to go. As the true Norman revealed more and more of himself, Reed found that his patient was—or *wanted* to be—a moral, gentle man. But at the same time, Reed sensed that there was something even deeper, farther below the surface, a darkness, an anger that was perhaps better left unseen, entombed in Norman's psyche. Buried with Mother.

Norman wasn't expecting visitors that afternoon. After his usual late-morning session with Dr. Reed and the visit from Nurse Marie with his lunch, Norman usually passed a few hours reading in his cell. They called it a *room,* but he knew what it was, with its thickly padded walls—it was like living inside a winter coat, which was fine with Norman. He felt as snug as a bug in a rug, like his mother used to say.

Wait. No thinking about Mother. Dr. Reed was helping him with that, showing him why he had to keep Mother out of his mind. He thought he was doing a pretty good job of it. She spoke to him less and less now. Still, even when she was quiet, there were times when he could hear her in there, scurrying around way down deep, as though lost in darkness and trying to find her way out. If he thought too much about her, he was afraid he would leave some kind of door open down there in the cellar of his soul through which she might be able to escape, and he was *not* going to do that.

He didn't *want* to listen for her, and he certainly didn't want to hear her speak to him again. She had only done so a few times since he told her to go away, and that made him feel strong, as though he were his own person again. They were talking about that, he and Dr. Reed. They were talking about more and more things now.

It felt good to talk, to be honest, and Dr. Reed was so easy to talk to. Norman couldn't remember ever speaking to anyone who relaxed him so much, to whom he felt so ready to share the things he thought, the things he'd experienced, both good and bad. It was as though Norman was *important,* as though Dr. Reed really cared about him and about what he thought, and Norman had shared more than he ever thought he could. As a result, he had figured out some things, important things.

Norman had told Dr. Reed that he knew that Mother was imprisoned with him, and that he would never let Mother get away from him again, because *she* was the one who killed. The way Norman figured it, if she stayed inside him, way down deep, then she'd never be able to kill again, since Norman was locked up. It was for the best, he realized, just as he realized he could probably never be free again. Dr. Reed had told him that he hoped that Mother could be made to go away, to leave Norman forever. And if that happened . . . well, maybe someday years from now, Norman could walk out of the hospital a free man. And alone.

Norman had liked it when Dr. Reed said that. But as much as he liked talking to Dr. Reed, he didn't talk much to anyone else, not even to Nurse Marie. He liked her very much, and he didn't need Mother to tell him that. But he was afraid that if he liked her *too* much, he might say or do things that he'd be sorry for, that would maybe make Nurse Marie not come to see him anymore, and he didn't think he could stand that. So the less he said to her, the better. He was always polite, saying *please* and *thank you*, just the way Mother had taught . . .

No. Don't think of Mother. As the old saying goes, "That way madness lies." And he was living proof of that, wasn't he?

The best way to forget about Mother—about *everything*—was to bury himself in a book. Dr. Reed had started to bring him volumes from the hospital library. Norman had timidly asked if they had any titles similar to those he'd enjoyed when he lived at home, but Dr. Reed felt it best that he spend his time reading fiction of a not too excitable nature. He first brought Norman a love novel by Grace Livingston Hill that Norman quickly found he didn't like. Sinclair Lewis's *Arrowsmith* and *Babbitt* were the next offerings, and they were better, though Norman requested something with a bit more action.

Though Dr. Reed didn't come right out and say it, Norman thought that action equated with *violence,* something Dr. Reed wanted to keep Norman away from, even on the page. Still, the day after Norman finished *Babbitt,* Dr. Reed handed him a copy of Owen Wister's *The Virginian.* There was as much love story to the book as there was Western action, but that was fine with Norman, and his praise for the book brought him several Zane Grey and then Max Brand novels. It seemed that Dr. Reed thought Westerns a relatively safe genre in which Norman might read, with their accent on moral men doling out justice in an earlier time, using violence only when necessary and only for good ends.

Norman was halfway through *Riders of the Purple Sage* when a peremptory knock sounded on the door of his cell, and he heard a voice say, "Norman?" through the open slot. Norman sat up as the door opened, and saw Dr. Reed standing there smiling.

Norman smiled back. "Hello, Dr. Reed," he said.

"Norman, I wonder if you'd be ready to talk to some friends."

Norman felt a sharpness in his throat. "Friends?" he said, hating how his voice had suddenly diminished in volume.

"Yes. Just for a minute."

He tried to say yes, but the word locked in his mouth. Still, he didn't want to disappoint Dr. Reed, so he nodded.

Dr. Reed smiled again, but the smile was crooked, as though he wasn't sure if he could count on Norman. Then he stepped back and allowed two men to enter the small cell.

The first was an older man, well over six feet tall. His hair was steely gray and cut close to his scalp. His gray beard was neatly trimmed as well, and he wore a dark suit and tie and a white shirt. He peered at Norman through a pair of thick, gold-rimmed glasses. The second man, short, balding, and chubby, followed. Norman recognized him. He was the doctor who had talked to Norman after the police got him, the one who had made him tell what Mother had done.

No, what *he* had done. What Mother had *made* him do.

Norman didn't like this doctor. He didn't want to talk to him again.

"You may remember Dr. Steiner, Norman," Dr. Reed was saying. "He talked to you when you first came to us. And this gentleman is Dr. Goldberg. He's the superintendent of the hospital." Dr. Reed stepped aside so Norman could see yet a third man, in a suit, younger than the others, looking in from the corridor. "And this is Dr. Berkowitz," Dr. Reed said. "He's a friend too. Dr. Goldberg would like to ask you a few questions, Norman."

The oldest man continued to stand, towering above Norman. Norman looked up into his face, then down again at the floor. "Norman," Dr. Goldberg said, and in that single word Norman knew that Dr. Goldberg wasn't from this country, at least not from any part of it that Norman knew. "How are you feeling today?"

Only it wasn't *feeling,* it was *feelingk,* like some sort of German accent. Norman thought that Goldberg was a Jewish name, so maybe the accent was Jewish. Wherever he was from, Norman didn't want to talk to him. Norman didn't look up, didn't answer the question.

"Norman?" Dr. Goldberg said again. "I asked how you're feeling."

"It's all right, Norman," Dr. Reed said. "You can talk to Dr. Goldberg. He wants to help you too."

But Norman didn't want to. He didn't know Dr. Goldberg, and he didn't feel comfortable with him. He only felt that way with Dr. Reed. He just wasn't ready to talk to other people. Didn't Dr. Reed understand that?

"Norman?" Dr. Reed said. Norman continued to look down. He realized he still had his book in his hand. It was an escape. He opened it to where he had been reading and looked at the words on the paper. He couldn't concentrate, since all his attention was fixed on the tall man standing over him, but he acted as though he were reading.

"Don't you want to talk to me, Norman?" Dr. Goldberg asked. He didn't sound happy. "Mr. Bates?" he said, but Norman didn't respond to that either. He heard Dr. Goldberg sigh, an exasperated sigh like Mother always gave to show that she was once again disappointed in him, and Norman saw the tall man's legs move to the door, past the other doctors and into the corridor.

Norman didn't look up, *wouldn't* look up as the others left his cell. The last thing he heard was Dr. Reed saying, "All right, Norman, you read. I'll talk to you later." The door closed, and Norman was alone. Almost.

My. That went well.

Be quiet, Mother. I'm reading. Go away.

And, to Norman's surprise, she did.

"Goddamnit, I *knew* he was going to do that."

"Felix—"

"It was idiotic to bring in a whole *panel* like that. It took him forever to get comfortable with *me*."

"I'm sorry, but Goldberg *requested* me to come."

"But it wasn't necessary, Nick! And bringing in the new resident too, well, hell, why didn't we just have a whole goddamned APA national convention in his cell?"

Felix Reed threw himself back in his chair and looked at Nicholas Steiner across the desk of Reed's tiny office. Steiner's cherubic face, usually wreathed in a quiet smile, was frowning. "I agree with you," Steiner said. "It was overkill. It should have been you and Goldberg only. Five people in a room that small, and *I* get claustrophobic. I can only imagine what poor Bates must have felt like."

Reed took in a deep breath and blew it out. He wished he smoked like Steiner did. Maybe it would help relax him. "I'm getting the feeling that Goldberg *wants* me to fail. That he can't wait to get Norman into electroshock therapy."

Steiner took a drag on his Camel before answering. "You may be right," he said. "Dr. Goldberg is very old school, after all. But, Felix . . ." Steiner leaned on the desk. "You *have* to show Goldberg an improvement in socialization skills. Now, I'm betting that he'll give you some more time, but on the other hand I don't think you can just keep Norman as your private pet in his cell. You've got to expose him to . . . other patients, perhaps. There's a reason for social hours, after all."

Reed considered it. "Well, maybe. He's far from ready for the dining hall. He's barely at the point where he's eating a meal by himself, let alone engaging in conversation while he's doing it."

"What about the social hall?" Steiner suggested.

"I just don't know, Nick. In spite of what Norman's done, he's such an innocent in so many ways. I keep thinking some of those other . . . *playmates* would eat him alive."

"Then keep a watch on him. Observe from a distance, but intervene only if completely necessary. See how—and *if*—he interacts with others. He's going to have to eventually. Goldberg won't stand for him to be alone in his room forever."

"Only one example, Dr. Berkowitz, of the many challenges we face here at the state hospital." As he sat behind his intricately carved wooden desk, Dr. Isaac Goldberg took a cigar from a wooden humidor and offered it to the new resident.

Elliot Berkowitz shook his head. "No, thank you, I don't smoke."

"We all have our vices, I suppose," Goldberg said. "Do you mind if I . . . ?"

Berkowitz shook his head again, faster this time. "Of course not." He was surprised that Goldberg would even ask. The superintendent had so much old-world charm about him that Berkowitz could imagine himself back in prewar Vienna, in the office of one of the early psychoanalysts, even of Freud himself, with whom Goldberg, it was rumored, had studied.

The music helped the illusion. As soon as they had entered the office, Goldberg had gone to a console record player at the far end of the room and put a disc on the turntable. A classical overture started playing—Mozart, Berkowitz guessed—and Goldberg had proceeded to his desk and his cigar.

"So tell me," Goldberg said, "a bit about yourself, *ja*? Not your scholastic record, that I know, but your own background, your family. Are they supportive of your career plans?"

Berkowitz smiled. "My mother is. My father is dead."

"Oh?" Goldberg cocked his head to the right as if he wished to hear more.

"He died in Germany. He and my mother were born there. But after the Nuremberg Laws were passed in 1935 . . . you know of them?"

"Oh yes, I know those laws well. The true beginning of anti-Semitism in Deutschland."

"Well, my father saw the writing on the wall. He sent my mother to America. She was pregnant with me, and I was born here. His plan was to stay in Berlin and keep working until he could afford to join us, but after he sent my mother money, there was never enough left for his passage. He never got to the United States."

"What happened?" Goldberg seemed to have forgotten his smoking cigar. His expression was sorrowful.

"*Kristallnacht.* He was arrested and placed in a camp. A friend wrote to my mother about it. She never heard from my father again. We're sure he died there, but we don't know how or when."

Goldberg shook his massive head. "*Ach,* so many. *So* many." He seemed to remember his cigar and took a puff. From his expression, Berkowitz thought it must have tasted bitter. "Your mother . . . did she remarry?"

"No. It was just the two of us."

"I understand," Goldberg said. "I have experienced much the same kind of loss."

Suddenly a burst of song came from the large speaker of the phonograph console, and both their heads turned toward it. Goldberg laughed. "The divine Mozart!" he said. "He never fails to bring levity to any situation! And believe me, my young friend, you will be in great need of levity in this place. Mr. Norman

Bates, whom we have just visited, is one of the more gentle tenants here. We have patients that the old, pre-Freudian world would have burned as demons, but it is our task to banish the demonic from them in whatever ways possible."

"I see," Berkowitz said to fill the silence in which Goldberg puffed meditatively on his cigar. "Well, Thorazine, imipramine, and clonazepam are excellent allies there."

"They are indeed. But there are other, nonmedicinal ways. Tell me, young man, your feelings on the various shock therapies in the treatment of such conditions as schizophrenia?"

Other residents who'd been at the state hospital had tipped off Berkowitz about Goldberg's preferences. "Well," he said, "even though the general move seems to be away from electro-convulsive therapy, it still seems to be beneficial for patients who meet certain criteria."

"It does indeed," Goldberg said. "During the many years I have worked in this field, I have seen no greater results than those derived from these therapies—even insulin shock, now hardly ever used, alas. The word *shock* is an unfortunate one, with its negative connotations, but the *results*—ah, the results are nearly always positive. If you accept that reality, I believe you will fare well here. Now, one other question, if I may be so bold. Regarding your faith."

Uh-oh, Berkowitz thought. What now? He'd noticed the menorah and the Star of David, but he wasn't sure what they meant.

"You are Jewish, are you not?"

Elliot hoped Goldberg wasn't about to offer the official secret Jewish-doctor handshake he'd never learned. He nearly grinned at the thought, but said only, "Yes."

"As am I, as you can see." Goldberg gestured to the Judaic items. "Are you an observant Jew?"

"If you mean do I regularly attend temple, no, I don't. I haven't since I left my mother's house."

"Any particular reason?"

"No. I still consider myself a Jew—I always will—but as far as observing the rituals, I'm afraid not."

Goldberg nodded slowly. "I understand. Don't be apologetic. It's difficult to be a good Jew out here. The nearest temple is seventy-five miles away, and as a result I too have become . . . a *private* Jew, shall we say. Even though our profession teems with our spiritual brethren, we are somewhat alien in this part of our fair state. As they say, it's just you and me, kid."

"Dr. Steiner?"

"No. Protestant. Although Steiner can be a Jewish name, let us not forget General Steiner of the Waffen-SS." Goldberg frowned. "He lives as a free man in Germany today. Sometimes one must question God's justice." Then a smile broke across the clouded face. "But know, Dr. Berkowitz, that although I am your supervisor, I am also *ihr Brüder* in the eyes of God." The smile grew even broader as Goldberg opened his desk drawer. "And now," he said, "would you care for a cookie?"

4

Norman had no idea how much time had passed between the day he was visited by all the doctors and the day Dr. Reed took him to the big room. During those days, the doctor spent much of their time together telling Norman that he wanted him to meet some other people. Norman, Dr. Reed said, kept to himself too much. That was why it was so difficult for him when the other doctors visited him. He wasn't used to seeing anyone but Dr. Reed and Nurse Marie and Ben and Dick, and he *should* see some other people. He didn't have to talk to them if he didn't want to, but it would be good for him to be around them.

Mother didn't seem to have any opinion on the subject, but Norman didn't want to meet other people. He was happy in his cell with his books and Dr. Reed and Nurse Marie. But Dr. Reed *really* wanted him to do it, so finally Norman said he would.

Dr. Reed led him down several corridors so that Norman lost his sense of direction. He had only been out to the showers, and there was a shower area close to his cell. "We're going to the social hall, Norman," Dr. Reed told him. "As I told you, there will be a lot of other patients there. Some may want to talk to you, and some may not. If they do, just be polite. I'll be on the other side of the room watching, so you won't get into any trouble, and no one will hurt you. After all, they have no reason to. You're a nice guy, right? . . . Right, Norman?"

Norman nodded. "I'm a nice guy," he said softly. "I'm a nice guy."

When Dr. Reed led him through the door of the social hall, Norman froze. There was too much going on to process all at once.

The room itself was benign enough. There was a green-and-cream tile floor, and against the opposite wall were several windows, covered by a diamond grid screen. Couches and easy chairs were scattered about the room, and several dozen wooden captain's chairs stood in lines against the walls. Die-cut, thin cardboard pictures of wreaths, snowmen, and Christmas trees hung on the walls, reminders of the season.

An upright piano stood at the end of the room to Norman's right, and a man sat on the bench, pecking at one key in a rhythm so uneven as to seem like Morse code. A few magazines dotted the tables, which in turn dotted the floor. At the end of the room opposite the piano was a large fireplace whose opening had been closed off. The wooden fireplace was ornately carved, darkened by years of smoke, the sole reminder of when the facility had been a sanitarium for the disturbed rich.

Now the room was filled with only the disturbed. There were perhaps two dozen men there, watched by two attendants, one at either end of the room. Some of the men were playing checkers, some were watching a soap opera on the black-and-white television set next to the dead fireplace, some were talking to each other, and several were talking to themselves.

One in particular, a lanky man who seemed more bones than

flesh and who wore a gray baseball cap with his gray prisoner's shirt and slacks, stood in the center of the room and babbled loudly and nonstop about Communists and how they were going to take over the country and one day everyone would wake up to find themselves enslaved by Communism. At least Norman thought that was what he was saying, since the man spoke so quickly, and seemingly without ever taking a breath, that Norman couldn't be sure of all the words.

Another man stood on his head, his feet leaning against the wall, and was chanting what sounded like a prayer. His shirt had fallen down around his chest, and Norman could see dozens of small scars crisscrossing the man's belly like the diamond grid on the screens that helped imprison them all.

An instrumental of "Autumn Leaves" was drifting from a portable record player next to the piano. It sounded like Percy Faith or Andre Kostelanetz or some other easy-listening bandleader, and was background only, there to soothe the loonies, Norman thought. With the music and the smoke that hung in the air, it seemed like a lunatic's version of a nightclub.

It was far too smoky for Norman's taste. He had never smoked, and at least half of the men in the room were holding or puffing on cigarettes. He wondered if all these madmen, possibly including pyromaniacs, were allowed matches, but he was relieved to see one of them go to an attendant for a light. Then he realized that Dr. Reed was speaking to him.

". . . go over there and read a magazine," Dr. Reed said. "Or watch the men playing checkers. There are other board games on that shelf. Maybe someone would want to play."

"I, uh . . ." Norman cleared his throat. "Maybe a magazine."

Walking into the smoky room, Norman felt as though he were leaving behind what little remained of the rational world. These people all around him, with their worn clothing, hacked hair, bad teeth, were all crazy in the eyes of the law. And then he reminded himself that he was crazy too, and, whatever they had done, what *he* had done was probably worse.

He walked quickly toward the closest table with magazines on it, and looked over the offerings. There were copies of *Life, Look, Reader's Digest,* and *National Geographic.* He picked up a *Geographic* and walked between the standing men, careful not to brush against any of them, and sat in one of the captain's chairs. Without looking up again, he opened the issue and started reading at random, trying to concentrate on the words and pictures rather than the fear he felt from being in this room with these people.

He had hardly covered a page when he felt the presence of someone sitting down in the chair next to him, and smelled breath so foul that it might have been air drifting out of a newly opened grave.

Ronald Miller recognized Norman Bates as soon as he walked into the social hall. He'd seen his photograph in the newspaper they allowed the inmates to read every Sunday, and had read as much of the story as they dared to publish. In fact, Ronald had torn out the article when no one was looking, folded it up, and stuck it down his underpants. He hid it in one of the books in his cell and read it late at night, by the dim light that seeped in through the slot in his door.

They weren't allowed to watch the news on television, so Ronald never knew if more details had come out about the story. It didn't really matter. He had made up his own details. He knew that Norman Bates had killed a young woman named Mary Crane and a detective named Arbogast, but he didn't give a damn about Arbogast. He thought about Mary Crane a lot. Ronald had never killed anyone, but he'd wanted to. He admitted to himself that he just didn't have the guts, because he didn't want to die.

Prison was okay, though. He'd been in prison before, and the state hospital was a whole lot better. He didn't think he was crazy, though he pretended to be. The insanity plea was always a winner if you could sell it. The danger was that you could stay in stir indefinitely, but when his lawyer told him about the lengthy sentence he could serve as the result of seven violent rapes in as many months, the wacky ward started looking pretty good.

So he lost no time in setting up a profile as a crazy bastard who'd rape anything that moved or had legs he could get between, including guards and fellow cellmates. Finally they'd put him in solitary and shoved his food through the door, and he'd talked to a lot of nice old doctors who tried to be professional but were scared as hell that he'd jump them next. He played it sweet, though, and got the gig he wanted. It wasn't paradise, but as long as he played it cool, so did the guards, and Ronald wasn't above a little ass kissing and wheedling to make things better for himself.

Problem was, you couldn't talk to most of the nutcases in here. They'd start out like anybody else, but eventually they'd begin talking screwy. But he had his memories to keep him company and, when that wasn't enough, his imagination.

And his imagination dwelt on what Norman Bates had done—what Ronald had always *wanted* to do. He liked hurting women, and he especially liked the feeling of having power over them. That was why he got so mean when he raped them. But to *kill* . . . well, that was something else altogether. That was the ultimate power, wasn't it? And to kill them while you were taking them . . . that meant taking *everything,* and Ronald couldn't imagine a better feeling than that. He really wanted to know what it was like.

In his waking dreams, he'd seen Norman Bates doing exactly that, plunging in the knife while doing what Ronald did, in all the different ways and permutations. Ronald could hardly think about it without getting himself all excited.

And now here he was, in the same room, in the chair right next to Norman Bates, who had done things Ronald had only dreamed of. He *had* to talk to him. He had to find out his secrets, hear the details, every last bloody, juicy one . . .

"How ya doin'?"

Norman didn't look up. The man was right next to him, his elbow touching Norman's on the arms of the chairs. Norman moved his arm over onto his lap. He could see the man's hand, the fingers long and skeletal, with yellow, cracked, untrimmed nails like talons.

"Whatcha readin', the *Geographic*? Not as good since they don't run them titty pitchers anymore, y'know? Man, growin' up I used to go to the library . . ." He pronounced it *liberry,* an error Norman had always hated. "I'd tear out the titty pitchers, take 'em home, look at 'em at my *leisure,* know what I mean? I didn't like them African coloreds so much, but some of them South Sea babes, and Indian ones—not U.S. Indians, but them Indians from India and around there, they were really all right, near as good as white girls."

Norman looked over toward where he'd left Dr. Reed. He was still there, but far out of earshot. He looked at Dr. Reed pleadingly, but the doctor looked back at him with no expression on his face, as though he was just *observing* Norman.

"Your name's Norman, right? So how you makin' out, Norman? My name's Ronald. Ronald Miller. Nice to make your acquaintance. Y'know, I was readin' about you in the papers. Got a little reputation goin', don't ya? Well, hell, so do I, though you may not know it." The man gave a little laugh. "My vics don't tend to talk much about it, but everybody knows yours. Maybe I'd got more publicity if I hadn't left 'em alive, y'know? But that's me, too damn tenderhearted for my own good. Now, *you* had the right idea. Shut 'em up, then they can't blab about you, right? 'Course, you got caught anyways, and we both ended up here, right? . . . Um . . . you followin' me, Norman?"

Finally Ronald Miller was quiet. It seemed he'd been talking for hours, and the sudden silence surprised Norman so much that he turned and actually looked at the man. What he saw wasn't pretty.

Piercing blue eyes stared at Norman out of a gaunt, scarred face. They weren't the kind of scars that come from cuts, however. These were red and puckered, and ran from beside Ronald Miller's right eye across his cheek, around his mouth, and down the center of his neck. His right eye squinted, and the right side of his mouth was pulled slightly askew. It looked as though someone had once splashed his face with liquid fire. Although the scarring still looked painful, Norman somehow knew it had been that way for a long time.

"Hey, Norm—you hearin' me?"

Norman looked back down at the magazine in his lap. What was this man with the terrible face saying to him? That he had forced women to . . . ? Norman suddenly felt guilty about reading this particular magazine, and slapped the pages shut.

"Whatsa matter? Don't you wanna talk to me? 'Cause I wanna talk to *you*."

Ronald Miller was talking more quietly now, but also more intensely.

"I wanna hear about what you done. When you done that girl. How'd you do it? I read you stabbed her, right? Were you doin' it while you stabbed her?"

Norman's head started to swim. He felt as though he might topple out of his chair. The man was whispering now, his scarred, twisted mouth against Norman's ear.

"What noises did she make, huh? Was she cryin'? Could you see the tears?"

Norman felt hot, feverish. The man's hissed words snapped against his eardrums. His stomach started to roil.

And then Ronald Miller asked a question so vile, so horrible, that Norman's mind rejected it. No one could ask such a thing. No one could think of finding that kind of pleasure in such pain and agony. But though his mind refused to process the question, his body reacted. Norman lurched to the floor on his hands and knees as everything in his stomach revolted against the words that had assailed him, and splattered onto the tile floor.

"Whoa, Nellie!" Ronald Miller said, leaping to his feet and backing up, both from the vomit that continued to spew from Norman's mouth and from the two attendants who were quickly advancing on them.

"What the hell," said one of the men. "What'd you do to him, Miller?"

"Nuthin', *nuthin'!*" Ronald said. "We was just talkin'—about the magazine and stuff, and he just . . . well, you seen it."

Then Dr. Reed was there, and he knelt next to Norman, who had stopped puking, and patted his back. "It's okay, Norman," he said. "We'll go back to your room now. Relax." And then the doc gave Ronald a look that told him he didn't like him. "What were you *really* talking to him about, Ronald?" the doc asked.

Ronald looked at the issue of *National Geographic* on the floor, with Bates's barf sprayed over most of its cover. On the untouched part, Ronald could see the names of a few articles. "Mexico," he said. "We was talkin' about the mummies of Mexico, like it says in there. I read that article too. 'Bout, uh, *mummies* . . . in *Mexico*."

The doc's face got funny, like he'd just thought of something. Then he helped Bates to his feet while one of the janitors showed up with a mop and bucket to clean up the puke. The attendants told Ronald to back off, while Doc Reed led Norman, his head still down, out of the room. The doc glanced back once over his shoulder, and looked at Ronald like he thought he was something dangerous.

When the doc turned away, Ronald grinned. Guess he was, at that. He certainly hit on something that bugged the hell out of little old Norman Bates. Maybe Bates didn't *like* sharing his memories. Or maybe he'd just gotten sick on the shitty food in here. Whatever the reason for the throw-up, Ronald wanted to talk to—or *at*—Norman again. If the little freak didn't want to share his happy memories, at least it'd be fun to tease him, find out what buttons to push to make him puke again.

In here, you got your pleasures where you could.

"Norman? I have your dinner. Are you feeling better?"

Marie Radcliffe, carrying a tray, came through the door that Ben Blake was holding open for her. She was sorry to see Norman sitting on his bed, no book in his shaking hands. He was gazing down at his lap, not looking up and smiling, like he usually did when Marie entered.

Dr. Reed had told Marie about the encounter with Ronald Miller in the social hall, and the sudden, violent burst of vomiting. The doctor had seemed both brokenhearted and angry, and

Marie felt the same way. Norman had come so far, and it was terrible to think of this incident causing any regression.

She was surprised to realize how concerned she was for Norman. Whenever she recalled what he had actually done, she had to suppress a shudder. But to equate those deeds with the substantial yet frail man who now sat trembling before her was nearly impossible. He seemed like a child who needed . . .

His mother? God, no, Marie thought. Anything but that.

What he needed was a friend. Dr. Reed was both friend and confidante, but Reed needed something from Norman—he needed him to *change,* to become less withdrawn and more of a social animal. It was a matter of professional pride to him. But Marie, though she didn't want to see Norman fall under the less-than-tender mercies of Dr. Goldberg and his treatments, needed nothing from him. Maybe she could just be a friend.

"Roast chicken and rice, Norman," she said. "Maybe you could get down a few bites? I know your stomach's not feeling well, but . . ."

She sat down on the chair and looked at him. "You had a bad day, didn't you?" He didn't look up, but he nodded, and his trembling subsided a bit. "Norman, when I was in school, I was shy and a lot of times I was scared. I had trouble making friends, and sometimes kids laughed at me. My dad gave me a gift that helped a little."

Marie reached into one of the pockets of her nurse's uniform and took something out. She held it out to Norman. "See?"

Norman was afraid to look at first, but, when he did, he saw in Nurse Marie's palm a small polished piece of what looked like stone. It was nearly round, and only the size and shape of the tip of his finger. It was gray in color, but tinged with purple, and veined with parallel threads of brown.

"It's petrified wood," Nurse Marie said. "You know what that is?" Norman nodded, unable to take his eyes off the little piece of wood. "See the lines? They're tree rings. It's oak from Louisiana," she said. "My dad said that it was something soft that got tough and strong, and that I could look at it and remind myself how tough and strong *I* could be."

She took his hand and put the piece of petrified wood into his palm, then closed his fingers around it. "I'm going to give this to you, Norman. You can keep it. When you feel scared, just reach into your pocket and hold it, and think about how strong you can be." Then he looked up at her, and she smiled. "You don't need your mother, Norman. Dr. Reed showed you that. You just need yourself, okay?"

Norman didn't speak, but he smiled. It seemed silly, but the feel of the small smooth stone in his hand *did* make him feel better, braver, and he nodded his thanks to Nurse Marie. Then he put the stone into his pants pocket.

"Be sure you put it toward the front of your pocket," Nurse Marie said. "Those pockets are pretty shallow—you wouldn't want it to slip out."

Norman nodded, did what she said, and patted the small stone under the cloth. Then he picked up the single utensil next to the food. He did feel a little hungry after all.

Time passed. Norman wasn't sure how much, since one day seemed very much like another. He had a session with Dr. Reed nearly every day in the afternoon. Norman didn't always remember what they talked about, because he was so relaxed most of the time. Mostly about his childhood, growing up, his school years, his relationship with Mother. Sometimes it was nice to remember those things, sometimes it wasn't so nice.

He hadn't gone back to the social hall, but every few days Dr. Reed would take him for a walk through the hospital, and they would also go into what they called the exercise yard, though Norman didn't see anyone ever exercising in it. It was a large outdoor area behind the building, bordered by the two wings of wards. Dr. Reed gave Norman a warm jacket and some gloves, because it was winter now, and it was colder outside.

Norman liked breathing in the cold air, and seeing the puffs his breath made. There were other patients in the yard, but they ignored Norman, which was fine with him. And he never saw Ronald Miller out there, which was good. Norman would walk around and look out into the woods through the chain-link fence with the barbwire on top of it, twelve feet up. It felt good to stretch his legs and see the sky, the clouds, the sun. Dr. Reed stayed nearby all the time Norman was in the yard, and Norman was glad for that.

When he and Dr. Reed walked through the building, Ben the attendant always came along, lagging a few steps behind. Ben seemed nice. They would walk down different hallways. Sometimes they stopped at the nurses' station and talked to some of them, or Dr. Reed would. They seemed okay, though Norman could tell they were a little uncomfortable when he was around. They still smiled, all except for Nurse Lindstrom. She didn't smile at all. She just looked at him, then looked away like she'd seen a disgusting bug. That was all right with Norman. He didn't want to talk to her anyway.

He didn't talk to any of them. Nurse Marie was the only one he'd talk to, and then just enough to get by. He didn't want to get into *any* trouble.

That was how his days went, along with the one or two books he read daily. So it was a real surprise when Dr. Reed came to visit him again one day, only this time long after dinner. There was a soft knock on the door, and he heard Dr. Reed say his name through the slot. Then the door unlocked and opened.

"Hello, Dr. Reed," Norman said, getting to his feet. Dr. Reed was alone. He came into the room and closed the door behind him.

"Good evening, Norman," he said. He hesitated, then motioned to Norman to sit back down. Norman sat on the bed and put a paper bookmark in the Louis L'Amour novel he'd been reading. Dr. Reed sat in the chair. He leaned toward Norman, hands between his legs.

"Norman, I . . . I have some news for you." Norman realized he must have looked worried, because Dr. Reed immediately raised his hands. "Now, it's not *bad* news or anything, it's just . . . well, rather *startling*. Unexpected. Very surprising. To you and me both."

Dr. Reed sat back and assumed the more relaxed position he took during their sessions. "Norman," he said softly, "we never touched on this in our talks, but did your mother ever mention *anything* about the existence of . . . a sibling you might have had? In particular, a brother."

Norman gave a little laugh. He couldn't help himself. He'd never heard of anything so ridiculous. "Dr. Reed, I . . ." He chuckled again. "I'm an only child. I don't have any brother."

"You, uh, you may have to rethink that . . . aspect of yourself, Norman. You see, a letter, with some copies of documents attached, came to the hospital. It was marked 'Regarding Norman Bates,' so it was given to me. It was from a gentleman who claims to be your brother. Your twin, actually. The documents were the evidence, and I have to say it's pretty compelling."

"But . . . Mother never mentioned *anything* like that . . ."

"Well, under the circumstances, that's understandable. May I tell you what the letter and the documents claim?"

Norman nodded. His hands were trembling.

"This man who claims to be your twin—nonidentical, I might add—says that when he saw your photo in one of the news stories in the paper he was struck by the similarity in appearance to himself."

"But if he . . . *we* are nonidentical, how . . . ?"

"Family resemblance, I suppose, and I have to say that he's right. You're very similar."

"Then you've . . . seen him?"

Dr. Reed held up his hands again. "Let's not get ahead of ourselves. I'll just say there *is* a resemblance. A very close one. *But* . . . this man decided to look into the possibility that you were related. He'd always been curious about his birth. He had been adopted, and there was nothing on record as to the circumstances. He'd been . . . a foundling, you might say, left anonymously at a charity home far from Fairvale. Actually left for dead, since he had a gross physical birth defect. A misshapen skull that suggested brain damage."

"Is he . . . ?" Norman tapped the side of his head.

"No. Not at all. He survived, he was—*is*—intelligent. Enough so as to be curious about his heritage. Curious enough to hire an investigator to go to Fairvale." Dr. Reed paused. "Norman, do you know where you were born?"

Norman nodded. "The house. I was born at home. Dr. Mayhew, our family doctor, delivered me. *Just* me."

Dr. Reed shook his head. "That's not what the investigator found. Dr. Mayhew died some years back, but his daughter still had his records. And at the entries on the date of your birth, Norman, was one that said that twin sons were born to Mr. and

Mrs. J. Bates, and that the firstborn, whose skull was partially crushed in the area of the left parietal bone, was taken to the Wilkins Charity Home for Babies and Children, to be cared for 'until its imminent demise,' I believe was the wording. Dr. Mayhew didn't expect it to survive the birth trauma."

"But . . . it did."

"Yes. And recovered. The investigator tried to find this Wilkins Home to match it up with their records, but there was an S&H Green Stamp redemption center at the old address. The home shut down decades ago, no records surviving. It's about a hundred miles north of Fairvale."

"Was this Wilkins place where the man was adopted from?" Norman asked.

"His parents would never tell him," Dr. Reed said. "They didn't want him to obsess over his background, so he says. He had no idea he might be a twin until seeing your picture. Then the thought occurred to him, and the rest . . ." Dr. Reed shrugged. "It looks as though it's a distinct possibility, Norman. I've seen the documents, and they're legitimate. I do believe this man is your brother."

Norman didn't know what to say. So he shook his head and tried to make a little joke. "Too bad for him. To finally track down your brother and find out he's a . . ." Norman gestured to his surroundings.

"He says it doesn't matter, Norman." Dr. Reed's face was serious and, Norman thought, a bit sad. "He says he wants to meet you."

Norman opened his mouth, but found he couldn't say anything.

"I've been considering it," Dr. Reed said. "You've told me that you felt very lonely during your childhood. Very isolated. I think if you'd had a brother, someone with whom you could have shared your childhood, well, things might have turned out differently for you." He smiled. "And when it comes to family, they say it's never too late. I've met your brother, and he seems to be a good man. He has a family, his own business, lives not all that far from here. He could visit you frequently, if that would be acceptable to you. And to him, of course."

Norman couldn't say anything. It was all too much.

"Would you like to meet him?" Dr. Reed asked. "Afterwards, you wouldn't have to see him again if you didn't want to. And you don't have to see him *now,* if you'd rather not. It's your decision, Norman."

"What . . . what do *you* think I should do?"

Dr. Reed took a deep breath. "He seems very sincere about meeting you. And I don't think it would be harmful for you. On the contrary, I think it would aid in your socialization skills, and that's something that we've been concentrating on. You also may find it very meaningful to be in contact with the person with whom you shared so much . . . yet so little. But as I said, it's your choice."

Norman sat for a moment, staring at the floor, then said, "A brother . . ."

"Yes, Norman. *Your* brother. He's here now."

"*Now?*" Norman's head shot up. He felt dizzy.

"Yes. It's after visiting hours, but he works during the day—on weekends as well. He and his wife have a diner, so he's kept pretty busy. I kind of bent the rules to accommodate him."

"What's his name?"

"Robert. Robert Newman. His foster family's name, of course." Dr. Reed cocked his head and looked at Norman. "Well?"

Norman felt his head nod, and he heard himself say, "All right."

Dr. Reed nodded back. "Good, Norman. I'll bring him in."

Dr. Reed stood up and walked out the door, closing it behind him so that it locked. Norman waited in the silence.

Only it wasn't completely silent. He sensed her before he heard her, like something scratching within his brain.

He's a liar.

Mother?

He's lying, boy! You had no brother! This man wants something from you!

There was so much rage in her that it surprised Norman. He hadn't felt such anger from her since . . .

Well, he didn't want to think about that time. No. Instead he thought about what she had done to his brother. What she would have done to *him* if he'd been born less than perfect.

I think you're the one who's lying, Mother. He tried to make his anger match hers, but cold rather than hot. *I think you gave him up. You left him for dead.*

There was no reply.

Are you ashamed, Mother? Are you?

The door opened, cutting off any reply Mother might have made, and Dr. Reed came in.

"Norman, this is Robert."

Dr. Reed stepped aside. Norman saw a man come through the door. Then Dr. Reed left the room and closed the door again. Norman was alone with his brother.

5

Robert Newman stood there smiling. It was a soft smile, a Norman kind of smile. In it, Norman recognized the lines of his own face.

He realized that Robert was what he might have become. What he had *wanted* to become. Robert Newman was Norman's height, but he was slim, his shoulders broad, his hair nicely cut, his face a shade of tan that Norman had always admired in movie stars. He wore a dark suit that hung perfectly on his trim frame. His shirt was blindingly white, accented by a silk tie with diagonal stripes of blue and silver. The silk shimmered as though it were alive.

"Hello, Norman," Robert said.

It was as though he'd spoken the words himself. The timbre and pitch of Robert's voice was so close to his own it was like hearing an echo. He looked into the man's eyes, the same hazel color as his own. There were crinkles at the corners, *smile lines,* he thought, and as the words came to him, he couldn't help but smile himself.

"Hello . . . Robert," he said, the name feeling strange in his mouth.

"I can't believe I'm actually here," Robert said, and Norman heard joy in the words, a joy that he hadn't heard from another person in a long, long time. "That I finally found out, not only who I was, but that I have a brother." He chuckled. "A *kid* brother. I was the firstborn, according to the doctor. I, uh, I like to think I cleared the way for you, you know?"

Norman laughed a little, just like Robert did. Then he cleared his throat. "I thought that it wasn't possible," he said in a voice that sounded small to him. "When Dr. Reed told me about you. It just seems . . ."

"I know. After all these years." Robert looked at the chair. "May I sit down?"

"Sure, sure. Please."

Robert sat, and now their faces were on the same level. The resemblance was uncanny, Norman thought. Though not identical, it was no wonder Robert had recognized in Norman's picture more than the dark monster the press must have made him out to be.

"I guess I ought to show you . . ." He patted the left side of his head. "More proof. Can you see it?" Norman looked. There seemed to be a slight indentation near the back of Robert's skull, as though the two sides didn't quite match. "You can touch it," Robert said.

Norman put his hand on Robert's head and felt a depression there, a small crater hidden by hair.

"That's the culprit," Robert said. "It doesn't look like much now, but on a *baby's* head . . . well, that's what made the doctor say I wouldn't make it." His smile faded. "And what made my mother and father give me up."

"I'm . . . sorry," Norman said.

Robert shrugged. "Not your fault. Not your fault at all . . . brother." He chuckled. "Gosh. It feels so strange to say that. In my adopted family, I was an only child."

Norman smiled back. "Me too. My mother never . . . I was the only one."

It was amazing, Norman thought, how comfortable he felt with Robert. After Dr. Reed had told him about his brother, he'd been terrified of seeing him. But now, sitting and talking with him just seemed like the most natural thing in the world, even more relaxing than talking with Dr. Reed when he was nearly asleep.

They each had over forty years' worth of life to catch up on, which meant a total of over eighty years to share. Norman insisted that Robert go first, and he told Norman about his boyhood in Michigan, where his parents had taken him after his adoption; about the surgeries that he'd had through his childhood to ease the pressure on his brain; about the sports he played in spite of his condition and how worried his mother had been that he might get hurt; about his graduation from high school with honors and his marriage to Mindy, his sweetheart, a year later; about his working as a new-car salesman; about his stint in the army during the war, where he saw action in Italy and returned unharmed to the arms of his wife; about his growing tired of sales, moving out of Michigan, and buying a diner fifty miles north of the state hospital; about their two kids, John and Susie, both in junior high; and finally about seeing Norman's picture and hiring the investigator.

"I have to tell you," Robert concluded, his face sobering, "that once we—Mindy and me—learned the truth, I didn't quite know what to think. I mean, you can probably understand that as much as I wanted to see my brother, I was shocked by what . . . had happened. I wanted to talk to the doctor in charge of your case, and Dr. Reed explained to me certain things, about why you were here instead of in a regular prison. He seemed pretty insistent that what had happened, well, that it wasn't really your fault. That you were . . . ill. And I thought, if that's what his doctor thinks, then that's probably what happened. So I decided that I should meet you."

Norman felt gratitude, sorrow, and joy all intermingled. "I'm glad you did," he said, his voice choked.

"Now tell me," Robert said, "about yourself. As much or as little as you want." His grin was comforting. "After all, you're among family."

So Norman did. He told Robert succinctly but fully about his life. He felt no hesitation in relating everything up until the death of his mother and her lover, but when he reached that point he stopped.

"This," he said after a moment, "is where things start to get really bad. I know I did some of these things, they *tell* me I did and it's true, but I don't have . . . much memory of them. Mother did some of them. But what *I* did . . . what I did . . ." Norman felt his eyes fill with tears. "Oh, Robert," he said, and his voice was thick with pain and grief, "I killed . . . I killed *our mother* . . ."

He broke down then and wept, for the first time in so long, and he felt arms around him, holding him close. He felt Robert's arms clutching him to his strong chest, felt Robert's hand on the back of his head, patting him, soothing him as he cried.

"It's all right . . . it's all right, little brother. I understand. It's all right. I forgive you . . .

"I love you."

After Norman's tears finally ceased, he was relieved that Robert didn't press him to tell any more about the deeds that had put him in the hospital. In fact, Robert mercifully changed the subject, saying how they actually had a lot in common, since they had both provided public services, one food, the other lodging.

Robert told Norman about some customers he had served at his diner and the funny things they said and did, and Norman thought back to when the Bates Motel was thriving, before the new highway was put in. He remembered and told Robert about some crazy and overly demanding customers he'd had to deal with, and some of the strange things they'd left behind. Robert laughed.

"Sometimes it just gets so insane," Robert said. He seemed to realize he'd made a poor word choice, and corrected it. "So *frustrating*," he said. "Problem with me is that I'm pretty easy-going. I let folks get away with too much sometimes. Mindy tells me I ought to sit hard on some of these people, especially the smart-aleck kids who come in at night after they've had a few beers. And she's right. Hell, sometimes I feel as if I'd like to . . ." He stopped and snorted as though in derision at himself. "It kinda scares me. I wouldn't want to get, you know, carried away. Really hurt someone."

There was a soft rap on the door, and it clicked as it opened. Dr. Reed cautiously put his head in. Norman wondered if he'd been listening through the door slot. With all his attention on Robert, he hadn't noticed if the slot had been open or closed.

"Excuse me," Dr. Reed said, "but I think you two should end your visit at this point. I'll wait out here while you say goodbye." The head withdrew.

"I'd like to visit you again, Norman," Robert said as he got to his feet.

"I wish you would," Norman said, standing as well. "I'd . . . like you to."

"We'll do it, then." Robert opened his arms and Norman

stepped into them. They hugged briefly, and Robert turned and left the room. The door closed, and Norman was alone.

The slot in the door was also closed, but Norman didn't know for how long. He stood, looking at the door, thinking about who was on the other side. Robert. His brother.

Suddenly his head swam, and he sat down heavily on the bed. His brother. And his *friend*. To have nothing, and then to discover that you had *someone*, someone who was blood, closer than a friend, someone who said that he *loved* you.

Norman didn't know how he could feel any luckier.

The next day Dr. Reed discussed Robert's visit with Norman. He said that Robert had indicated that he'd like to see Norman again—regularly, if possible. Dr. Reed told Norman that if it was all right with Norman, it was all right with him. He said that such visits would be therapeutic for Norman. Norman quickly agreed.

So it was arranged that Robert would come to see Norman on whatever evenings he could. Since the visits were outside regular hours, Dr. Reed suggested that it might be best if Norman said nothing of them to other staff members.

"I've told the evening attendants that Robert is a friend and colleague of mine," Dr. Reed said, "and that's enough to get him in, as long as he's in my company. I'd rather that Dr. Goldberg . . . you remember him?" Norman did, all too well. "I'd rather he not know about Robert, not just yet. I think your brother is going to have a very positive influence on you, Norman. And I don't want anything about our . . . situation to change until that occurs, you understand?"

"Sure," Norman said. "Mum's the word."

Dr. Reed chuckled, and Norman couldn't blame him. *Mum* was *generally* the word where Norman was concerned.

His spirits were much higher now, and when, three days later, Dr. Reed asked him if he'd like to try visiting the social hall again, Norman swallowed hard and thought about it. He knew that Dr. Reed would be proud of him if he did (and managed to keep down his food), but he also thought that it would give him something to tell Robert about on his visit that evening, and maybe Robert would be proud of him too.

That afternoon, when Dr. Reed walked with him to the social hall, he said, "Norman, I'm very sorry, but I can't stay with you today. I have a staff meeting I have to attend."

Norman felt a chill pass through him, and he looked at Dr. Reed with panicked eyes.

"Now, Norman, I think you'll be fine. If someone begins a discussion you don't want to have, just walk away from them. Remember, the attendants are there to keep everyone safe, so you don't have to be afraid. But you *do* have to learn to cope with other patients." Dr. Reed slowed their pace and turned to Norman. "You can't just stay in your room indefinitely. We have to integrate you into a social life here. Eventually you'll be eating with other patients in the dining hall, doing activities with them, being on a work detail—janitorial or grounds or laundry or . . . maybe the library. Would you like that?"

Norman nodded.

"Of course you would, and I think that would be a good position for you. We'll see. But before any of that happens, you have to become more social, make some friends. And this is a start."

They were at the door of the social hall now, and Dr. Reed held it open for him. Norman nodded. "All right," he said. "I'll try."

"Good for you. I'll see you in an hour or so. Read, watch TV, play a game if you like. But don't be frightened." And then the door closed, Dr. Reed was gone, and Norman was in the social hall.

There were more Christmas decorations taped to the walls, and in a corner was a scraggly tree with tinsel and lights but no ornaments. That made sense, Norman thought. Broken glass in the hands of some of these patients could be dangerous.

He recognized some of the people he had seen before, but not the man who had been so horrible, who had asked him those terrible questions. Norman coughed at all the smoke in the air, and walked over to a table that held magazines. He really didn't want to talk to anyone, but if someone came over and talked to *him,* he'd try to respond politely.

No one did, and Norman read magazine after magazine. He had thought he might catch up on current events, but all the magazines were from before he'd come into the hospital, so he read old stories about politicians and celebrities. Some pages had been torn out, and Norman wondered if it was because the stories were about crime.

He was actually starting to get comfortable when he heard shuffling footsteps behind him, and a soft drawl. "Well, well, if it isn't my old buddy Norman . . ."

Norman didn't turn around. He knew all too well who it was.

He saw an arm reach past the right side of his head and pick up a magazine from the table, then vanish again behind him. He heard a wooden chair creak as Ronald Miller sat in it. "How's your tummy today, Norman?" the voice went on. "Feelin' a little better? Really sorry that I made you sick, but I thought it'd take a lot more than that to upset *your* stomach. 'Specially after some of the things you done. Tell me, you chop 'em up afterwards? That's gotta be pretty messy, huh? Or do you like chop and puke, then chop some more?"

Norman clutched the magazine in his hand and stood up, looking through the haze of smoke for a haven. Across the room in the corner was a faded and worn easy chair, stained in a dozen places. Holding the magazine, he got up and quickly walked toward the chair and sat, facing his adversary. He reached into his pocket and felt the piece of petrified wood Nurse Marie had given him, rubbed its smoothness with his fingers, and thought about being strong.

Ronald Miller had turned to follow Norman with his gaze. When he saw that Norman had moved, he shook his head sadly, stood up, and strolled over to the corner with the easy chair. Norman looked at the closest attendant, but the man's attention was elsewhere.

Ronald Miller stopped a yard away from Norman and started looking at some of the cardboard Christmas decorations on the wall. "Can't get away from me, little Norman. You've really gotta tell me some things. I wanna know everything, pal. Unless your mama doesn't want you to tell."

Norman hissed in a breath.

"Oh, yeah, that got ya, huh? Word travels fast. 'Bout you killin' your mama, 'bout the way you stuffed her—" Miller stopped abruptly. "Oh, I just *got* it. Why Doc Reed looked so funny when I lied to him and told him we were talkin' about *mummies;* hell, yeah, your *mama* was like a mummy, huh? That's pretty weird, Norman. I wanna hear about that too. And you're gonna tell me. Or you know what, Norman? One of these days, when they get you back in with us, when we eat together and take *showers* together, y'know? Well, hell, I got a reputation for bangin' anything that moves, and that could easy include your chubby little ass, Norman. Now *spill.*"

The man moved closer. Norman, trembling, could feel the heat from Ronald Miller's body.

"Okay, Norman," he whispered. "Tell me. Get it out of your system. Tell me the worst thing that happened, the worst thing you did, get it over with, and we'll go from there, huh?" A little laugh came from Miller's throat. "So tell me, before you stuffed your mother . . . did you *stuff* your mother?"

What happened next surprised Norman. He didn't throw up, and he didn't hit Miller. He wanted to, but he knew that would be terribly wrong, and that both Dr. Reed and Robert would be disappointed in him. Not knowing what else to do, he started to softly cry.

"Aw," Miller whispered, "is Mama's baby boy *cwyin'?* Did mean old Wonnie make him sad?" The man chuckled. "You think you're cryin' *now,* wait'll I get you alone, Norman. And I will. I'll either make you talk or make you squeal, ya freak."

Miller looked around at the attendants to make sure they weren't looking, then leaned down and pried Norman's right hand off the rolled magazine he was crushing. He took Norman's hand in his own.

"Guar-on-teed. Let's shake on it, buddy . . ." The long cracked nail of his right middle finger sliced across the soft side of Norman's hand, and Norman winced at the pain, though he didn't cry out. "Somethin' to remember me by," Miller said, dropping Norman's hand and standing erect. "You think about it, buddy, and the next time you see me I wanna hear some good stuff, okay?"

Ronald Miller smiled down at Norman. "You think about what you wanna tell me, and you better not be makin' it up. I want the real deal, Norman." Miller turned and walked away, over to the windows, where he looked out at the cold, cloudy afternoon.

Norman stopped crying and looked at the side of his right hand. A thin line of blood marked where Ronald Miller's fingernail had sliced him open. He released the stone he'd been holding in his left pocket, and nestled the small wound in the palm of his left hand. There he sat, looking down at the floor, until Dr. Reed finally returned to take him back to his room.

It wasn't until they were there that Dr. Reed noticed the way Norman was sheltering his hand. He asked to see what was wrong and Norman showed him. Dr. Reed sent Ben to get some antiseptic and bandages, then asked Norman how it happened, and Norman told him. Dr. Reed frowned.

"I'm sorry, Norman. That was inexcusable on Miller's part. He'll be reprimanded. We'll take away his access to the social hall, starting tomorrow." Dr. Reed sighed. "Do you think you can eat dinner after our session?"

Norman's stomach felt queasy. "I'm . . . not sure."

"You really should, you know. Robert's visiting you tonight. If you don't eat something, you won't feel well when he's here."

Norman agreed to try to eat. When Ben returned, Dr. Reed treated and bandaged Norman's scratch, which had stopped oozing blood. Then Norman lay back on his bed, and they began their session. When they were finished, Norman felt more relaxed.

Nurse Marie brought his dinner, he ate, then sat in his room and read before Robert arrived. Finally Dr. Reed knocked and entered. "Robert's here," he said. "Are you ready?"

"Sure," Norman answered, putting down his book and sitting up, and Dr. Reed smiled and disappeared.

Robert came in a moment later, and Norman heard the door close on them. "Hey, little brother," Robert said as he gave Norman a hug. Then he sat down and they started to talk. It didn't take long before the subject of Ronald Miller came up.

"Dr. Reed told me about your trouble with that guy today," Robert said, shaking his head. "Man, it's gotta be tough in here.

When I think about that son of a bitch, I just feel like . . ." He paused. "Is this guy a lot bigger than you are?"

"He's . . . tall," Norman said, fearing what Robert might be getting at. "But he's skinny. Still, I couldn't . . ."

"No. No, of course not. But people like that . . . I mean, they make me realize why people like you go over the edge. So many times I've run into idiots like him, and I want to hand them their heads, you know? But I just don't have the guts, I guess."

They sat quietly for a moment. Then Robert said, more softly, "It helps me understand *you* more when I feel like that, feel that urge to lash out. Sometimes I . . ." He shook his head. "I can understand what you did."

"What I . . ." Norman was confused. "What I did?"

"In a way, I respect you, little brother, for having the courage."

"To do . . . what?"

"To kill people when you felt you had to."

The silence sat heavily in the room. Norman thought he could hear his heart beating, faster than before.

"I didn't . . . ," he said. "It was . . . Mother who killed those people."

Robert nodded, and his mouth twisted into a crooked smile. "Sure. It was our mother. But she was inside *you,* Norman. She may have been the . . . inspiration, but it was your hands and your mind that killed. Just like it was your hands and mind that killed our mother. And her boyfriend, that Considine guy. Mother didn't have anything to do with *that,* did she?"

"I—" But before Norman could say what he wanted to, he heard her.

Maybe this is my son after all.

Mother?

He sees the truth. He sees that you killed that girl, not me.

"I have to admit, Norman," Robert said, "I do respect that."

He sees the truth, Norman. The truth about the killings. I've told you it wasn't me, but you're not man enough to admit what you did, are you?

Be quiet, Mother!

You killed me and my lover—yes, my lover, Norman! It wasn't me inside you then! Have the gumption to face the truth, boy!

"You had guts, Norman," Robert said. "Dr. Reed told me all the details. You knew our mother was betraying you, and that Considine was stealing her away, and you had the guts to do something about it."

Now this *boy has got the gumption to face the truth even if you don't, Norman!*

Shut up, Mother!

"And as far as killing the girl, I don't know why—but you must have had a good reason. She was a criminal, right? She stole all that money? Maybe you didn't know at the time, but there was probably something about her, wasn't there? Or did she lead you on and then try and back out? I can understand how that could make you sore."

"No, it wasn't like that, she was—"

"And the detective, well, hell, he came snooping around, who could blame you for getting rid of *him*? It may have been wrong, but I understand it, Norman, I do."

Robert was looking at him with the most serious gaze Norman had ever seen. After all Robert had said, Norman expected his eyes to be wild, even crazy, but they were coldly sane.

"I can't help but think," Robert said slowly, "that doing what you did—killing in that way—must be somehow . . . liberating, freeing. When people *deserve* death, to mete it out to them, that must be . . . quite satisfying. Is it?"

"I . . . don't know. I don't really remember . . . doing it."

"Sometimes," Robert said, "I wish I had the nerve. To see what it's like."

"*No,*" Norman said. "You don't want to wish that. Not ever. Why would you want that? Why?"

Robert didn't answer for a long time. "Maybe to feel some power, for a change, in this world. Maybe to make a difference." He smiled. "Maybe to understand my brother a little bit better."

"But you have a *good life*. You have a wife, children, a business. What do you mean, *power?* And making a difference? You already have! All *I've* done is cause people pain and grief." Norman leaned toward his brother. "All you have to understand from me is that killing is wrong, Robert. It's what put me here. If I could go back and make things right, bring people back to life, I'd do it in a second."

Robert looked at him, then spoke. "They say that twins are bound. Psychically. Have you ever heard that?"

Norman nodded. His readings in the field of psychic phenomena had been extensive before his incarceration. "Yes," he said cautiously. "They say that twins have a closer connection than other people. That if one experiences something highly traumatic, the other can experience aspects of it too, even though they're far away. It's as though their minds are bound psychically, maybe bound by blood."

"Norman, we're bound by more than blood. If you were able to kill, then I am too. If you felt it necessary to kill, then I might feel it necessary too."

"No . . . ," Norman said, but the word was weak, dying as it left his mouth.

"You did do something wrong, but it wasn't killing alone. It was killing people who were too close to you. You got lucky with our mother and Considine. You got away with that—or would have if it hadn't been for the others. That's where you made your mistake. You killed someone who was too close to you—a guest in your motel. And you killed someone else who other people knew was coming to see you. It should have been more random—or at least *looked* random. It should have been someone with whom you had hardly any connection at all.

"Norman, if you could go back and make things right? I think you'd do exactly what you did before. But this time, you'd do it more carefully."

Oh, God, Norman thought, oh, dear God, this was Mother's son, all right. This was most certainly his brother.

6

Ronald Miller liked the dark. It was his friend and his collaborator. It kept his scarred face from being seen, and it had hidden him from his victims.

He liked to lie in his darkened cell and remember what he thought of as his past triumphs. He could picture each one in specific detail. He could feel their skin, hear their whimpering moans, recall the sensations that had pleasured him while bringing them pain. He turned the black wall of his cell into a movie theater and replayed the films over and over, whichever one appealed to him most that night.

And they thought he was crazy. Hell, he wasn't crazy, he just knew what he liked, and he had to get it *some* way, didn't he? The problem was that he liked *pretty* women, and the pretty ones would never look at him, not with *his* face. As for whores, forget about it. He'd never seen a single one who didn't look hard as a hammer, and the ones he could have afforded would probably give you a dose of something that would make your equipment fall off before you could use it again.

When Ronald talked to the doctors, he blamed his face, and so did they. He told them that when he was a kid, the guy his whore of a mom was living with had gotten drunk, poured rum on his face, and lit it up with a Zippo. Poor little Ronald had gone through a childhood full of people either cringing from him or making fun of him. *No wonder I got all screwed up in the head . . . no wonder I became a rapist, right, Doc?*

He never actually said those words. He was smarter than that. He just let them *think* it. It was a perfect case—kid has a lousy childhood, kid grows up sick and twisted, right?

The thing was, Ronald had a great childhood. His folks weren't rich, but they were good to him, and they stayed together till his mom died, and then his dad started grieving and drinking until he drank himself to death. But by that time Ronald was long gone. He'd gotten his face burned when he was twenty. He'd broken into the cabin of a woman whose husband was in the war, and before he could get done what he wanted to do, she'd grabbed a kerosene lantern by the bed and smashed it over his head. The fire went everywhere. He managed to get out. She didn't. The dumb bitch got what she deserved. But the souvenir of that night had been visible on his face ever since.

Ronald still had dreams about it, about the terror and the awful pain, pain that stayed with him for months and never fully went away. It just made him angrier when he took the women. It made him feel they needed to pay him back with *their* pain.

Forget about it for now, he told himself. The image of the fire had intruded, as it sometimes did, upon the more pleasant images, like a black-and-white war newsreel shown in the middle of a happy Technicolor musical. Let's get back to the good times, Ronald thought, and forced his mind to the happy place.

Happy for *him,* anyway. He felt the girl under him, her flesh on the cold stones of the alleyway, but his flesh warm on hers.

Ronald's right hand moved down his body, finding what he wanted as the memories excited him. He was constantly amazed at the details he could remember, even after years. He could swear he heard the scratching of her fingernails on the stones as he held her wrists above her head.

Or *was* that scratching?

The projector bulb inside his head darkened. His right hand stopped moving. He listened.

Except for the occasional screams of the crazed, the cells were always dead quiet after dark. Other inmates had told him they'd heard things in the depth of the night—footsteps, the sound of breathing, sometimes even voices, or moaning and weeping. Some blamed it on the ghosts who were left over from the days the hospital was a sanitarium. Others swore it was the spirits of the people they themselves had killed.

But that was their guilt talking. Guilt and the fact that everybody in here except him was crazy as a loon. Ronald had never felt guilty. That wasn't part of him. If he ever got out, the first thing he'd do after going somewhere far away—maybe even another country—was exactly what he'd been doing when they caught him.

Still, he could *swear* he'd heard something.

He sat up and listened more intently. No. Nothing.

Ronald stood, walked to the door, and peered through the open slot, through which just enough light was leaking to define the outlines of his few pieces of institutional furniture. The corridor appeared empty, and no sounds came to his ears. None of his fellow nuts were croaking their midnight songs.

Just his imagination, then. As he trundled back to bed, he wondered if he could re-create his victims' whimpers as realistically.

He lay back down in the nearly black cell, and the thoughts of whimpering made him think of that whining pile of crap Norman Bates. To think he'd admired the newcomer at first, before he'd realized what a weepy little baby he was. Amazing that he'd ever had the guts to do what he did. Ronald couldn't imagine Norman doing what *he* did. Instead he saw Norman thrashing out with his knife, crying and blubbering as he killed, making a mess of everything, and then dissolving into a puddle of tears.

No, he had a strong hunch that a knife was the only thing Norman Bates had ever penetrated a woman with. His fantasies about Norman had been just that. And the more he lay there and thought about it, the more Ronald realized that they were the kind of fantasies he himself would like to make reality.

After all, what did he have to lose? An act of rape and murder couldn't make him any crazier than they already thought he was, could it? Maybe he'd get a few days or weeks or even months of more extreme punishment, but wouldn't it be worth it? To get somebody like Nurse Marie, or that little receptionist he saw sometimes when they were taking him between the wings?

To stab someone while doing what Ronald often did. To feel them die under him while feeling so many other things as well . . .

He closed his eyes and imagined something he had never done, and reveled in it. And his imagination was so strong, so overpowering of all his senses, that he didn't hear again the sound he had heard previously, didn't sense a change of air in his cell, or the presence of another creature, either ghost or human, near him.

He didn't hear or see or feel or smell anything until the blade went into the soft spot of flesh under his heart and then up into it. It was then that his eyes opened to see a deeper darkness hovering above him. He heard the wet sound of his own death as the knife withdrew and his blood and his life began to leave him. He tried to breathe, but had forgotten how.

The final thing he knew was a pain greater than any even he could imagine, a flash of blazing heat, a bolt of fiery cold, and then he was dead.

Norman Bates had a dream in the early hours before dawn. He dreamed that he was going down a long tunnel. He had no idea if it was wide or narrow, because it was so dark. He was naked, and he kept walking and walking, never bumping into the tunnel's sides, but still somehow knowing it was a tunnel.

Finally he saw a light ahead, and he started to walk faster. The light grew brighter, and the tunnel narrowed until it was just the size of a doorway. He walked up to it and looked in.

Though the light that had come through the doorway had been blindingly bright, the room itself was lit in a red glow, and Norman could see what had *made* it red. There was blood everywhere.

The room was ovoid, narrow at the top, widening as the walls came down, then thinning again until there was a narrow gutter at the bottom. Thick red blood coated the room, dripped slowly like molasses from the ceiling and walls, ran down the curved sides and puddled on the floor. Norman could hear the *drip* . . . *drip* . . . *drip* in a dozen different places.

A man stood in the center of the room, his back to Norman. His strong legs straddled the central gutter, whose surface was hidden by the swamp of blood. The man was coated with it as well, so that his naked flesh was deep red. The shape of his torso was the antithesis of the room, wide shoulders curving down to a trim waist, then out again to muscled buttocks. His thick arms were outstretched, and in his right hand Norman saw a long knife pointing upward.

Though Norman didn't feel his legs moving, he drew closer to the man, the way one moves in dreams, until he was only a few feet away. Though the blood was dripping all about him, he felt no sense of wetness on his shoulders or head. He seemed encased in a bubble that kept the blood from touching his body or his feet, even though he felt he must be wading ankle deep in it.

He didn't *want* to draw closer to the terrifying apparition of the bloodied man, but he had no choice, and no power to refuse the dream's demands. The hair on the back of the man's head was matted with blood, so that it appeared as a textured helmet of shining crimson. Slowly the head turned, and suddenly it was as though the bubble burst around Norman, and the hot rank odor of blood rushed into his nostrils, gagging him.

And still the head turned, and Norman saw the brow, the chin, the cheek, a tip of nose, the deep red hollow of an eye, a cruel edge of mouth, and he thought he recognized the face, thought he knew, through the lineaments of gore, the identity of the brutal, commanding figure.

But just as he was about to see the creature full face, the ceiling opened like the sky itself, and torrents of foul, steaming blood flooded down on Norman, blinding him and washing the man from his sight. And now he *could* feel the drowning tide of blood embracing him, choking him, deafening him, and he screamed, over and over again, until his own screaming woke him from the dream and he opened his eyes to the beam of light coming in through the open slot in the locked door.

Oh, what the hell now, Tom Downing thought as he slowly got to his feet. There were screams and there were *screams,* and by this time he was able to identify most of them.

Harry Tibbetts, the ax murderer, was good for at least one outburst a month, yelling that the "green men" were in his room again. Tom would have to get whoever else was on night duty in Wards A and B, go into Harry's room, drag him out of the corner and calm him down before he'd stop yelling.

And Ralph Vincent would start singing "Rags to Riches" every week at three in the morning. It was the song that was playing on the jukebox when he'd taken his shotgun into the bar and blown away his wife and her boyfriend, then kept reloading and firing at other patrons until an oil worker caught him between reloads and laid him low. Usually he could talk Ralph down without having to unlock his room door, and Ralph would lower the volume and sing to himself quietly in bed instead of sharing it through the slot with the whole corridor.

Tom Downing was a connoisseur of screams, but this was a new one to him. As he slowly dragged his bulk out of his station chair in the short hallway between Wards C and D, he hoped to hell that it was one time only and didn't mark the beginning of a new regular. It was sort of easing off now into a frenzied panting, as if the loon had gotten tired of screaming. Tom hoped so as he rounded the corner and went down the corridor known as Ward C.

Damned if it wasn't coming from Norman Bates's room, which surprised Tom. Bates was one of the quiet ones, or *had* been up till now. Tom went up to the door and tried to peer through the slot, but didn't put his eyes too close. He'd made that mistake back in '49 and wound up with a faceful of piss thrown by "Mad Dog" Hennessey, who'd died of cancer a year later with no mourners at all.

"You okay, Bates?" Tom said, and took his flashlight out of its sheath, flicked it on, and shined it through the slot. He could see Bates in bed, shielding his eyes against the sudden light.

"Yes . . . yes . . ." The voice sounded weak. "Had . . . bad dream. Sorry . . ."

Thank God, Tom thought. Once and done, unless those bad dreams kept up. But hell, everybody had them now and again. And Norman Bates had a lot to have bad dreams about.

"You gonna be okay?" Tom asked.

". . . Yes. Sorry."

"All right, well, make sure you're good and awake before you go back to sleep. Think of something nice."

Yeah, right. What the hell was there *nice* to think about in a place like this? Tom sheathed his flashlight and started back toward his station, then figured he might as well walk the length of the corridor to be sure that none of the other birdies was going to start chirping in response to their fellow wackadoodle.

Every hour he was supposed to walk the Ward C corridor as well as Ward D, which paralleled C, but he hardly ever did. Hell, the doors were all locked, so it wasn't like the patients were going to go for a little midnight stroll, and if any of them went bonkers in their cell, he'd hear them easy enough. Still, might as well do his duty for a change.

He moseyed along, listening at the open slots, hearing nothing but breathing or snoring, and sometimes nothing at all. As he neared the far end of the corridor, he slowed down. Ahead, two doors from the end, was Ronald Miller's room. He'd never heard any screams from in there, but he *had* heard some loud grunts and moans. Once he'd asked Miller what he was doing, and Miller had answered, "Communin' with the gods!" Tom knew he was just jerking off in there. Most of the patients did, but Miller was never quiet about it, the creepy bastard. He could be at it most anytime day or night. Tom smiled to himself. Maybe he'd actually catch the creep doing it.

Tom walked as softly as he could up to the slot in Miller's door, drawing out the flashlight and lifting it to the slot, aimed it where he knew its beam would fall on Miller in his bed, then turned it on. To Tom's surprise, the bed was empty, and he involuntarily lurched back, as if expecting Miller's fingers to come through the slot toward his eyes.

But there was no movement within, and no sound. The bed was neatly made, as though it hadn't been slept in. "Miller?" he called, but there was no answer.

Tom Downing considered what to do next. He didn't want to open the locked door on his own, since Miller could be pressed against the wall next to the door, ready to jump him as he entered. It would be best to get Eddie Abbott, the attendant on Wards A and B. The two of them could handle Miller, all right.

Pure instinct made Tom check to be sure Miller's room was locked before leaving the corridor, and he grasped the handle and pushed it gently. To his amazement, the door moved inward.

He gasped and pulled it back toward him. It clicked shut, but didn't lock. Someone must have used their key to unlock the door to Miller's room. On the off chance the man was still inside, Tom fumbled with his key ring, jammed the proper key into the lock, and turned it until he heard the comforting click.

He had two choices at this point: one was to go get Eddie so that the two of them could investigate Miller's room, and the other was to go balls out and pull the security alarm. Not wanting to waste a minute if Ronald Miller was on the loose, Tom chose the latter.

Within minutes guards and attendants filled the corridor. With the arrival of reinforcements, Tom unlocked Miller's cell, and they found it empty. Some of the men checked the doors to the outside and all the fences to see if anyone had escaped the facility, and others examined the doors of every patient's room to make sure they were locked.

In another half hour, the big guns had shown up, including Dr. Goldberg himself and Myron Gunn, who looked at Tom

Downing as though he wanted to kill him. "What the hell went on here, Downing?" Myron growled at Tom. "You telling me Miller's door was *unlocked?*"

Tom explained once more exactly what had happened, while Myron Gunn looked more and more furious, and Dr. Goldberg's brow furrowed even further.

"And you didn't hear a *thing?*" Myron asked.

"No . . . I did all the checks, like always," Tom lied. "Nothing funny going on at all, not till Bates started yelling."

"All right," said Dr. Goldberg. "The important thing now is to find this patient. He poses a great danger to anyone he may come across. First of all, I want to make sure that all the nurses are accounted for and safe. Then I want this facility searched from bottom to top. Protocol dictates that we immediately inform the state police. We'll inform the local police too. If there is *any* possibility Miller may have gotten off the grounds, they need to know so that they can begin their own manhunt. Myron, you and your men take care of all that, *ja?* Quickly, please."

"You got it, Doc," Myron said, and, with one more baleful look at Tom, ran down the hall.

It had been four in the morning when Tom Downing discovered that Ronald Miller's room was empty. By dawn, the building itself had been thoroughly searched from bottom to top, as Dr. Goldberg had ordered. Even every patient room, occupied and vacant, was unlocked and checked. Ronald Miller wasn't found. No barred windows had been sawn through, no exterior doors had been forced. Yet it seemed that Ronald Miller had waltzed out of the building as easily as he had left his locked room.

Both state and local police arrived shortly after Myron Gunn called them, and a cadre of uniformed troopers searched the grounds, examining the perimeter for any sign that someone had either climbed over or burrowed under the stone walls, or cut their way through the chain-link fence topped with concertina wire that cordoned off the exercise yard.

Inside, in Dr. Goldberg's office, two tall men sat in the chairs in front of the doctor's massive desk. The younger man was Captain Banning of the state highway patrol. The older was Jud Chambers, Fairvale's sheriff. Goldberg had shown them the empty cell, and had then taken them to his office to discuss the next steps.

"All right," Banning said, taking control of the situation. He leaned forward toward Goldberg, his big head jutting from his thick neck. "So *how* could this Miller have gotten out of this cell himself? You say it was unlocked when the guard found it?"

"Yes," Goldberg said, "and I have no idea whatsoever how that could have happened. All rooms are locked by an attendant. When lights-out occurs at ten o'clock, every door to every room is checked again to be certain they are locked. This protocol is unbroken."

Jud Chambers scratched his curly gray hair. "Doc, could this Miller have stuck somethin' in the door to keep it from locking?"

Goldberg sighed theatrically. "Hardly, Sheriff. These are not those kinds of doors. We are responsible for keeping some of the most violent and dangerous men in the state imprisoned. All the doors have deadbolts. Once they are locked, they are impossible to open without a key."

"So then we've got to conclude," said Banning, "that somebody else unlocked that cell *with* a key."

"I can't imagine that happening," Goldberg replied. "There would be no reason to do so. Miller is disliked by everyone, including the attendants. He has no surviving family members, and no money, so the motive of bribery is extremely unlikely. I can't imagine anyone being willing to aid in his escape."

"Well, somebody sure did," Banning said. "That lock didn't open by itself. Who was on duty in that ward tonight?"

"Thomas Downing," Goldberg said. "He has been here a long time. His alarm and concern over Miller's escape seems quite genuine."

"Yeah, maybe *seems* is the word. He might've been faking."

"Captain Banning, I have been in the field of psychiatry for longer than you have been alive. I can tell when a man is lying."

"And I became a captain at the age of thirty-five, Doc. I know criminals too. I want to talk to this Downing guy."

"We'll arrange that."

"If I can put in my two cents' worth," Jud Chambers said, "what I'm most concerned about is catchin' this guy before he rapes somebody else. You think that's what he's likely to do, Doc?"

Goldberg steepled his fingers. "I think that if rape were his primary concern, he might have attacked one of the night nurses. They are all well and accounted for, so I believe his first goal was escape from this hospital, which he seems to have accomplished. I suspect that he will not want to stay in this area, and will wish to flee far from where he is being sought. However, once he is away from here and feels secure, *ja,* I have no doubt that he will resume his crimes. But since he is indeed a psychopath, he is still unpredictable, and people should be made aware of the threat he poses."

"Which means you really don't know what he plans to do," Banning said.

Goldberg frowned at the captain. "What I am certain of is that, once he feels secure, he will rape again. Or do something even worse."

Banning stood. "Then we better catch him before he can do it."

Jud Chambers stood as well. "I'll get my boys movin' too. And I'll let the *Herald* and the radio and TV station know. We'll get this fella's picture out there and either catch him or put him in the ground."

"Bringing him back here will be sufficient, gentlemen," Goldberg said.

Just before Jud Chambers followed Banning through the door, he stopped and turned back. Banning stopped as well. "Doc," Chambers said, "it seems pretty dang hard to get out of this place, but what about getting *into* it?"

"What do you mean?" asked Dr. Goldberg.

"Well . . . what if somebody wanted to get in here—to *take* Miller out, help him escape. Or maybe even some husband or boyfriend who wanted to do the opposite—maybe kill him for what he did. Could they get in to do it?"

"An outsider coming in, getting past security, getting the proper keys, and then taking a patient out would be even more difficult than a simple escape, Sheriff," Goldberg said.

"And as for killing him," Banning said with a smirk, "I think there'd be a body around if that happened. Unless they took it with them when they left."

The sheriff nodded slowly. "Got a point," he said, and walked out of the office.

Ben Blake told Marie Radcliffe about the disappearance of Ronald Miller as soon as she got to the hospital at eight that morning. He'd been called several hours before and had come in early to help search the facility for Miller. "I thought about calling," Ben said, "but I didn't want to wake you, and I figured even if Miller escaped . . ."

"What?" she asked.

He sighed. "I was just worried about you. With somebody like Miller, you know . . . still, I figured there was no way he was going to find where you lived."

"Oh, Ben, he wouldn't have come looking for *me*."

"Crazy people do crazy things." Ben shrugged. "You're right. I just don't know what I'd do if anything happened to you." He glanced up quickly to make sure no one was coming down the hall and gave Marie a quick kiss. They'd been going out together regularly for the past several weeks. It had gotten to the hand holding and kissing stage, but no further.

"I'm fine," Marie said. "Has Dr. Reed been in yet?"

"Haven't seen him, but he was at Delsey's last night." Delsey's was a roadhouse and bar on the road from the hospital to Fairvale. It had good food and cold beer. "Saw him when I stopped in on the way home. We talked a little, mostly about the way Miller messed with Norman again. I know Reed was planning to discipline him somehow."

"You think that could be why Miller ran?" Marie asked.

"Naw," Ben said. "I don't think it was anything spur of the moment. Miller must've planned this in advance. Too many people and locked doors and fences he'd have to get through. You don't just up and leave a place like this."

They both turned at the sound of footsteps coming rapidly down the hall. Dr. Reed was walking toward them holding a briefcase and a cardboard cup of coffee. "Ben," he said, "I just heard. What in God's name? How the hell could something like this happen?'

"Don't know, Doc. They'll catch him, though. Got a whole manhunt going, from what I hear. They're bringing dogs in to see if they can pick up a trail anywhere around the fence."

Dr. Reed shook his head. "Of all the people I'd like least to be on the loose, Ronald Miller tops the list. He's sick, but he's also *mean*. If we can ever cure the sickness, I suspect the meanness will still be there." He gave a thin smile to both Ben and Marie. "Sorry for the pessimism, but ours is a far from perfect science. I hope they catch him soon. And be careful, both of you—he could still be around here somewhere. Heaven knows what he might do . . ." And Dr. Reed continued down the hall to his office.

Norman Bates learned of Ronald Miller's disappearance later that day, when Dr. Reed arrived at his room to take him to the social hall. When Dr. Reed told him why he was there, Norman lowered his head and softly said, "I really don't want to go today. I don't feel very well."

He felt Dr. Reed's hand on his shoulder, and heard him say, "I know why you don't want to go, Norman, and I understand. It's Ronald Miller you're worried about. But you don't have to be. He won't be in the social hall today."

Norman looked up. "Why not? Did you punish him?"

"No, Norman. I'd been planning to, but he . . . left the hospital last night."

"Left?"

"He escaped from his room, Norman. And then he apparently got outside and somehow made it over the fence."

"He's . . . he's not here anymore?" Norman knew that he should be upset about someone as bad as Ronald Miller being on the loose, but he couldn't help but be glad that Miller wasn't there to bother him.

"He's not, Norman. So I think you can feel more comfortable in the social hall, yes?"

"Do you think they'll catch him?" Norman asked.

"I think they will, Norman. But when they do, it's going to be a long time before he's in the social hall again. If ever. Okay?"

Norman smiled and nodded. "I do want him to be caught, Dr. Reed, it's just . . ."

"I understand perfectly. Things will be a little more pleasant with him not around, is that what you mean?"

"Yes. It is."

"Are you ready to go then?"

Norman was.

Once in the social hall and knowing that he was going to be free of the presence of Ronald Miller, Norman actually walked around the room several times. Though he didn't engage in conversation, he listened to some. A few were completely nonsensical. One was about Communism and how "Communists are running this asylum, goddamnit!"

Another conversation dealt with Ronald Miller's escape, although that wasn't what these two patients considered it. "Escape, my ass," said one. "Nobody escapes from here. I seen 'em try, but it don't happen. You know what *did* happen, don'tcha?"

"Whut?" said the other man. He wasn't looking at the first. He was looking at the ceiling, as though he was watching things crawl across it.

"Ghosts," the first said. "Those damn ghosts got him. I hear those bastards all the time."

"Naw."

"Yeah. Talkin' and wailin' and cryin'; hell, ain't you heard the stories? How long you been here?"

"Five weeks."

"*I* been here near five *years*. Heard about 'em when I first came in, then started hearin' 'em for real. They're way old, y'know?"

"How old?"

"Like way-back-turn-of-the-century old. When this place was a crazy house afore the state got it. Was private. For crazy rich folk. 'Stead of us crazy *poor* folk, ha!"

The first man watched the second man move his gaze back and forth across the stained ceiling tiles for a while. Then he said, "You'll never catch 'em, y'know. They crawl right into them little holes in the tile." But the second man kept watching.

Norman looked upward but saw nothing moving on the ceiling, even though the other men seemed to.

"Boy, that's one's fast, huh?" said the first man.

"And *big*," said the second. "I don't fer the life of me know *how* they get in them little holes . . ."

Norman sat down in one of the easy chairs and thought that maybe he wasn't all *that* crazy. At least he didn't believe in ghosts.

But ghosts were on the minds of more people than just Norman Bates and two mentally disturbed men in the social hall. Among the patients, nurses, and support staff, the old stories were rearing their heads again. The facility had been considered haunted by the superstitious for many years, going back to its early days as the Ollinger Sanitarium. Many locals worked in the state hospital, and since the tales of hauntings and horrors were a half-century old, these residents of Fairvale and environs had grown up with those stories, shivering at them under their covers when they were children. Even though they may never have experienced any direct confrontation with the supernatural in the state hospital, their atavistic instincts convinced them of the *possibility* of such things.

In the years between 1918 and 1939, when the facility was deserted and only high stone walls kept out vandals, it was a favorite place for young roughnecks to come with their ladies, to both terrify the womenfolk and demonstrate their own courage by going right up to the gate and shouting at the spirits that still dwelt within to show themselves.

The spirits never did, though the animals that had found their way onto the grounds through chinks too small for humans often played proxy for the reluctant ghosts, and their rustles in the high grass and sudden bursts of speed when startled by human voices frightened many, even the roughnecks, to their great chagrin. So it was that the actions of these unseen but all too real creatures preserved and maintained the authenticity of the legends of the unresting dead, legends that once again became the subject foremost in the minds of many at the State Hospital for the Criminally Insane on this day.

One such example was Judy Pearson, who jumped several inches straight up from her chair when Marie Radcliffe entered the break room. "Judy!" Marie said. "I'm sorry—I didn't mean to startle you."

Judy relaxed, or tried to. Her tiny frame seemed to shiver with the effort. "Oh, God, Marie, *I'm* sorry, I've been on pins and needles all day, what with Ronald Miller escaping, and the guys *know* that all that ghost talk scares the heck out of me, and they just kid me more now, and it's starting to get dark, and it gets dark so early now I hate it, and . . ."

Judy's monologue was nearly unintelligible to Marie, though she was able to pick up bit and pieces. Judy never spoke much louder than a stage whisper, and when she was away from the hospital's reception desk, the tempo of her words increased to rocket speed.

". . . and having to go into the coatroom alone, because nobody's done at the same time as me, and the parking lot's so dark, and then I get home and there's nobody in my apartment—"

"Judy," Marie said, "I don't blame you. I'm sure one of the guys would walk you to your car. I can ask Ben."

"Oh, would you? That would be great! I keep picturing Ronald Miller hiding under my car and reaching out and grabbing my legs and yanking me off my feet!"

"He's far gone from here, Judy."

"I just hope he didn't go to my apartment; oh, God, I wonder if he knows where I live; you know the way he looks at every woman he sees, like he'd like to . . . oh, God, when the attendants would take him through the lobby past my desk, the *look* he'd give me . . ."

"Well, be cautious, of course," Marie said, "but everybody thinks he just wants to get out of the area, far away from here."

"Oh, God, as if the ghosts aren't bad enough, now we have to have a . . . a *monster* on the loose . . ."

7

June 12, 1911

To my great delight, Spiritual Repulsion Therapy has proven to be a successful treatment for those who have committed trespasses against their fellow men. When these patients are confronted in the deeps of the night with the spiritual manifestations of those they have wronged, the guilt they feel is nearly always a purging one, searing the evil from their souls as fire drives out impurities of the flesh.

One patient, W.S., is a prime example of the efficacy of the treatment. W.S. was committed here by his father, a man of no little means, after the youth pummeled a Mexican girl to death because she would not yield to his advances. It is questionable as to whether or not he slaked his dark lusts after he had rendered the girl unconscious, but that is neither here nor there. What is certain is that he took an innocent life in a moment of rage.

Being that the girl was Mexican, the authorities took the crime less seriously than if a white woman had been slaughtered, and it was arranged that W.S., in lieu of a prison sentence, would be committed here at the Ollinger Sanitarium. Of course this re-

quired that I testify that the act was committed as the result of a mental aberration, which I had no hesitation in doing. The beating to death of a young woman who had done nothing but withhold herself sexually is, by its very nature, the act of a madman. And it was my work to drive the madness out of that young man.

We had numerous discussions before I utilized Spiritual Repulsion Therapy, and I found W.S. to be sly and dishonest in his intercourse with me. At times he told me what he suspected I wanted to hear, but his insincerity was obvious. In the few moments when I could draw from him the truth in his soul, I was appalled at what I found: a complete lack of guilt and responsibility for the death he had caused. I had no doubt that, were he to walk free again, it might not be long before he would take another life, perhaps even under the same circumstances, and that must not be allowed to happen.

In total, W.S. received three treatments of Spiritual Repulsion Therapy, in ever increasing "dosages." The first was audible only; the second visible only; the third a combination of the two. Specific sedatives in increasing doses were given W.S. in his evening meal each time, which made him not only less likely to have a response of attack, but made him more suggestible to the phenomena to which he was exposed.

By the end of the third treatment, he was weeping tears of contrition, which continued until the morning, when an attendant came to take him to the dining room for breakfast. He begged to see me, and when I arrived (quite expectantly, I confess), he told me that he finally realized the gravity of his deed and repented of it. Dickens's Scrooge, after the visit of the three spirits, was no more sincere than this poor lad, who had been struck to the heart by the therapy he had received.

And it was then, with the thought of Scrooge in my mind,

that I wondered if Mr. Dickens had been my ultimate inspiration for this therapy. Nothing I had heretofore done with this youth had proven as effective as the "visitation of spirits" he had experienced.

At this point, I ended that so successful therapy and spent several months in more traditional channels. Just this week I pronounced W.S. cured, and today his father came to take him home. The youth has lost his rebellious, angry sprit completely, and now evinces a withdrawn, timid countenance, with more feminine than masculine emotions. Indeed, when his father came to retrieve him, he wept to see him, and when the father embraced the prodigal, the boy continued to weep and moan his apologies to his father, his victim, and the world. They left the facility, the father's arm around the still-weeping boy.

There have been a number of similar outcomes, some as dramatic, others less so but still successful. However, to be honest, I have experienced a few cases that were less than successful. While it is true that mankind's primitive fear of the dead is a primary staple of my therapy, when that particular fear overwhelms all else, it can persuade what may be a mild aberration to become something worse. I wish to imbue my patients with moral responsibility for their actions, and if making them more timid and tractable is a by-product, then that is completely acceptable. But when the fear becomes so great that it turns to uncontrolled and incurable terror, the treatment is too harsh. It does no good to render a patient tractable, if they are also to become so distant as to be uncommunicative.

Perhaps I shall relate some of these cases in the future, but they are too painful to revisit now. I must be optimistic regarding Spiritual Repulsion Therapy. Like any other treatment, mistakes can be made. Dosages can be too great. It may be found that some patients are more susceptible and suggestible to such therapy, *sometimes too much so, and we shall be able to identify them anon. But this is a great experiment, and as with any experiment, there are bound to be sacrifices that must be made so that we can learn.*

I most sincerely pray that the sacrifices will be few.

What in the name of sweet baby Jesus was happening to this place? Myron Gunn wondered. Let one nut disappear, and it affects the whole damned fruitcake.

Ronald Miller's escape had made the good patients not as good, the bad ones worse, and the worst ones terrible. And the kicker was that they hadn't *caught* the creep yet. That gave them all ideas that maybe *they* could escape somehow. And that just made them harder to handle.

But, Myron was quick to remember, they were *crazy,* and their reactions could be crazy too. Take Wesley Breckenridge. Quiet little guy who had gone nuts and chopped up his wife one Christmas Eve, then put the pieces back together so that she was sitting on the couch when family company came. He brought them into the living room, then sat right next to her and held her hand, which wasn't attached to anything else. Now *that* was a Christmas to remember.

Wesley, however, had one of the strangest reactions to Miller's departure. He was certain that the ghosts of the old sanitarium had gotten Miller somehow, but that wasn't the strange part, since a lot of the patients (and even some of the staff) believed that. What made Wesley's case strange was that he was convinced the ghosts who took Ronald Miller away *ate* him.

"They got to get strength somewhere," he said quietly when he explained his views to Dr. Steiner. "Ghosts gotta eat too. I wanna get so skinny that they won't want me."

Dr. Steiner had nodded his head, as though pretending Wesley's theory sounded quite logical. Then he said, "I understand that, Wesley, but you have to eat *something*, or you'll starve to death, and we don't want that, now do we?"

Myron thought, Hell, yeah, one less loony to deal with, but kept his mouth shut.

"Wesley," Dr. Steiner went on, "you haven't eaten a thing in three days, and you're not a very big person to begin with. In another day or so, your body will essentially start feeding on itself, and since you have very little stored body fat, your liver and other organs could be affected, and you could suffer permanent damage, even death. So you see, you *have* to begin to eat again."

Wesley shook his head. "Nope. Sorry, Doc, but I'm not gonna do it. I don't want them ghosts to get me."

Dr. Steiner reasoned with Wesley for several minutes. Wesley admitted that he was hungry, and that, yes, certain foods would taste very good, but he wasn't going to eat. Finally he promised to eat if a ghost showed up in his cell at night and refused to eat him because he was so thin. *Then* he'd have a little something. Not much, but enough to satisfy his hunger.

"Wesley," Dr. Steiner said with a smile, "we can't afford to wait until a ghost comes and refuses you. You must eat. I would rather not order that you be force-fed, but if you refuse to eat I see no alternative. I don't believe you've ever been force-fed, have you?"

Wesley shook his head no.

"It's not very pleasant. Myron and some other attendants will have to place a lubricated tube into your nostril and down your throat into your stomach."

Wesley furrowed his brow.

"And then they'll slowly pour a semi-liquid, which is very soft and nutritious, down the tube until they're assured that a certain amount is in your stomach."

Wesley frowned.

"They won't take out the tube right away, because they want to make sure that you won't vomit up the mixture, so it will stay there for about half an hour Then they'll carefully remove the tube. This will be done every day until you decide to eat again."

The frown on Wesley's mouth turned to a grim, straight line before he spoke. "You do what you gotta do. I'm gonna do what *I* gotta do. And I ain't eatin'."

All right, Myron thought. At least this day won't be a complete waste.

The disappearance of his nemesis, Ronald Miller, made Norman Bates feel much more at ease mingling with the other patients. Though he hadn't as yet spoken to any of them, other than a single *yes* or *no* now and then, he had smiled and listened as some of them talked, and they had welcomed him into their circle. They may have thought his silence strange, but it was certainly no stranger than some of the more active quirks of other patients. A nontalkative man was a godsend for those who wished to expound upon their unorthodox theories and views, so Norman was found to be good and receptive company. His smiles and nods showed agreement, even if his words didn't.

Norman was getting more and more exercise as well. He spent time every day in the exercise yard when weather permitted, and when it rained or was too cold, Dr. Reed allowed him to walk the long corridors in the company of an attendant, climbing the stairs from floor to floor.

He got to know the building better as a result, from the

treatment rooms in the basement to the offices on the first and second floors, to the wards on all four floors. When walking inside, each attendant had instructions from Dr. Reed to walk with Norman for thirty minutes. Norman liked some of the attendants better than others. Ben was a good guy, he thought. Ben would talk to him about the weather or about the food in the hospital, joke about it, really, so that he made Norman laugh more than once. And he didn't seem to mind that Norman didn't talk back. Norman liked going for walks with Ben, and Dick, who Ben worked with a lot, was okay too.

Some of the others, however, weren't fun at all. They acted like it was a real task to walk Norman around, and although they were never really mean to him, he sensed their disdain.

Even so, it felt good to stretch his legs, and Norman had gotten to like the daily routine of time in the social hall followed by a half-hour walk. It was almost fun to see the different people, doctors and nurses and attendants, through the building, and some of the nurses smiled at him. When they did that, he smiled back, but quickly looked down. He didn't want them to think he was having bad thoughts about them, and he tried very hard not to.

The basement, Norman thought, was a bit creepy. It felt damp down there, and it had stone walls, and some of the rooms were missing doors, so that there was just darkness inside when you passed. It reminded him of the cellar at home.

One end of the basement had some treatment rooms, but the doors were always shut when he walked by, and he didn't know what they did in there. It seemed less damp at that end, and he guessed that was why they put the rooms there. Down one basement wing was a large industrial laundry for all the sheets and blankets and uniforms and similar items used in the hospital. The machines were nearly always on, both washers and dryers, and Ben usually let Norman stop and look in the room while the machines whirled, spun, and clattered.

It smelled clean in there, like soap with a hint of bleach, the way it smelled in his basement years ago when Mother washed the clothes and let him watch her put them through the wringer. One time, when he was five, he had curiously put up his fingers to the thick rotating rollers, and she had grabbed his hand and held it in her wiry grip. *Don't ever put your fingers in there, Norman,* she had told him. *It'll suck your whole hand in. And then your arm. It'll crush everything.*

In his other hand Norman was carrying a doll with a china bisque head, which he never let out of his sight. His mother grabbed it, said, *I'll show you, boy,* and then let the wringer pull in the doll's foot. Norman had watched, fascinated yet horrified by the way the rollers crushed first one leg, then the other, then the torso and arms. But when it reached the head it had stopped, and Norman heard gears grinding. Then the implacable machine jerked in the remaining cloth, threads ripped, and the china bisque head fell to the hard earth of the cellar floor and shattered.

Norman had started to cry then, and his mother had shaken him and said, *Better that doll than you, Norman! That's a lesson you'll never forget! Besides, you're getting too old to play with dolls . . .*

She was right, of course. Mother was almost always right. She hadn't spoken to him for a long time, and now that he had banished her from his psyche, he sometimes found himself nostalgic for her. It surprised him. There were bad times, but there were good times too. Still, the times had never been so good that he wanted her to come back. No, Mother was as dead as dead could be, and she could be alive in his memory when he wished it so, but in no other way.

Today, as he walked down the hall, the attendant named

Frank right behind him, he wasn't thinking of his mother at all. He was thinking of seeing his brother again. Robert was coming tonight, and Norman was glad. Even though Robert had scared him with all that talk about killing people, Norman was sure that talk was all it was. Maybe Robert had just wanted Norman not to feel quite as bad about what he had done. It was a strange way to do it, since it made Robert look half crazy himself, but Norman understood that sometimes brothers did things for brothers that they wouldn't do for other people. Maybe Robert was talking about how he wanted to kill people just to be nice.

Now *that* was a silly thought, and it made Norman chuckle. Frank turned and looked at him. "What's so funny?" he said.

Norman dropped his smile and shook his head apologetically, then looked down. He didn't want to annoy Frank and have him end their walk early. There were always things to see . . .

"Okay, Wesley, I gotta tell you, this is your last chance."

Wesley Breckenridge lay on his back on the metal table on which a towel had been placed. Even so, lying there in his underwear, he was cold. Around each of his wrists was a tightened leather strap, and two attendants held them firmly at his sides. His legs were free. There was no pillow, so his head was slightly back, his nostrils raised.

"You gonna eat or not? You can drink this stuff, y'know. Make it a lot easier for all of us, you included."

"Uh-uh," Wesley said through chattering teeth.

"Your choice." Myron Gunn held a rubber tube, several feet long, in front of Wesley's eyes. "This is it. No?" Wesley didn't respond.

"Open the door. It's hot in here," Myron said, and one of the attendants did, and returned to hold down Wesley's left arm. Myron held the end of the tube and put it into a large jar of petroleum jelly. He pulled it out, removed the jelly from the hole at the end of the tube, then smeared the first few inches of the end with the jelly until it was covered, wiping his fingers on the edge of the towel that lay beneath Wesley.

Then Myron Gunn stuck the greased end into a small flask of what smelled to Wesley like alcohol. "Gotta make sure we don't get any germs down there. 'Cause it's gonna go all the way down." Myron chuckled, then looked at the attendant standing at Wesley's head, holding a leather strap. "I think we should just use lard to grease this thing—get a little more food down his throat."

The attendants laughed a bit, and Wesley's throat hitched.

"Now don't start that yet," Myron said. "I haven't even stuck the tube in. But it's time."

Myron nodded at the man at Wesley's head, and Wesley felt the leather strap go across his forehead, holding his head tightly to the surface of the table so he couldn't move it, either up and down or side to side. Then he saw the brown, greasy hose moving toward his face, and shut his eyes.

He felt the end of the hose enter his left nostril first, going in a few inches until it stopped. The tip pressed against the back of his throat, tickling the root of his tongue, and he started to gag.

"I think that side's a little too tight," Myron said. "Got an awful lot of hose to get down there. Let me try the other."

The tube slipped back out of Wesley's nose, and he gasped at the sudden pain. His sinuses felt like they were exploding, and there was burning behind his eyes. He opened them and saw the tube moving toward him again, and again he squeezed shut his now tearing eyes.

The rubber tip probed into his right nostril now, and it hurt, but not as much as the first time. "Aw, that's a *lot* better," Myron said as Wesley felt the tube snake down the back of his throat, deep, deeper, and he choked again.

"Just *swallow*," Myron said. "Nothing to it if you just swallow."

Wesley tried, and it helped, but the sensation was one that he had never before experienced, even in a nightmare, and the tears dripped from the corners of his eyes.

"Now, you don't have to cry—this is gonna be *good* for you."

Wesley opened his eyes, and through his tears he could see Myron Gunn looming over him, with still many inches of tubing in his hand. "Isn't that deep enough?" one of the attendants said.

"Nope. It's gotta go in up to this line," Myron said, pointing on the tube to a red line still several inches from Wesley's face. "Gotta get in the stomach, otherwise he could puke it all up, and, my friend, we don't want that. Now watch and learn . . ."

Wesley shut his eyes again and tried to pretend he was somewhere else. He thought about being outside on a summer day, sitting next to his wife before the terrible thing happened, and trying to remember how pretty she was, but it was difficult to do that as the tube continued to roll into him and tickle its way down his own tube, the one that led from mouth to stomach.

"All right, up to the line," Myron said after what seemed hours. "You can open your eyes, Wesley. You don't want to miss this."

Wesley opened them slowly, and saw Myron holding a glass quart jar filled with a thick greenish liquid in his left hand. In his right, he was holding above his head the end of the tube, which now had a plastic funnel inserted in it. "Dinnertime," he said, and he raised the jar up to the tube and poured in the green mixture.

Wesley didn't feel it going into his nose or down his throat at all, but he could feel it when it slopped into his empty stomach. It felt cold, not having been first warmed by his mouth and gullet. His stomach started to revolt against it, and he began to panic, wanting to reach up and grab the tube and rip it from his nose, but the attendants held his hands tight, and the man at his head pressed down even harder.

"Now, now," said Myron Gunn. "This is what you get when you won't eat your dinner like a good boy . . ." Myron's voice became softer and more dangerous. ". . . *and* when you chop up your wife with an ax."

Wesley opened his eyes and saw the hate in Myron's face.

"That's right, Wesley. This is what you get for your sins. This is how you only *begin* to atone for what you did, you little monster. Think this'll drive the demons out of you? Maybe not, but it's a good start."

And Myron Gunn poured the rest of the green liquid into the funnel until it was full.

Norman heard the moaning a long time before he and Frank reached the open door. He slowed his walk so that Frank got ahead of him and looked back. "Come on," Frank said. "Just guys doing their work."

Norman followed, getting closer to the sound that was coming from a door ahead on the left. Frank stopped when he got there and looked in. "Hi, guys," he said, and Norman heard the men inside respond, but the moaning didn't stop. He walked to where Frank, his arms crossed, was standing, and looked into the room.

Norman gasped. A nearly naked man lay on the table, held down by the others, while Myron Gunn held up a funnel and tube, a tube which, Norman saw, led into the man's now bleeding nose. The man was fighting against the three who held him, all his spindly muscles straining against the straps, but to no avail.

Then Myron Gunn fixed his gaze upon Norman, and Norman froze at the sight of his basilisk glare. "Well, well, if it isn't

Nor-man," Myron drawled, and gave Norman a smile that was no more than a smirk at the corner of his mouth. "Have you had your lunch, *Nor*-man? Maybe you'd like to join our boy Wesley here. I think we could rustle up an extra tube somewhere, couldn't we, boys? Whaddya say, Norman?"

Norman said nothing. He just gave his head a short shake. Myron set down the now empty funnel and walked slowly over to Norman, until their faces were nearly touching. The man's breath smelled of onions and something sour. Norman, trembling, looked down at the cement floor. Myron whispered so that only the two of them could hear.

"No? No, thank you? Well, don't worry, pal. I'll get you here eventually. Or maybe some hydrotherapy, like they did in the old days. Would you like that? Would you like me to hold you under-water until you can't breathe? Would you like me to hook up the electroshock to your fat head and leave it on maybe just a *little* bit too long? Maybe fry the Devil right out of you?"

Norman kept looking down and shook his head again, just a little shake to say no but not enough of a refusal that it would make Myron madder than he already was. At least Norman hoped not.

"Well, we're all done here, Norman," Myron said, moving back to the table and picking up the funnel. He detached it from the hose and looked down at the man lying on the table. "Taking out the tube is like taking off a Band-Aid, Wesley—you do it fast enough, and it only hurts for a second."

Then Myron took the end of the rubber tube and yanked. Norman watched as the tube flew from the man's nose, leaving a trail of blood, mucus, and something green. He felt tears sting his eyes as Myron took a wad of cotton and shoved it, none too gently, up the man's nose to stop the blood that was moving across his cheek like a small red snake.

Then Norman heard a voice he knew.

"What's going on here?"

He turned, feeling as guilty as if he had been one of the people torturing the man on the table. It was as though watching it was as bad as doing it. Nurse Marie was just behind him, and the look on her face was one he'd never seen before. She looked furious, and was glaring at Myron.

"How *dare* you do a procedure like this in front of another patient?" she said in a voice that was soft yet filled with anger. Not waiting for an answer, she turned to Norman. "Are you all right, Norman?" she asked, the anger gone from her tone.

Norman nodded, then looked down again, feeling like a child caught in an impossible situation.

"He's *fine*," Myron said. "He was *interested*. And I was explaining the procedure to him. Wasn't I, boys?"

The other three men nodded, and Nurse Marie looked at Frank. "Why didn't you take him away?" she said. "Go back the way you came?"

"I didn't know what was going on," Frank said. "The door was open."

"And *why* was it?" Marie said, whirling on Myron again. "These procedures aren't for open viewing!"

Now Myron's eyes narrowed and the smile left his face as he walked, his head out like a vulture's, toward Nurse Marie. Norman was suddenly afraid, not for himself, but for her. "The room," Myron said, stopping in front of her, "was warm. Hot as the pits of hell. And why I should even have to tell you why I opened the door is beyond me. The way I see it, you're just a nurse. I'm the head attendant. I'm the one who tells people what to do and when to do it, not you. Chain of command, Nurse."

"And do you think Dr. Reed would be happy about exposing his patient to this kind of"—she gestured to the blood on the table next to the man's head—"barbarity?"

"Force-feeding isn't pretty," Myron said, sneering. "A *lot* of what we do isn't pretty here. But we saved that man from starvation, and if he gets a bloody nose as a result, that's God's will. Now why don't you get your little busybody self out of where the *men* work, and if you want to squeal to Dr. Reed, go right ahead." He frowned at Norman. "His being here was an accident. If anybody's at fault, it's Frank. Right, Frank?"

Frank nodded. "Yeah, Myron, I just shoulda taken him back the way we came. Sorry." He turned to Marie. "Sorry, Nurse. I'll, uh, I'll make sure it doesn't happen again."

"There," Myron said. "Now everything's peachy again, isn't it? Frank, why don't you escort Nurse Radcliffe and *Mister* Bates back upstairs while we finish up with *Mister* Breckenridge here . . . unless the *nurse* would like to stanch the bleeding for *Mister* Breckenridge." He raised his eyebrows at Nurse Marie.

She looked at Frank. "Please take Norman upstairs." Then she walked into the room and over to the man on the table. "I'll be happy to take care of the patient," she said.

Norman felt Frank's hand on his arm, turning him toward the end of the hall. As they walked away, Norman looked back to see Myron Gunn leaning out the doorway into the hall. He waved goodbye to Norman with his fingers, then disappeared back into the room, closing the door firmly behind him.

8

"So, Dr. Berkowitz," Dr. Goldberg said, leaning back and luxuriating with one of the cigars he always seemed to be smoking in his office, "how have *you* found your first weeks here at the state hospital?"

Goldberg had just finished giving Elliot his observations on the resident's performance during the short time he had been at the hospital, and Elliot had been pleased by the laudatory qualities of it. Dr. Goldberg had a few suggestions, but seemed pleased by Elliot's performance so far.

"It's fascinating work, Doctor," Elliot said. "I was surprised to find that it really does feel like a mental hospital rather than . . . a prison. The correctional aspects are there, of course, but I've found that the doctors and staff, for the most part, are really interested in bringing about cures for the patients' various conditions. And they *seem* like patients rather than prisoners."

"I'm glad to hear that," Goldberg said. "That is what we strive for here, even though, like most state institutions, we are severely understaffed. Still, one must never forget that our patients are potentially quite dangerous, much more so than in the private facilities in which you have trained." Goldberg's face grew cloudy. "Our recent escapee is a prime example of that."

Elliot nodded. "There's been no trace of him?"

"Nothing. He seems to have vanished off the face of the earth. At times, considering the harm of which he is still capable, I almost hope that is true. I wait in fear of the reports of his next victim."

"Are you really afraid he'll rape again?"

"Yes. He was undergoing electroconvulsive shock treatments, and they were slowly making him more . . . civilized. But obviously not civilized enough. I think with several more months' work, we might have had a breakthrough." Goldberg paused and chuckled. "*Civilized*. That is what I wish to see every patient here eventually become, that is my dream." He raised his head and listened to the music playing softly from the other side of the room. "Opera," he said dreamily. "Perhaps we should give all the patients *opera* treatments. Were they to aspire to understanding and appreciating the finest, most all-encompassing of the arts, a blend of music, drama, dance, and art, then they might truly become civilized. I know of no opera devotee who ever went insane . . . oh, some of the *divas,* perhaps, but that's an occupational hazard."

Elliot laughed politely, though the comment was actually funny. It wasn't hard to appreciate Goldberg's bon mots, and Elliot found himself really liking the man. "You are a *big* opera fan, aren't you?" he said, as he gestured to the oversized shelves near the record player.

"I have been an aficionado since my youth in Vienna. I heard Mahler conduct, you know. One of the greatest Jewish composers and conductors. What a shame that he never composed an opera." Goldberg stood and walked toward the shelves holding several rows of boxed sets of long-playing records. "Come. See if there are some that you know."

"Well," Elliot said, standing and following him, "I have to confess I'm not all that familiar with opera. My mother would play the Saturday Met broadcasts when I was at home, so I've heard a lot of them, but at that age you don't pay too much attention. It was beautiful music, that's all I knew."

"And that is all one needs to know to start. A lifetime of joy awaits you." Goldberg displayed his collection with a gesture. "See what there is here that you might remember from childhood."

Elliot dutifully cocked his head to the right to read the titles on the boxes, and named several operas he remembered hearing. Then he paused. "You have a lot of Wagner."

"*Ja,* two different Ring cycles, and at least one of all his other operas, except for the very early ones."

"I'm . . . kind of surprised that you like him," Elliot said.

"You mean, of course, because of his virulent anti-Semitism."

"Well, yes. I mean, Israeli orchestras won't even play his music, will they? After all, he was Hitler's favorite composer. From everything I've heard, Wagner's music was the sound track for the Third Reich."

Goldberg nodded and took a puff on his cigar. "That is all true, but it is also true that Richard Wagner died half a century before Hitler became chancellor. He could not protest at the way his music was used, nor was he responsible for the way our people were treated." He sat in a chair next to the record player. "It has taken me many years to learn to separate the art from the artist, but I have done it, in Wagner's case, at least. His music is sublime, no matter what your faith or your race, and I feel that he, in his *art,* was touched by God, as were Mozart and Verdi and Puccini. I listen to the music, which is the finest manifestation of

Wagner's soul, not his anti-Semitic screeds. I have forgiven him his sins and celebrate only the beauty he has created."

Elliot smiled. "That's rather a good way to consider it."

"Is it not like our profession?" Goldberg said. "We do not seek to judge. We seek to observe, to appreciate the good."

"But," Elliot said, "we also try to unearth the bad, and, by understanding it and helping the patient understand it, we help to heal."

"Yes. To cure that sickness and thus dispel what people think of as evil. *Ja,* that is a good way to put it. Wagner's anti-Semitism was an illness. If we had been able to get him on the couch, who knows?"

"Perhaps the history of Germany would have been very different," Elliot said, thinking of his lost father.

"Or," Goldberg said, "perhaps he would have proven to be another Ronald Miller, and escaped as soon as we turned our backs."

There was a soft rapping on Dr. Reed's office door. "Come in," he said, glancing up from his patient reports. The door opened and Nurse Radcliffe stood there.

"Excuse me, Doctor," she said, "but do you have a moment?" Reed beckoned her in and motioned to the wooden chair in front of his desk. She sat. "You're seeing Norman late this afternoon, is that correct?"

"Yes."

"I think you should know there was an incident in the basement. Between him and Myron Gunn."

Reed straightened up. "What happened?"

Marie told him what she had come across; Norman witnessing Wesley Breckenridge's force-feeding and Myron's not-so-veiled threats to Norman. "I've never seen him so upset," she said. "And Myron was merciless—with Wesley too. I stayed to stop his nose-bleed after Frank took Norman upstairs, and . . . and Myron shut the door and just *watched* me as I worked. Not a word, but he looked at me like . . . well, it wasn't pleasant."

Reed shook his head. His mouth was a grim line. "Jesus . . . *Jesus,* why did Frank let him watch in the first place?"

"The door was open, and—"

"Well, right *there's* a breach of the rules!"

"And I think Frank . . . well, he's not as compassionate as some of the other attendants are."

"All right. I'll talk to him. And from now on only Ben and Dick take Norman on his walks—if I can ever get him to want to take a walk again. *Damn* Myron Gunn . . ."

Marie paused for a moment. "I don't know how to put this, since it's not really my place, but . . . would there be any way to file a complaint against him?"

"I've tried. Just between you and me, I've talked to Dr. Goldberg about his cruelty, but the doctor finds that his good qualities—his ability to control patients, oversee the attendants, and keep things contained when situations with patients have gotten chaotic—outweigh his negative qualities. I disagree, but then I'm not the superintendent." Reed stood up. "Thank you for letting me know, Nurse. I'll see what I can do. I think the first thing is to see Norman."

Norman was sitting on his bed, still trembling. He had tried to read a paperback Western by a man named Elmore Leonard, but, though he liked it, he couldn't keep his attention focused on the story of bounty hunters and their adventures. Norman couldn't get the picture out of his mind of that little man on the table, being held down while Myron Gunn yanked out that horrible piece of hose. It was so long.

Norman shuddered. And Myron Gunn had told Norman that he would do that to *him* someday, or drown him in one of those old tubs. Both ideas terrified him. And he believed that both things could come true. Myron Gunn seemed to have all the power in the hospital, more than Nurse Marie and Dr. Reed and Ben and *anyone* who was kind to him.

When the knock came on the door, Norman jumped straight up from the bed, even though the rap was gentle. He hugged himself to stop shaking, then said, "Yes?"

The door opened slowly, and Dr. Reed stood there. "May I come in?" Norman tried to speak, but found he could only nod. Dr. Reed entered slowly and sat in the chair. "I understand you had an unpleasant experience today. In the basement."

Norman nodded, and was able to finally get out a whispered, "Yes."

"That should *not* have happened, Norman. And none of it was your fault. It won't happen again."

"He . . . he said he'd do it to me . . . choke me like that . . . and drown me . . ."

"Myron Gunn, yes? He won't do anything of the sort. I'm in charge of your treatment, you know that, and I wouldn't let that happen to you. Now, you've got to try and relax and let that go. I know it's hard, that what you saw was very ugly, but that's not going to happen to you, I promise."

Dr. Reed reached into his pocket and Norman tensed, but he pulled out a pill wrapped in paper and then picked up the tin water cup on Norman's small table. "I'd like you to take this, Norman. It'll calm you down. Both because it's time for our talk today, and also because Robert will be visiting you tonight."

Norman gave a small gasp. In his alarm, he had forgotten that his brother was coming. Then he breathed out, took the pill, and swallowed it with the water.

Dr. Reed spoke very quietly during their therapy session. He asked not only about Norman's fears, but about what he liked here in the hospital, and whether anything made him think of home. When they were done, Norman felt better.

He still didn't eat very much of his dinner that night, and Nurse Marie frowned sympathetically when she took away the tray. Then he made himself read the book and waited for Robert to come.

Finally, later in the evening, Dr. Reed knocked again, opened the door, and said, "Norman, Robert's here," and stepped back so that Robert could enter, and then closed the door behind them.

"Hey, little brother," Robert said.

"Hey, *big* brother," Norman replied.

"Hear you had a bad day."

"Well . . . yeah, sort of."

"Doc told me about it. About this guy, what's his name, Gunn?"

"Myron Gunn."

"Yeah. Doc Reed didn't tell me what time it happened, but let me take a guess. Maybe around . . . two-thirty this afternoon. What do you think?"

Norman didn't have a watch or a clock in his room, but he thought it would have been around then, since the attendants usually came to the social hall at two to get him for his exercise. "That's right," he said. "How did you know?"

"Remember what I told you before? About us being psychically linked? You know what happened to me at two-thirty today?"

"What?"

"We were between lunch and dinner, just one or two customers were in the diner, and I was taking it a little easy. Sitting back in the kitchen reading the morning paper. What with people coming in all through the morning, I never have time to read it till after lunch. Anyway, I was reading the funnies, you know, the comic strips? And I'd gotten to 'Dick Tracy' when all of a sudden I went cold all over. I guess I kind of, I don't know, blacked out for a minute, you know? And I saw this . . . this stone tunnel, like underground somewhere. And these stone walls are on either side of me, and it's dark, but I hear somebody moaning.

"And then this face comes up in front of me, and it's ugly, and this face is grinning at me, but not a happy grin. It's like the toothy grin of some monster that wants to rip me apart, and I know damn well that if I don't do something, like turn and run, that this thing is really gonna get me. So I turn to run away, and the sudden jerk wakes me up. And there I am in the kitchen again, with my eyes on 'Dick Tracy.'"

Robert leaned in to Norman and put a hand on his shoulder. "I think I was here with you when that happened, brother. I think I was seeing—or maybe *feeling*—through you. I think you got so upset, your emotions were so strong, that I felt them, and saw something of what you were experiencing." Robert gave a little laugh. "Sounds crazy, doesn't it?"

Norman didn't know what to think. He remembered the dream *he* had had, about the tunnel and chamber filled with blood dripping from the ceiling, and he wondered if somehow he had seen through Robert's eyes. But no, that was impossible. Robert wasn't a killer, no matter how much he talked about it.

Then, as though Robert was reading his mind, his brother said, "Have you had anything strange like that happen to you lately?"

"I . . . I don't think so. Some bad dreams, that's all."

"Bad dreams? When was that?"

"A while back . . ." Then he remembered. It was the night that Ronald Miller had disappeared.

"What was it about?"

"It was . about blood. A room filled with blood."

Robert looked more serious than usual. "Old memories?"

"I . . . don't know. I'm not sure . . . but probably, yes. All those bad things that I have so very little memory of."

"*Old* bad things?" Robert asked. "Or *new?*"

"New? There's nothing new like that . . ." Norman thought for a moment, remembering some of the things that Dr. Reed had talked to him about, how the things and people he was afraid of, like Ronald Miller and Myron Gunn, could creep into his subconscious mind and give him bad dreams. They could even depress him when he wasn't even specifically thinking about them. They were still there all the time.

"Did you ever think," Robert said, "that just like I might have seen what was inside your head, you might sometimes see what's in mine?"

Norman looked at his brother's face, and felt dizzy. Could the figure in the room of blood of which he'd dreamed actually have been Robert?

"Who was in that room with you in your dream, Norman? Did you see anyone?"

"I . . . yes. There was a man . . . but I couldn't see his face."

Robert smiled. "Do you think it could have been me?"

"I . . . don't know. But why? How *could* it have been? I'm not afraid of you, you're my *brother.* Why would I have nightmares about you?"

"Who's to say it was a nightmare?" Robert asked.

Norman waited for him to say more, but he only sat there smiling. Finally Norman said, "I think we should talk about something else. Let's talk about . . . your family. How's Mindy?"

Robert leaned back, and some of the tension went out of him. He told Norman about what Mindy had been doing, about her helping with a bake sale as part of the Rotary Women's Auxiliary (Robert was treasurer of the local Rotary), and about how John and Susie were doing in school (John was having some trouble with math, so they'd hired a tutor, and Susie really liked a new boy in seventh grade whose family had just moved to the area). He also related some stories about certain characters in the diner that made Norman laugh.

But as his brother talked on, Norman found himself thinking about what Robert had said about his dream possibly mirroring reality. Did Robert mean to suggest that he had actually killed someone? It seemed that way. But why? And who? Maybe, he thought as he had before, Robert was just trying to—what was the word that Dr. Reed had used?—*bond* with Norman by identifying with Norman's past deeds. But that was stupid, wasn't it? Since it was those very deeds that had brought him here, and that insured he would never again be a free man.

Robert finished a story that Norman barely heard but chuckled at anyway. "You getting tired?" Robert asked.

Norman shrugged. "Oh, maybe a little. It was kind of a stressful day."

"Right. With that Myron Gunn. Don't worry. He won't hurt you."

"It's not just me I'm worried about," Norman said. "He threatened Nurse Marie. She's my friend. I'd hate to have anything bad happen to her."

Robert took Norman's hand in his own. "Little brother, nothing bad is going to happen to her. Or to you. I'm going to make sure of that. Anyone tries to hurt you or your friends, well . . . let's just say they'll be sorry."

A knock came on the door, and Robert let go of Norman's hand and stood up. "Time for me to go."

They said goodbye, the door opened, and Norman saw Dr. Reed in the hall as Robert walked out. The doctor smiled at Norman and closed and locked the door.

It was quiet in Norman's room. He didn't even hear Robert and Dr. Reed's footsteps as they went down the corridor. He lay back on his bed and closed his eyes. But as soon as he did, he became aware of something. It was like a mouse scuttling somewhere at the edges of his brain, and he realized that it was Mother.

Norman . . .

No. She wanted to come out again, but he wouldn't let her. He had put her away, and she would stay there, deep down in the cellar of his brain. No one would open that door again to let her out. He pushed it shut and held it tightly until the echo of her voice faded away.

9

The next morning, Eleanor Lindstrom was sitting in her office smoking her third cigarette of the day and halfway through her first cup of coffee when there was a knock on her door. She knew who it was. She'd put a note in Marie Radcliffe's box last night telling her to come see her as soon as she got in the next morning. Eleanor didn't acknowledge the knock right away. Let the bitch stew a little, she thought.

Finally she inhaled and exhaled her last drag, stubbed out her smoke, and said, "Come in."

The door opened, and Radcliffe was standing there, the note in her hand. "You wanted to see me, Nurse Lindstrom?" She seemed nervous. That was good.

"Yes. Close the door." Eleanor didn't invite her to sit down. Let her stand. "Now. I understand you had a run-in with some of the attendants yesterday. In a treatment room."

"Yes, ma'am."

"And I also understand that you were giving them orders—including orders to the head attendant, is *that* right?"

"I . . . was rather forceful in expressing my feelings," Radcliffe said. "I don't recall if I actually gave any *orders*—I think not."

"But you were highly critical of them."

"They were performing a forced feeding with the door open, allowing another patient to witness it, and that *is* against procedure. And, I might add, the treatment given the patient being fed was harsh, with little attention given to his well-being."

Radcliffe's face was red, and Eleanor smiled at her, but it wasn't a pleasant smile. "The attendants were in charge of force-feeding, not you, and it's essential that there be no antagonism between attendants and nurses. We all depend on each other in this hospital. If there was a breach of protocol, you should have reported it to me, as your immediate superior. That's how it works here. Now, I've talked through this whole situation with the head attendant, and you were *way* out of line with what you said and did. I'm giving you a warning, which will go into your file. If there should be any repetition of such actions, you will be let go. Do you understand me?"

Radcliffe looked as though she wanted to punch Eleanor. She was trembling, and grabbed her right hand with her left to stop Eleanor's note from shaking like a leaf in the wind.

"Do you?" Eleanor said.

"Yes, ma'am."

"Then I want you to write a note of apology to the head attendant, regretting your reaction and assuring him that you won't behave like that again."

Radcliffe was quiet, but it appeared that she was seething inside. "All right. If that's what you want," she said.

"Good. Bring it to me tomorrow and I'll see that it's delivered. That's all."

Radcliffe left the office, closing the door behind her so gently that Eleanor almost wished she had slammed it shut instead. At any rate, that should take care of that stuck-up little bitch for a while.

Eleanor picked up her coffee and sipped. She couldn't wait to see Myron's face when she handed him that apology. He had been nearly apoplectic the previous evening when he'd told her about Radcliffe's intrusion. He'd had to be cool when his men were around, but he'd really let it rip when he was with Eleanor. They'd gone down to the empty laundry area again so he could vent, and it didn't take long before she turned his anger into hard lovemaking, which was just what they had both known she would do.

There was only one other person who knew about Eleanor's feelings for Myron Gunn, and that was Tess Asher. Tess and she had come to the state hospital together and formed a friendship right away. Myron was just an attendant then, but Eleanor had made no bones about being attracted to him, married or not, and had confided such to Tess. She hadn't slept with Myron until some years later, after she was divorced from that useless husband of hers. By that time, her ambition had taken her to the position of head nurse, and she had grown apart from Tess, but she always suspected that Tess knew of her lengthy and ongoing affair with Myron. She could tell from the way Tess looked at the two of them as they walked the halls together, and once, when Tess was on night shift, she had seen Eleanor and Myron coming up from a tryst in the cellar, Eleanor's face still flushed, and Myron wearing his satisfied-more-than-usual after-sex smirk.

Still, she'd never even mentioned it to Eleanor during the few conversations they had, which were now mostly business. Eleanor was grateful for that, and she'd never had the temptation to tell Tess or anyone else what was really going on between her and Myron. She knew he could be difficult, but she loved him just the same. If he got impatient with the patients—and hell, they were *criminals,* after all, weren't they?—who could blame him for that? Christ, she got pissed off often enough herself at the loonies. You had to be a saint not to.

Eleanor always wanted more from Myron, though. They'd played their little screwing-in-the-cellar game (and occasionally in an empty patient room, though that was riskier) for years, and neither of them was getting any younger. She knew that Myron had no relations with his wife, but his damned religion kept him from leaving her, and she couldn't understand why. He wasn't even a Catholic.

She kept hoping he'd change his mind, finally have had enough of living with a stick, and tell her he wanted them to be together all the time. Just in case, she romantically had a packed bag in the trunk of her car, with a sexy negligee and enough clothes to last several days if and when Myron ever told her that he wanted to be with her. Then they could hop in a car and go somewhere for a weekend or a whole week, as a start to their lives as a real couple.

It was foolish, she knew, but it gave her hope. They could be happy together, if Myron would just realize it.

Several nights later, a strong storm had come up across the land from the Gulf. The cold air, driven by the winds, was bone-chilling, but just below the edge of forming ice or snow. Huge raindrops fell out of the dark swirling skies onto the windshield of a car at the back of the parking lot for the State Hospital for the Criminally Insane. The car was black, and was dark inside as well.

A man was seated behind the wheel. He wasn't smoking, not wanting to risk drawing attention to himself by the flash of a match or the burning glow of a cigarette, if it could have been glimpsed at all through the maelstrom outside.

Such caution was probably unnecessary, anyway, since the few people he had seen leave the facility were holding umbrellas in front of them and keeping their heads down so as not to receive a face full of icy raindrops. Not once did any of them even glance in his direction.

Still, he was able to see them, at least when they opened their car doors and the dome lights illuminated their bodies and sometimes their faces. The man was watching for the person he thought of as his quarry, but he hadn't seen him yet. He wondered if he would. He had to get a sense of his prey's schedule, and he suspected that it wasn't a regular one, that under certain circumstances he would stay longer, leave earlier, perhaps even stay all night.

It wasn't easy to take the quarry. One didn't just waltz in and do it. That was how one got caught. And the man didn't want to get caught. He hadn't before, and he didn't intend to now.

What he intended to do was to take his man and make him pay for what he had done. Pay with his life.

The winds increased. The rain fell more heavily, drumming on the steel roof of the black car. The man leaned toward the windshield, turned the ignition key, and flicked on the wipers. Someone was coming into the parking lot with an umbrella over him . . . *wait* . . . over him and a woman huddled close to him. He took her to a car and held the umbrella over her as she got into the driver's side, then waved goodbye as her car started and she drove away.

As the man with the umbrella started toward his own vehicle, the man in the black car recognized him. It was Dr. Felix Reed. Not his quarry. He turned off the wipers and leaned back on the seat, waiting for the next person to leave.

At this point, the man in the car wasn't sure where he would take his quarry, but once he had a better sense of the man's schedule, he would make the decision. Perhaps it would simply be best to do it as he had done it the last time. That had been efficient. And satisfying. It had been *deeply* satisfying. Vengeance always was. And vengeance was what he would take. Not for himself directly, but for those who shared his blood.

The storm continued through the night and into the next day, filled with buffeting winds and drenching rain. There were periods when it lessened in ferocity, but by early the following evening it had returned in its full strength. Thunder and lightning had been added to the mix as well, and the patients had been restless all day. A number of nurses and attendants had been asked to stay late and earn overtime, adding to the usually reduced night shift.

Naturally Eleanor Lindstrom and Myron Gunn were working late, overseeing their charges both professional (the nurses and attendants) and medical (the patients). Both had their hands full. With every new crash of thunder, certain rooms produced cries, bangings, and hammerings, and nurses armed with pills and hypos filled with sedatives were escorted by burly attendants into those rooms to administer medicinal calm, voluntarily received or not.

Most of the disturbed patients were talking about ghosts. It was as if the thunder and lightning had made them recall all the other tropes of horror films they might have seen when they were free, as well as ghostly tales they'd heard in their youth and there in the confines of the state hospital. The facility was rich in spectral lore and history.

The majority of patients bore the storm as anyone else would, but that still left dozens of terrified men in need of calming, and it took some time. Myron Gunn seemed to be everywhere at once, lending authority and muscle wherever they were needed. He was none too gentle with the patients, actually sitting on some of the recalcitrant ones who refused to submit to an injection.

Marie Radcliffe was concerned about Norman Bates, and

when she saw Dr. Reed in one of the corridors, trying to lend some order to the chaos, she asked him if he wanted her to check on Norman. "Not necessary," the doctor said. "I just did, and the thunder and lightning don't seem to be bothering him at all. His light's off and he's sleeping like a baby. Let's not disturb him." Reed looked at his watch. "How long are you all here?"

"They asked the overtime people to stay until midnight. The storm is due to move out around then," Marie said. "Although most of the patients are tractable at this point."

"They seem to be. I think I'll head home. It's been a long day, and there really isn't anything else for me to do here. Maybe I'll grab a burger at Delsey's if they haven't been washed away. Did Ben stay tonight?"

"Yes," Marie said with a smile.

"Good. Then you've got someone to walk you to your car." He grinned. "Someone who might do a far better job than me."

She laughed. "At least I remembered my umbrella today."

"I doubt you could have left your house without it. See you tomorrow, Nurse." And Dr. Reed disappeared down the hall toward his office.

Despite Marie Radcliffe's optimistic estimate, it took until nearly midnight for all the patients to settle down. Dr. Goldberg received the reports from Nurse Lindstrom and Myron Gunn, told them to dismiss everyone except the night staff, then retired to his office, where he would spend the night, as he often did.

Myron had always thought that was pretty cushy, to have a big office with a daybed and a bathroom with a shower. If he had that kind of setup, he would *never* go home to that dry, unloving bitch Marybelle, and he would bring Eleanor into his office with him

too, and they could make love on something other than a big pallet of towels.

As he and Eleanor separated, she to find and dismiss the overtime nurses, he to do the same with the attendants, he thought
that tonight might be a good time for him and Eleanor to get together in the basement again. It was much later than when they
regularly left the hospital for the night, so there would be fewer
snooping eyes. He had already called Marybelle to tell her that
he didn't know when he'd be home, and Eleanor had no one to
call anyway. They could do it the whole night if they really
wanted to.

The more he thought about it, the more he wanted it to happen. Eleanor was a hell of a woman, and sometimes he thought he
really loved her. She understood him in a way Marybelle never
had, and he could see spending the rest of his life with her. It was
a much prettier picture than growing old with Marybelle. That
woman would continue to dry up until all that was left was hide
and bones, and eventually even that would turn to dust and blow
away. But it would be a long, long time before that happened.

Maybe Jesus wouldn't mind too much if he left Marybelle.
Maybe he'd understand, even if Pastor Oley Crowe wouldn't. It's
not like he'd be the *first* member of the First Baptist Holiness
Church to get a divorce. Chuck and Joanie Medford had split up a
few years back after Chuck caught Joanie with the Fuller Brush
man, and Chuck still came to church and everybody treated him
okay, even though they said behind his back that he deserved it for
marrying a woman twenty years younger than him. And Jimbo Pe-
ters divorced his wife so he could marry the bookkeeper at his Ford
dealership, and nobody groused about it much, especially after he
donated enough for the church to buy a new electric organ.

Well, it wasn't a decision he had to make right away. He and

Eleanor had been doing the deed for years now, and she never pressured him much. Might as well take your happiness where and when you can. Tomorrow would take care of itself.

At last he rounded up all the overtime attendants, most of whom had gathered in the staff break room, which was filled with cigarette smoke by the time Myron got there. He dismissed them all, and gruffly, almost grudgingly, offered thanks for their work, as though embarrassed that he needed their help to subdue the patients during the storm.

As they filed out, he got a cup of coffee from the machine and sat sipping it. He suspected that Eleanor would come to the break room looking for him. He could have gone to her office, but he didn't want to act like a dog in heat. And besides, after all the activity of the evening, he welcomed a chance to just sit down with a cup of java before exerting himself again, no matter how pleasurably. He stretched his muscles, thinking that he wasn't as young as he used to be. Hell, he wasn't young at all anymore. Fifty-two. All the more reason to think about making whatever changes he needed to make before he became too set in his ways.

By the time Eleanor came in, he had finished his coffee, and the brief rest had reinvigorated him. She stopped in the doorway when she saw him, and smiled a close-lipped, sultry smile.

"Evening, ma'am," he said. "Buy you a cup of coffee?"

She leaned back into the corridor and looked both ways, then stepped back into the room, walked over to him, put her hand on his shoulder, and squeezed gently. Clever girl. She was thinking exactly what he was.

To further prove her cleverness, she was carrying a clipboard with papers on it, something they could look at and discuss if anyone saw them in the corridors. "So here we are," Myron said, "just staying late and taking care of business after a crazier than usual night."

"Working hard to make the State Hospital for the Criminally Insane as safe and efficient as it could possibly be," Eleanor said.

"We ought to get citations," Myron said, in a rare moment of humor.

"We ought to get *some* reward for such a hard night," she said, squeezing his shoulder again.

"You know," Myron said, getting to his feet, "maybe we ought to check the basement to make sure we didn't miss anybody down there. Hate to have someone think they had to stay when they could be on their way home."

"You're all heart, Myron," Eleanor said. "Let's go do a good deed." And they walked together out of the break room and down the hall toward the stairway that led to the cellar.

Though she had been in the cellar thousands of times since she began working at the state hospital, Eleanor Lindstrom never really liked it. The stone walls and the hard floor were oppressive. It always felt like a dungeon to her.

She especially didn't like it at night, which she realized was ridiculous, since there were no windows down there, so day and night were both the same. Still, it felt different at night, and she always recalled the stories she had heard over the years about the ghosts of insane and demented men and women who inhabited the building all those years before. She tried to tell herself that the *living* creatures who resided there now were far worse than any ghosts, but she still couldn't keep the short hairs on the back of her neck from trembling when she had to go down there alone at night.

Now, thank God, she wasn't alone. Myron, the strongest and toughest man in the entire facility, was with her, so she didn't need to fear ghosts *or* patients. And, she reassured herself, she didn't need to fear being discovered making love by any wayward nurse or attendant. No one ever came down here this late, not until the laundry people started showing up at six in the morning.

The laundry area was far less disconcerting than the other parts of the cellar. For one thing, it was warmer. Heat from the washers and dryers gathered and remained in the rooms, so that even hours after the machines stopped running, it was still balmy.

The surroundings were less depressing as well. The rooms were painted white, and when Myron flicked on the overhead lights, the brightness, the smell of fresh laundry, and the memories of past lovemaking sessions eased Eleanor's mind. She could feel the tension flow out of her as Myron embraced her from behind, and she took in a deep breath of relief.

Together they walked toward a pallet of white towels. They were worn and thin, but an abundance of them made for wonderful softness beneath. When they stopped, Eleanor was surprised when Myron kissed her, not hard and roughly, with his usual brutal need, but almost tenderly, as though . . .

No. She wouldn't allow herself to think that. She would take this for what it was, nothing more, no matter how much she wanted it to be. Still, she kissed him back with as much passion as she felt coming from him. Holding her, he looked steadily into her face and started to unbutton her uniform blouse. She almost drew back, and he saw the question in her eyes. "Let's be naked," he said with a rasp in his voice as he continued to undo the buttons. "Let's finally be naked."

They had always made love partially clothed before, both for the sake of convenience and out of concern for being discovered, but there was no rush and no one to discover them now. Eleanor looked up at the shining fluorescent lights. "It's so bright . . ." Her protest was feeble, but Myron acted on it. He went to the bank of switches and turned off nearly all of them, so that only the constant light from the corridor illuminated their love nest.

Then he returned and continued to undress her while she did the same to him. When they were wearing only underwear, Myron lowered Eleanor to their bed of towels, lay over her, then slipped off her panties, while she helped him with his shorts.

"Dear Lord," he whispered, "you're so beautiful. I had no idea how much."

"Oh baby," she said, pulling him down toward her, "oh, my sweet man . . ."

They really made love then. It wasn't just sex, as it had been so many times before. She felt something different in him, something new, and she realized with joy that while things might never be what she wanted them to be, they would be much better from now on. When the moment came, she closed her eyes and let the feeling take her. It was wonderful, and she felt Myron shudder at the very same time, shiver like everything in him had poured out at once and left him weak and exhausted.

And lifeless.

Startled, she opened her eyes and in the dim light she saw Myron's face above hers, in a familiar rictus that had always signaled his moment of arrival, but now, she saw, meant something quite different. Blood was trickling from Myron's open mouth, and his eyes were wide in shock. He coughed once, and warm blood splashed into Eleanor's eyes, blinding her, so she didn't see him roll off of her, but nonetheless felt him withdraw from her and list like a mass of dead flesh off her right side, off the pile of towels, flopping onto the cold cement floor.

Eleanor rubbed her eyes and blinked wildly, trying to clear her vision, but Myron's salty blood stung them too badly. She could just make out a human shape standing above her, shadowed against the light from the corridor. Her ears were filled with Myron's gasping as he struggled to breathe, and then words came out in whispers, borne on the shallowest of breaths: ". . . Oh,

Jesus . . . so sorry . . . f'give me . . . f' my . . . sins . . . Lord . . . oh . . ."

The last sound dropped into the darkness that surrounded Eleanor, and the shape began to descend upon her, shutting off the light from the hall; descend upon her, as Myron had done with his gift of love, but the gift this shadow carried was much, much different.

With a sudden burst of strength, Eleanor threw her body to the side and fell off the pile of towels directly onto Myron. The huffing groan he gave told her he was still alive, and she felt the wetness of his blood as she tried to push herself away from him and scuttle farther from death on her hands and knees. His hand grasped her ankle as though clinging to her meant clinging to life, and she kicked hard with her other leg, felt her heel hit his face, heard the crunch of bone, and for an instant hated herself for having done it. Then self-preservation took control once more, and, now free, she crawled farther into the darkness with no plan but to hide, like a child escaping the bogeyman.

There was no place to hide. She heard footsteps behind her, and pushed herself to her feet, planning to run, but she saw only a dark wall ahead of her. Fight, then. She was naked and vulnerable, but she could fight.

She whirled around, arms raised, fists clenched, ready to strike. But it was already too late. The shadow was in front of her, and she felt one hand grasp her neck and the other hand drive into her soft stomach that long, sharp thing whose shape she had glimpsed. She felt it worm its way up like a living creature inside her, and her fists fell to her sides. When the knife slipped out and the hand released her throat, the rest of her fell as well, down to the hard floor. She died within two seconds of her head striking the cement.

———

Myron Gunn wasn't so lucky. The knife had entered his back, severing his spinal column and rooting about in his left lung before it was withdrawn. He knew why he was dying. God had sent an angel of death because of Myron's sins, because he had not only betrayed his wife by becoming an adulterer, but also because he had fallen in love with Eleanor, and the thought had come to him, sure and strong, of leaving Marybelle for her. That had been the last straw for Jesus, Myron was certain. You couldn't keep defying the laws of God with impunity. His sins had found him out at last.

He was lying on his back now, looking up into the blackness of the ceiling. It seemed as though dark clouds were gathering up there. Though he could no longer speak, he prayed silently that those clouds would break open into the sunshine of heaven.

But instead, a darker cloud drifted across his view, a black moon that he realized was his killer's head. It descended close to his, only inches away, and then, in spite of all his other pain, Myron felt something tickling at his nostril. At the first prick, he knew it was a knife.

And as the blade slipped up into his nose, he remembered Wesley Breckenridge, and he prayed harder than he had ever prayed before.

The man drove the car down the nearly deserted road, the high beams on. When he saw the sign for the motel he slowed. He'd seen it before, but not at night, and was concerned he might miss the turnoff.

There it was, the long strip of rooms, the office at the one end, and up above stood the house, abandoned now, the windows empty eyes in the gaunt face of peeling boards. He drove the car around the back of the motel and up the gravel drive toward the house. But he didn't stop there.

The driveway went around the rear of the house and stopped at a dilapidated wooden shed that had been used as a garage. The man looked carefully and discerned, just beyond the shed, a pair of grooves in the brown grass, worn nearly flat by tires over the years. The path led into a field. On a clear night, the lights of the car might have been visible from the road, but rain was still pattering down, and a dense fog had formed in the wake of the night's earlier, savage storm, so the man used the low beams, and the rough road was visible if he watched intently.

At last the car reached the edge of the swamp. There was an incline leading down to its miry surface, and the man suspected it was the same place at which Norman Bates had dumped the car belonging to Mary Crane. The man stopped the car several yards from where solid ground turned to quagmire, pushed the "neutral" button on the automatic transmission, pulled the parking brake, and opened all the windows. Then he got out, closed the door, and reached back through the driver's window. He grasped the steering wheel and turned it until the tires were aimed straight ahead into the muck.

He opened the door, took off the parking brake, and pushed the "drive" button, getting out quickly and slamming the door shut. Then he ran behind the already moving vehicle and pushed with all his might, helping the transmission move the car slowly forward toward the thick mire of the swamp. He pushed until the front tires went in, and continued to push as the entire front of the car started to submerge. Not until the tips of his shoes dipped beneath the muddy surface did he stop pushing.

By then, gravity was doing his work for him. The car was going down, though slowly. He watched as the swamp muck poured in through the open windows, making the car even heavier. He had no doubt it would sink fully. It had worked for Norman, so why not for him?

Still, he felt a bit of trepidation, the same tension Norman had felt, no doubt, when the sinking of the car slowed to almost a standstill. It wouldn't be the end of the world if the car was discovered, but it was bound to make things easier if it wasn't.

Ah, it was going down faster now. It was incredible, he thought, how deep the drop-off must be between ground and swamp. Only the top of the trunk was showing. It was as though it was driving down a very steep ramp in the swamp. Finally there were what sounded like a phlegmatic inhalation of breath through a gigantic throat and a series of thick bubbles from displaced air far below, and the car was gone.

The man smiled and pulled up the collar of his waterproof coat as further protection against the rain. His hat had kept his head relatively dry, but he had a long way to walk through the wet, chilly weather. Still, he was glad for the rain. It would certainly erase all the tire tracks by morning.

He hunched his shoulders against the wind and started to walk toward the road.

Norman Bates awoke and switched on the light. Despite the warmth of his room, he was trembling with cold. He'd had another dream, but this one had been less explicit than the previous one about the figure bathed in blood.

In the dream from which he had just awakened, he couldn't recall where it had taken place, but it was certainly not the ovoid room in the earlier dream. All he remembered, all he had *seen,* really, were two faces, faces that were strangely familiar but that he couldn't place. They seemed out of context, somehow, and he thought about when he was a boy and had seen his schoolteacher, Mrs. Hoffman, at the grocery store when he'd gone in with Mother. It didn't make *sense* to see Mrs. Hoffman anywhere other than the schoolhouse, and he had stood there stunned while she smiled down at him and Mother asked what on earth was wrong and why was he acting so moony.

Was it like that now? Norman wondered. But he was sure the faces were from where he was now, the hospital, and not his life before. If it wasn't a different place, then, could it be something else? Could it be . . . ?

Their expressions.

There are certain people whose expressions never change, at least when they're in certain places or doing certain things. There are people, Norman thought, who are so used to acting one way that when you see them acting another way you don't even recognize them.

People who are strong and tough and mean. You wouldn't know who they were when they were terrified, would you? When their faces were trembling and tears were coming from their eyes, like the two faces in the dream. You wouldn't know them. Unless you thought about it . . .

And those were the reflections that led Norman to the realization that he had seen Myron Gunn and Nurse Lindstrom in his dream. Once he recalled who they were, he remembered the details of the dream more clearly. There had been a nimbus around their heads, a glowing aura of . . . red, yes, red like the previous dream, and instead of their white uniforms, their necks and shoulders had been bare. But their faces—that was what had been so terrible. To see such strong, unyielding personalities cringing and shuddering, *fearing,* was upsetting to Norman, even though he had no love for either of them.

And perhaps, he conjectured, that was what caused the dream—his *wanting* to see them suffer as they'd made others suffer. He'd never had any personal experience with Nurse Lindstrom, but her attitude had always been chilly toward him, and he'd heard stories in the social hall and the exercise yard about things she did to certain patients who displeased her. Maybe that was why his subconscious mind had placed her in such peril in his dream.

He'd have to tell Dr. Reed about it during their next session. It would be something to talk about with Robert too.

And then he remembered Robert, and what Robert had said to him about Myron Gunn, about how if anyone tried to hurt Norman or his friends, they would be sorry.

How sorry? Norman wondered. Could it be possible that Robert had actually done something to Myron Gunn? Lay in wait for him when he left the hospital? And had Norman seen part of what had happened through that psychic connection Robert had talked about? But then why was Nurse Lindstrom in his dream or vision or whatever it was? Had she been with Myron Gunn at the time? Had Robert hurt them both? Hurt them to try and keep Norman safe?

The thought that people might have suffered for something he'd said to Robert made him sick to his stomach. He didn't like Myron Gunn, but he didn't want any harm to come to him. No, he'd had enough of that. Still, he felt a sense of guilt settle heavily on his shoulders, as though *he* had been responsible, if what had happened in his dream had been reality, and he looked at his hands as if expecting to see them stiffly coated with dried blood.

But Norman's hands were clean, even his cuticles and under his nails. And there came to him the words of that story by Poe, "The Tell-Tale Heart," that he had read so often as a boy and later as a man:

. . . no stain of any kind—no blood-spot whatever. I had been too wary for that. A tub had caught all—ha! ha!

Norman shuddered at the words, looked at his spotlessly clean hands once again, turned off the light, and tried to go back to sleep.

10

The following morning the state hospital was abuzz. If one supervisor hadn't shown up for work without calling in sick, it would have been inconvenient enough. But when *two* people, in particular the head nurse and the chief attendant, failed to appear at their usual times, the organizational house of cards threatened to topple.

When he was informed of the no-shows, Dr. Goldberg quickly appointed Senior Nurse Wyndham, a fifteen-year veteran, to oversee the nurses, and Ray Wiseman, who had been an attendant since the hospital had opened in 1939, was chosen to act as temporary head attendant.

Judy Pearson, at Goldberg's request, kept calling both Nurse Lindstrom's and Myron Gunn's homes. Just before 10:00 a.m., Marybelle Gunn answered. No, Myron hadn't come home at all last night, and she had no idea where he was—she'd just been over to her mother's house telling her about it, which was why she hadn't answered the phone. No one answered the phone at Eleanor Lindstrom's house, but Judy tried every ten minutes.

Doctors Goldberg, Steiner, Reed, and Berkowitz met in Goldberg's office, and Goldberg told them that he didn't think the disappearance of Gunn and Lindstrom was a coincidence. "I have long suspected," he said in his thick accent, made thicker by morning phlegm, "that the relationship between Mr. Gunn and Nurse Lindstrom may have been more than purely professional. As long as I was given no proof of this, and since it did not affect their work, I chose to turn a blind eye. But now, gentlemen, we must don our investigators' deerstalkers as well as our usual hats, and ferret out what our two missing colleagues may have done and where they have gone. It may be something simple, or it may be scandalous, if such a thing as scandal still exists in this most modern world.

"So while Miss Pearson continues to try and contact our missing pair, let us see what might be in their offices—if they have emptied them out—whether or not their automobiles are here—see if they hinted to anyone of their individual or joint plans . . . yes, Dr. Steiner?"

Steiner lowered his raised hand. "In light of Ronald Miller's recent escape, should we . . . well, do you think it might be advisable to contact law enforcement?"

Goldberg looked puzzled. "I don't understand the connection."

"Well," Steiner said, "there's been no trace of Miller either nearby or farther away. He could still be in the area. His case file suggests an extreme sadistic personality, and if a personality such as that has a desire for vengeance as well . . ." He shrugged.

"So you are suggesting that Ronald Miller might have . . . what? Kidnapped or harmed Myron and Nurse Lindstrom?"

"It's possible."

"I suppose it is, but there have been no indications of foul play of which I am aware. While there *may* be indications of a lovers' tryst. Also, in the absence of such evidence of violence as what you suggest, Dr. Steiner, I believe the authorities require one to wait a certain length of time, twenty-four hours or so, before opening a missing persons investigation, is that not right?"

Dr. Berkowitz cleared his throat. "Excuse me, but that's a common misconception, Doctor. If there's any indication of violence, or unusual circumstances, the police want to hear about it. The sooner their investigation starts, the easier it is for them to pick up the trail."

Goldberg beamed. "Ah, *mein jüngerer Bruder,* you have knowledge of more than psychiatry. And what you say makes sense. But before we contact the authorities, may we at least search the two prodigals' offices and also see if their cars are present, for I am sure the *Polizei* will wish to know that. And who knows, perhaps we may find a note saying that they decided to go together to a psychiatric conference in Omaha." Goldberg chuckled, and the rest gave feeble laughs. "Also, I have already asked Mr. Wiseman to have all the attendants search all floors of the building thoroughly to make sure that the couple is not here, the same kind of search that was carried out after Miller's escape. And I'm sure that if there are any indications of violence, we will know quickly."

The parking lot was found to contain Eleanor Lindstrom's green Buick Skylark, though Myron Gunn's black DeSoto Firedome was absent. In Myron's small office, barely larger than a closet, they found his waxed cotton cap with earflaps and the red plaid wool hunting jacket he wore in cold weather, but his car keys weren't in the pocket.

Dr. Berkowitz and Dr. Reed entered Nurse Lindstrom's office, where they found her purse along with her overcoat. "Strange," Berkowitz said. "A woman runs off with a man, she hardly leaves her purse behind."

"*Or* her coat," Reed said. "Not in this weather. Are her car keys in her purse? The police might want them."

Berkowitz opened it and dug around, then came up with a ring of half a dozen keys. "Bingo."

The doctors met back in Goldberg's office. While it was conceivable that Gunn and Lindstrom had left in Gunn's car without their coats ("Maybe they ran off to Florida," Goldberg jokingly suggested), it was unlikely she would have done so without her purse.

"*Unless,*" Berkowitz said, "it was an impulse, a spur of the moment thing where they . . . threw caution to the winds."

Steiner nodded. "Possible. Also possible that they didn't intend to be gone for long, that they planned to do something together and then come back."

"But do what?" Reed asked. "Her car is here, his is gone, so if they're not still here, apparently they drove away together, but to what end?"

"Sex?" Steiner said.

"A nasty night for coupling in an automobile," Goldberg said with a frown. "Where could they have gone for a . . . what do you call it, a quick one?"

"Not Gunn's," Steiner said. "He's married. That would leave Nurse Lindstrom's house—or apartment."

"House," Goldberg said. "She once spoke of it to me."

Reed raised a finger. "May I suggest that at this point we call Sheriff Chambers, tell him what's happened, and ask him to check on Eleanor Lindstrom's house? If that's where they went, and it turns out to be . . . well, a crime scene, I'd much rather have the law discover it than one of us." A heavy silence fell. "I'm sorry to suggest that, but what Nick here said about Ronald Miller . . . well, I guess it got my imagination working. I hope I'm wrong."

"I think that is a capital idea," Goldberg said as he picked up the phone and called Sheriff Chambers, to whom he explained the situation.

Chambers called back a half hour later. "Had a deputy stop by the Lindstrom woman's house," he told Dr. Goldberg. "Myron Gunn's DeSoto wasn't in the driveway or anywhere on the street. My man knocked, but there was no answer, so he radioed me and I told him to force the lock. House was empty, with no signs that anyone had made a speedy exit. You, uh, want us out there?"

Dr. Goldberg paused before answering. "*Ja,* if you wouldn't mind, Sheriff. There are a number of elements that are . . . questionable. Perhaps with an organized investigation, interviewing our staff, you may be able to learn things we have not. Would you want to get Captain Banning involved?"

"I'd rather not bring in the state boys just yet," Chambers said. "We don't even know if a crime was committed, after all. We can call them if we need them."

"You know best, Sheriff. It may be best to handle this situation discreetly. There may be nothing more to it than two people running away together, who knows?"

After Goldberg hung up, Steiner said, "You really believe that could be a possibility, Doctor?"

Goldberg sighed. "After a long life studying humanity and its behavior, Nick, nothing would surprise me. I can envision the two of them getting in the car on impulse and driving to a motor lodge, leaving all else behind in the throes of passion, having sexual relations, and then, away from the facility in which they have previously shared all their time together, come to a joint realization—or illusion—that one cannot live without the other. They then decide to leave together, run away for a brief time, or for forever, who knows? They simply get in the car and drive. Unlikely? Yes. Illogical? Yes. Unexpected? Of course. But passion and love make people do such things. So it is not *impossible*. As Conan Doyle said in the words of the world's greatest consulting detective, 'When you have eliminated the impossible, whatever remains, however improbable, must be the truth.'"

"So," Steiner said, "is the involvement of Ronald Miller impossible?"

"Certainly not," Goldberg answered. "There are still a great many things that are not impossible. Perhaps the police will discover some possibilities we have overlooked."

But the police, consisting of Sheriff Chambers and two deputies, found little. They gathered all personnel together in the break room and Sheriff Chambers asked anyone with any personal knowledge of Myron Gunn and Eleanor Lindstrom to please stay there to be interviewed, and dismissed the rest. Several stayed, among them Nurse Tess Asher and Ray Wiseman. While Chambers talked to them, one of his deputies took the car keys that Berkowitz had found in Eleanor's purse and went outside to look in her car.

Ray Wiseman seemed comfortable with Sheriff Chambers. He'd lived in Fairvale his whole life, and knew the man. "So, Ray," Chambers said. "What can you tell me about these two?"

"Look, Jud," Wiseman said, "you didn't hear this from me. Myron comes back, I don't want him thinking I been telling tales on him, y'know? Man can hold a grudge."

"Our secret," Chambers said. "What do you know?"

"They had . . . well, they've *got* a romance going, all right. Have for years. I heard them one time, couple years back, in an empty patient room at night, but I think they do it mostly down in the laundry room. Warmer, and nobody goes there after six. They're not the only ones who use it, but we're just talking about those two now. I actually saw them once. I'd gone down for some cleaning supplies, and I heard them before I come across them, thank God. I was on the darker side of the corridor, so I peeked, and there they were, Myron and Santa . . . uh, Nurse Lindstrom. Had most of their clothes on, but it was pretty obvious what they were doing. On a big pile of clean towels." Wiseman's face soured at the thought.

"You say anything to anybody about it?" Chambers asked.

"No, sir. Not my business. If it was somebody who was working under me, why then, I might've later. But tell my boss I saw him like that with the head nurse? No, thank you. I'd like to stay working here a little longer."

Some of the other people who remained had similar stories, and some were just gossips, telling what they'd heard about but never seen. Nurse Tess Asher was more helpful in that she could actually confirm the relationship. "Eleanor was in love with Myron from the first day he walked in here. It was only a matter of time. And I *knew* when they first started . . . doing it."

"How?" Chambers asked.

"Oh, a woman knows."

"And, being a woman, you did."

She did, she replied, in no uncertain terms.

When the deputy returned from checking Eleanor Lindstrom's car, he had found only one item of interest. It was a small suitcase he had taken from the trunk. When Chambers unlatched it, he found several blouses and skirts, some bras and panties, and a black lace nightie.

"Well," he observed to the deputy, "if she was planning on running away with this guy, she didn't take her supplies along."

Chambers had no sooner closed the suitcase than his other deputy, whose job had been to canvass the building for anything out of the ordinary, returned. "Find anything?" Chambers asked.

"Not hardly," the deputy said. "No signs of struggle, no bloody hatchets lyin' around."

"Not funny," Chambers said.

"Sorry. Only thing kinda out of whack was some missing towels."

"What?"

"Yeah. The guys down in the laundry said that about half a dozen clean towels disappeared from some piles they have on pallets down there."

Chambers thought about the laundry, and about what Ray Wiseman had said about Gunn and Lindstrom having sex on piles of towels. "Let's take a look."

When they got to the laundry, the clean towels had already been taken away in wheeled baskets for distribution to the patients. Chambers asked where exactly the missing towels had been, and one of the workers showed him the now empty wooden pallet. There were other empty pallets near it, but each of them was covered with a large cloth.

"Was there a cloth cover on this pallet too?" Chambers asked the man.

"Sure. Can't put clean towels on rough wood like that."

"So was the cloth cover missing on this one along with the towels?"

"Yep."

Chambers lifted the bare pallet and looked underneath it, but saw nothing on the painted cement floor other than the usual scratches and gouges. Then he looked at the wood of the pallet itself.

"Whatcha lookin' for, Sheriff," the deputy said, "bloodstains?"

"Nah, I'm just lookin'," Chambers replied. Finding nothing, he set the pallet back down and started examining the rest of the floor and the nearby walls. Nothing there either. The floor around the pallet appeared to be cleaner than the surrounding area, though not by much.

"How often this floor get mopped?" he asked the man, who had lit a cigarette to watch the police in action.

"Once a week or so."

"Done recently?"

"Couple of days."

Chambers nodded and dug out a cigarette of his own. He stuck it between his lips and lit it. "Can you think of any reason," he asked the man, "for somebody to steal some towels? Or that cover?"

The man shrugged. "I don't know. People take stuff sometimes. But towels, they'd be hard to sneak out. Still, these are pretty thin. Guess you could always wrap them around yourself and put your coat over them. If you needed towels that bad. As for the cover, I don't know. They're just old sheets, really, too worn for the patients to use."

Chambers nodded and looked around again. "Okay, that's all here," he said, and he and the deputy walked back upstairs.

Dr. Goldberg was doing some paperwork when Chambers entered his office again. Music was playing on a big record player at one end of the room. It wasn't loud, but Chambers winced at the high voices, and Goldberg noticed. "You don't care for opera?" he asked.

"That what that is?" Chambers said. "I can stand it. Wanted to tell you what we found—or didn't." Goldberg nodded and leaned forward. "Mr. Gunn and Nurse Lindstrom were most definitely an item. Plenty of proof of that. We found no signs of any violence or foul play, only thing strange is that somebody stole some towels last night."

"Stole some towels?"

"Yep. But I don't see that it has much to do with this disappearance. Just kinda goofy, though." He paused. "You want to know what I really think?"

"Of course."

"I think they went off together. I think it was unplanned, and I think that once they did it, they liked it. Maybe it's just something they had to get out of their system, I don't know, you're the headshrinker. But I'd bet that once they realize what they've done, they'll come back, maybe today, tomorrow, next week, but sometime. You say they were in their late forties, early fifties? People get desperate at that age sometimes. Sex makes them do crazy things, but you know that, right?"

"That is, as you say, putting it mildly," Goldberg said. "So you suggest nothing be done at this point?"

"Well, as far as we know, they haven't done anything illegal and aren't in any danger. If Gunn's wife wants to file a missing persons report, she can. At least that'll get other law enforcement to keep an eye out for the car. I'll drop over to her place, tell her what we found, and suggest she do that. 'Course, under the circumstances, she might want to keep it quiet."

"I doubt that's going to happen," the doctor said. "So many of our staff live in Fairvale that the story will be widespread."

"You're probably right. Well, let me know if you hear anything from either of them. I've got no doubt that they'll show up eventually, a little embarrassed and worse for wear."

November 17, 1916

The unease I feel grows every day. The gemstone in the crown of the Ollinger Sanitarium, my Spiritual Repulsion Therapy, has begun to show cracks. *Cracks? Rather I should say fissures.* It seems that for every patient who is aided by the therapy, there is another who is damaged by it, and, in some cases, destroyed.

The therapy itself is not at fault, I have no doubt concerning that, oh no. I suspect it is the zeal with which some of the trusted nurses and attendants who play the roles attack their parts. There is a vast difference, I tell them time and again, between correction and abuse, and to always err on the side of the former. But, in the unbalanced minds of our patients, the dividing line is fine indeed. Should the portrayer of the correcting spirit become too filled with vengeful fury, the already attenuated mind of the patient snaps, and rather than achieving recognition of guilt and the resultant redemption, what we are left with is an altogether broken spirit, some of which have proven irreparable.

To be specific, the case of one M.R., who was committed here by his family after beating his mother to death with a silver hand mirror after she had discovered him in her bedroom wearing her undergarments and performing self-abuse. After the usual legal arrangements were made, he became my patient, but proved to be fully uncommunicative. I urged him to discuss his transvestism (as the German Hirschfeld has named it) as a starting point, but he gave no response whatsoever. He was not mad, and I do believe that he understood every word I uttered, but he would only look at me, as if he held me beneath contempt.

Nevertheless, I spoke to him of the wrong he had done, not so much in his sexual deviance as in his killing of his mother. Try as I might, even to the point of pleading, I could not persuade him to admit to the gravity and permanence of his actions, or to claim the responsibility for his mother's death. After the more traditional treatments failed, I felt that only Spiritual Repulsion Therapy remained as a possibility to cure his illness.

The usual preparations were made, the patient moved to one

of the proper rooms, and that evening the sedative administered. Sometime after midnight, the ruse was undertaken. Along with one of the stronger attendants, one of the elect cadre who are privy to the full details of the therapy, I lingered in the dark passage as the nurse entered in full and faithful re-creation of the unfortunate mother of M.R. What occurred then was greatly surprising and alarming.

At the first word (M.R.'s Christian name) uttered by the nurse, the patient, who should have been sedated to the point where such activity was impossible, leapt to his feet, strode across the small chamber, and with a fearful shriek fell upon the poor woman, fingers clawing and teeth biting at her face, bearing her to the floor. The attendant and I entered upon the instant, and pulled the patient off his victim, but he continued to scream and thrash about, trying to bite the attendant and myself with his ravening teeth.

The attendant putting him in an unbreakable hold, at last M.R.'s struggles subsided, though he continued to scream, with tears pouring down his cheeks and his eyes rolling in his head. I was able to see to the nurse, and found that her face had been severely scratched and her cheek lacerated by the patient's snapping teeth. I helped her out of the room through the way we had entered, thankful that she was still conscious, and the attendant followed, flinging the now prostrate body of M.R. onto his bed and exiting quickly, making sure the passage door was tightly shut (how could it have been otherwise?).

The nurse recovered with only slight scarring. The story was that she was attacked by a patient, which was, after all, the truth. Those of us who are fully aware of my still as yet secret therapy did not disclose the exact circumstances of the nurse's injury to the many others who are not privy to our confidences.

The case of M.R. was the first of the negative results of

Spiritual Repulsion Therapy. There have been many since; though, with the increased dosage of sedatives I felt necessary, there have been no repetitions of attacks on nurses or attendants. I have thus far not described the fate of M.R. after the failure of therapy, but I fear I must.

The man has not regained what little sanity he had when he came here. On the contrary, he has become what an earlier, less enlightened age would call a raving lunatic. When he is awake, he screams until he grows hoarse. When asleep, he twitches incessantly in despairing dreams. I have had his sedation increased, and that has helped to calm him, but when it wears off the screaming returns.

There are six other such patients now. And these failures do not augur well for the future of the facility. M.R.'s father, upon visiting him and seeing his condition, was livid with rage at the change in his son, and called me a mountebank, threatening to never again visit, to stop all monthly payments, and to slander my reputation were his son to remain in this condition. This, unfortunately, has been the reaction of most well-heeled relatives who find from one visit to the next that their loved ones have gone irretrievably mad.

Three so far have discontinued payments, and when I asked if they wished to have their wards transferred to another facility, I have received such responses as, "Do what you like—I wash my hands of him and you," "I find her malady brought on by the sanitarium's maltreatment, and wish to hear of nothing other than her return to sanity," and, simplest of all, "I do not give a d——."

I can only believe that these original supporters of my work wanted a place to lodge their criminal children rather than have them go to prison. Now that these patients' lives have become equivalent to those sufferers at Bedlam, they withdraw their support and their interest, writing off their former loved ones for good and all, telling themselves that they tried to do their best for their son, daughter, uncle, father, husband, wife, so they need feel no guilt and may go on with their lives.

But what to do with these "errors," these sacrifices made on the altar of mental health? Their shrieks disturb the other patients day and night, and it becomes dangerous to enter their rooms. Therefore I have decided that, once their patrons have deserted them and visits cease, they should all be placed together in a less luxurious ward, where they may be overseen by a minimal staff, and where their ravings will disturb only each other.

There is a quite large room, as yet unused, in the cellar. Beds may be placed in there, perhaps in small individual cage-like cells, which would eliminate the need for constant restraints. It will be best to keep this area from visitors, though it is not likely these particular patients will receive visits. Should that occur, they can be brought up and placed in one of the regular patient rooms during the visit.

I regret this deeply, but I see no opportunity for improvement in these poor creatures. In fact, I fear for the very future of the sanitarium itself. The consortium of businessmen who have financed the facility are receiving complaints, some from within their own ranks, and the inspectors from the state board come more frequently. As of yet, the facility has received their approval after each visit, but none of the inspectors, indeed, no one except for a portion of my staff and myself, even know of the existence of my Spiritual Repulsion Therapy.

I only pray that those with the knowledge remain steadfast and silent, so that I may continue in what I still consider to be my life's great work, and the gift to mankind that Providence has intended me to make.

———

No one told Norman Bates about the disappearance of Myron Gunn and Nurse Lindstrom. He learned of it through a conversation he overheard after lunch in the social hall. The two men who had previously discussed ghosts and somehow saw bugs in the ceiling tiles were talking.

"I say they run away together," said the one, his eyes on the ceiling as before. "They was sweet on each other."

"That's true enough," said the other. "I seen Santa give Myron Gunn the eye over and over, and he looked back at her sometimes and I almost seen him smilin' once. But that don't mean they run away."

"Well, neither one of them's here. You think they're hidin'?"

"Nope. You know damn well what happened to 'em. Same thing as happened to Ronald Miller."

Just for a moment, the man looked away from the ceiling at his friend. "You're not tellin' me . . ."

"Yep. The ghosts got 'em. They're gone. Ain't never gonna find 'em."

Norman felt a sudden chill. Myron Gunn and Nurse Lindstrom were missing. And last night he had dreamed . . .

"Well," said the other man, looking back at the ceiling, "whether they got 'em or they run away, I don't care neither way. They was both mean sons a bitches."

The other man said, "I just hope they don't turn into ghosts themselves now. Can you imagine Myron Gunn as a ghost? Can't think of anybody I'd rather have haunt me less'n him."

"That'd be one goddamn mean ghost," the ceiling man agreed, then pointed upward. "*That's* a good one!"

"Nah," said his friend. "I don't like the blue ones."

The longer Norman sat and thought about Myron Gunn and Nurse Lindstrom, the sicker he felt. He hoped he wouldn't throw up again. He stood up, walked to the window, looked out at the trees in the distance, and thought some more.

First Ronald Miller, whom they still hadn't found. And now Myron Gunn and Nurse Lindstrom. Every one of them had posed a danger to Norman. Though the nurse had never actually threatened him, he knew she was a friend, and apparently a lover, of Myron Gunn's, and would be on his side in whatever he did.

And now all three of these people were missing.

Anyone who tries to hurt you or your friends, well . . . let's just say they'll be sorry.

Robert's words came back to him clearly. And:

Who's to say it was a nightmare?

Norman felt that if he kept these secrets inside of him, his heart would burst. There was only one person he could talk to about this, one person he could really talk to at all, and that was Dr. Reed. He would try and stay calm until four o'clock, which was the time scheduled for today's therapy. He picked up a magazine and tried to concentrate on it, but it was no use.

It seemed an eternity until four. His walk took forever, but finally he was back in his room, and the minutes dragged on until Dr. Reed knocked, then opened his door. He asked the doctor if he could talk about something that was concerning him rather than start his therapy right away.

Dr. Reed replied, "Of course, Norman. Therapy is really just talking about what concerns you. Now, what is it?" Dr. Reed settled into the chair, smiling at Norman.

Norman told him everything then—how he had learned of the disappearance of Myron Gunn and Nurse Lindstrom, how he'd had dreams about seeing them the night before, and Robert's reassurances to him that no one would harm him. "I just can't help but wonder, Doctor, if . . . if Robert could somehow be responsible for . . ."

"For the three disappearances?" Dr. Reed finished. "Norman, I can understand how you might connect these individual occurrences, especially since you've been emotionally involved with two of these three. But let's look at this logically. First, your dreams have an explanation. We've already talked about the man in the red room, remember? The violence that was a part of your life doesn't just go away. It remains in your subconscious. And where do dreams come from?"

"The subconscious."

"Correct. Your recent confrontation with Myron Gunn, and your fear of him *and* Nurse Lindstrom, is in both your sleeping and waking mind. It could easily be that your wish not to be dominated by them could result in a dream where *they* feel the same emotions of fear and anxiety that *you* do."

Norman nodded. "I guess that makes sense." He frowned. "But what about Robert saying that he'd protect me from anyone who tried to hurt me?"

"It's only natural for your brother to want to reassure you, even if he might not be able to do anything physically to keep you from harm."

"But he . . . suggested that my nightmares . . . might not be dreams."

"He may have been joking. Or it just might have been an observation of some kind regarding this psychic link you said you two talked about. If that link exists, which we have no valid proof of, you . . . could have been seeing something your brother was *thinking* rather than doing."

"But maybe . . . he *did* do it," Norman said softly.

"Let's turn to logic again, Norman. Ronald Miller first. Now, for your brother to get Ronald Miller out of here—or, let's say for the sake of argument, *do something* to him—he would have to get back into the facility, and that's not going to happen. He has no credentials, and I always have to accompany him in and out of the building. Once he leaves, there's no coming back.

"But even if he were able to get back in, in the case of Ronald Miller he would have had to get the key to Miller's cell and take him out bodily through locked gates and past attendants and the outside guards. Because Miller—or his body—wasn't found in the facility.

"As for Myron Gunn and Nurse Lindstrom, Robert would have had to do the same thing, only with *two* people, either removing them from the building or doing something to them here and then getting out. Myron's car is gone, so he would have had to take that too. It's just physically impossible that an outsider could have done any such thing. Does that make sense to you?"

Norman nodded again. He felt a little better. "I guess so," he said. "It's just that the combination of different things . . . I put them together. In my imagination."

"And that's all it is, Norman. Your imagination. And there's nothing wrong with that. It's part of our human makeup to look for patterns, and, if none exists, we sometimes create them. We see clouds that look like horses, or faces in the bark of a tree. That's what you've done. It doesn't mean the horse or the face is really there." Dr. Reed sat back and crossed his arms. "Would you feel more comfortable not seeing Robert for a while? I could offer him a reason that wouldn't offend him if you would want visits to resume after a time."

"No, no," Norman said. "It's just . . . I enjoy his visits, they're great, and it's not his fault I get these ideas in my head, he just . . . well, I think he wants me to feel comfortable with him, to feel that he understands what I . . . what I went through. Am *going* through."

"I'm sure he does. But if you feel disturbed by some things

that Robert says, don't hesitate to tell him so. Ask him to change
the subject. I'm sure he will." Dr. Reed smiled at Norman. "Now.
Since we've got that out of the way, shall we continue with our
session? Lie back and relax . . ."

After his session with Dr. Reed, it was time for dinner. Nurse
Marie came in, Ben behind her, and he was happy to see them
both. He hoped that Myron, if he had indeed run away with
Nurse Lindstrom, would *stay* away. He didn't like the way Myron
talked to Nurse Marie, and had been worried about her when
she'd stayed in that room where the man was being force-fed.

She seemed to be fine, though, and greeted Norman warmly.
He grinned at her, and she looked at him oddly, but still smiling.
"You look happy today," she said. "I wonder if it's because you
heard some news."

"Yes," Norman whispered, then said, "Myron."

Nurse Marie raised her eyebrows in surprise. Norman assumed it was a response to his relative volubility. Other than
please and *thank you,* he'd never said more to her. "That's right,"
she said. "And . . . ?"

"Nurse . . . Lindstrom."

Nurse Marie turned and smiled at Ben, who smiled back.
Then she looked back at Norman as she took the cover from his
tray of food. "They may be back eventually," she said.

The food smelled good to Norman. It was beef stew, which he
liked. The good spirits he felt sustained his talkativeness. "Maybe
not," he said with a smile. And then, in spite of what Dr. Reed
had told him, he pictured the faces of the two that he had seen in
his dream.

"Maybe not," he whispered, but now he wasn't smiling.

He was, he thought later, more right than he could imagine.

11

A week passed, and Myron Gunn and Nurse Lindstrom still hadn't reappeared at their homes or the hospital. Marybelle Gunn had filed a missing person's report, and the highway patrol was on the lookout for Myron's DeSoto, but the car hadn't been sighted.

Nurse Wyndham and Ray Wiseman retained their temporary positions as head nurse and head attendant, and the state hospital went on with its business as before. In fact, it proceeded even more efficiently, since neither Wyndham nor Wiseman had the sadistic bent that their predecessors had. They were strict and stern, a necessity when dealing with criminal madmen, but they seemed to feel no pleasure in enforcing discipline. It was part of the job.

Rumors abounded among the patients:

One of the more violent residents had murdered and chopped up both Gunn and Lindstrom, and the affair had been hushed up and a cover story established, though no one could explain why . . .

The pair had run away together, but Ronald Miller had been waiting for them and killed them both, then stolen Gunn's car . . .

The ghosts of the old sanitarium had claimed them when they went into the cellar to have sex, and their bodies would never be found, their souls captured and tortured forever . . .

Even the staff discussed the possibility of these disparate scenarios, though the consensus was that Myron and Eleanor had run off and then continued running, and wouldn't be heard from again. This, however, was not the opinion of Judy Pearson, receptionist and Dr. Goldberg's secretary, who was certain that Ronald Miller had never left the hospital and was still hiding in the facility, skulking between various rooms and closets, stealing food to survive, and biding his time. Myron and Eleanor had come across him, and he had killed them to shut them up and hidden their bodies somewhere. Now he was still on the premises with blood on his hands, prowling for his next victim, which Judy was afraid was going to be her.

So when, just before she was due to leave for the day at six o'clock, Dr. Goldberg asked her to retrieve one of the older patient files from the cellar storage room, she felt more than slight trepidation. It was already dark, and odds were that no one would be in the cellar at this time of day.

What made things worse was that the file room, one of the few rooms in the cellar that was humidity controlled, was down a short hall off of the main one. Once she went down that hall, she'd be trapped, if anyone (and by anyone, she thought of Ronald Miller) followed her.

She stopped by the break room first to see if any of the attendants would go with her, but the only one there was Cappy Reilly, who grinned when he saw her. "Hey, Judy!" he said. "How ya doin'? Heading over to Delsey's—join me for a beer?"

Cappy had asked Judy that a dozen times since he started

working at the hospital, and she had always declined, each time a bit chillier than the time before. She had thought he'd finally gotten the message, but apparently not. "I can't," she said. "I have to get some files from the cellar. Um . . . I was wondering if maybe you'd come with me?"

"Well, now that's an invitation I've been waiting for." His grin grew broader and toothier. "I knew you'd come around eventually."

Her anger conquered her fear, and she gave her head a hard shake. "Never mind," she said, turning to walk away. "I'll be fine on my own." At the door she turned back. "You're *disgusting*," she said, and walked out.

"Your funeral, honey," Judy heard him say as she stalked down the hall.

Your funeral. Oh, *damn* it, she thought, then gritted her teeth and headed for the stairway. Going down there and finding the files would take ten minutes, tops. And it wasn't like she was going down there by candlelight, like one of the heroines in those Gothic romances she always read. The lights in the hallway were plenty bright. She'd be fine. Ronald Miller was probably long gone. Probably.

She hit the switch at the bottom of the stairs, and the cellar hallway was illuminated all the way down its length. She almost started to call out *hello,* but wasn't sure if she wanted to make her presence known any more than it already was. Maybe whoever might be there would think she was a big, burly attendant and stay hidden.

The short hallway that led to the office was halfway down the hall, and she walked carefully, trying to make no sound, her heart pounding. Some of the doors on either side of the corridor were closed. Others opened into darkness, and she walked against the opposite wall when she came to those. Not planning to go without a fight, she clutched her key ring so that the points of the keys stuck out from between her fingers like claws.

When she got to the short hall, she slowly put her head around the corner, almost expecting something to jump out at her, but it was empty. She walked the few yards to the door, unlocked it, pushed it open, and immediately turned on the light.

Fortunately the room wasn't very big, and the filing cabinets were all against the far wall, so that there was nothing for anyone to hide behind. Judy kept the door open, not wanting to have to open it again to whatever might be in the hall when she left. She went directly to the *T–Z* file and removed the folder Dr. Goldberg wanted. It was when she was checking the contents to be sure the file had been correctly labeled that she heard the sound.

It was a quick scuffling noise from the doorway, and she whipped around just in time to see a movement of something passing in the main corridor, from right to left as she viewed it, going in the direction from which she had come. In the fear that swept through her and wrapped ice around her throat, she couldn't see the face or make out what the person was wearing, but they had shot by as if not wanting to be seen.

She listened, but didn't hear anything else. No footsteps, no breathing except her own. Then she heard what sounded like a door thudding shut.

What was happening? Was he hiding in one of the rooms now? She put the keys back into her hand the way she had before, ready to claw out the eyes of any attacker. Then, holding the file under her arm, she quietly closed the drawer with her free hand and walked toward the door. Before she locked it behind her, she would peek out into the hall to make certain no one was still there.

Just as she reached the doorway, a large figure suddenly appeared, shadowed against the light from the hall.

Judy gave a quick yelp, leapt back into the room, and slammed the door closed behind her, turning the catch so that it was locked. She stood leaning against the door, panting in panic, feeling sweat coat her face, hoping that her ratcheting heart wouldn't burst. What could she do? There was no escape from this room. She looked around wildly for air vents, thinking that she could suffocate if she had to stay there too long. But she couldn't open the door, not now, not ever, even if the air ran out—

She jumped at a soft knock on the door. "Judy?" a voice said.

It was familiar to her.

"Hey, it's me, Cappy. Sorry I scared you. I came down to apologize. I really acted like an idiot up there. I know you were a little scared to come down here alone, so I figured I'd just keep you company; that's it, really."

Cappy. God *damn* him. But at the same time, God bless him. "Okay," she said, but her throat was so tight the word didn't come out. "Okay," she said again, and wiped the sweat from her face before she opened the door.

Cappy stood there, smiling sheepishly. "I really am sorry." Then he noticed how white her face was. "Are you okay?"

"Not really." The words raced out of her, and she moved past him to look down the hall. "Somebody was down here. I heard them, like they were trying to move fast and not have me see them. Did you see anyone when you came down?"

"No, not a soul. When did this all happen?"

"Just now!"

Cappy shrugged. "I know I would've seen anybody there, but there wasn't—or on the stairs."

Judy thought for a second. "He must have gone into one of the rooms. I heard a door close!"

"Which way did he go?" Cappy asked.

"That way," she said, pointing down the hall to her left.

"That's how I came down," he said, "but I didn't see him. We gotta check these rooms."

"What do you mean, *we?*"

He chuckled. "I mean *we* as in some of the guys. Look, let's walk to the end of the hall, then you run up the stairs and get two, maybe three attendants to come down here. Tell 'em possible escape. I'll stay here and keep an eye on the hall to make sure nobody slips out of a room, okay?"

Judy nodded, pushed open the door to the stairs, and ran up them. She quickly gathered several of the men from their evening posts and led them back down, all the time clutching Dr. Goldberg's requested report under her arm. Then she waited while the attendants went from one room to the next, using master keys to open the locked doors.

When they reached the short hall that led to the records room, Cappy said, "You're sure he didn't go to your right, Judy?"

"No, he'd be in one of these rooms," she said, indicating the portion of the hall they'd already searched.

"Well, he's not in any of them. And I was coming down the stairs, so he either disappeared or we missed him."

"We didn't miss him," growled one of the men.

"*Or,*" Cappy went on, "it was maybe your imagination?"

"I know what I saw, Cappy," she said. "And what I *heard.*" She tried to keep the anger out of her voice. "Thanks for checking anyway." She walked down the short hall to the records room, turned off the light, locked the door, and walked past the men to the stairs.

When she took the file folder from under her arm, she saw that it was damp with sweat. She waved it in the air to try and dry it as she walked to Dr. Goldberg's office, feeling embarrassed, slightly relieved, but still frightened.

———

Robert hadn't visited Norman for a long time, and Norman missed him. He wasn't exactly sure how long it had been, as he lost track of days, since each one was the same and seemed to blend into the other. Norman really had no religion, so Sunday didn't have the significance for him that it did for others, and he never attended the morning services on that day.

It wasn't until he mentioned to Dr. Reed that he missed his brother that he knew how long it had really been. "Over two weeks," Dr. Reed said. "Robert called me just today, in fact, and asked me to apologize to you for not having come in. He said he's been very busy with both work and family. Apparently his children have been ill with the flu, and he's had to handle his diner alone while his wife takes care of them."

"Are they all right?" Norman asked, alarmed by this news of his niece and nephew.

"They're fine," Dr. Reed said. "They're going back to school tomorrow, in fact, and Robert said he'd come visit you tonight, if that's all right with you."

"Sure!" Norman said, delighted by the prospect.

When Norman saw Robert walk into his room that evening several hours after dinner, Robert seemed as anxious to see Norman as Norman had been to see him. Robert hugged him and sat down, keeping his hand on Norman's shoulder. He apologized for having taken so long between visits, and promised that he would see Norman more frequently, now that the kids were no longer ill.

"I, uh, understand that you've had a burden lifted from your shoulders," Robert said with a soft smile.

"You . . . you mean that man? Myron Gunn?"

"And an exceptionally annoying head nurse as well, I believe."

"How did you . . . ? Did Dr. Reed tell you about it?"

"He did. He knew how concerned I was with the way you've been treated by some of the staff here."

Norman nodded. "People are saying they ran away together," he said, suddenly unable to meet Robert's gaze.

"And do you believe that?" Robert asked. His voice had gone flat. Norman didn't answer. He looked down at the floor between his feet. "Did you have a dream, Norman?" Robert asked. "The night they disappeared? Did you . . . *see* anything?"

Norman didn't answer right away. Then, softly, he spoke. "I didn't . . . *see* anything. I had a dream, that was all."

"And what did you dream?"

"I dreamt about him. Myron Gunn. And Nurse Lindstrom. I dreamt about them. I saw their faces, that was all."

"And how did their faces look?" Robert asked.

"They looked . . . scared."

Norman looked up at Robert, who nodded, that same soft smile on his face. "I told you not to worry, didn't I? That I wouldn't let anyone hurt you. I meant that, Norman. No one here is going to hurt you."

"Do you think . . . will they come back?"

"They're not coming back, Norman. They ran away together, and they're *staying* away. They won't bother you again. Not ever. So don't worry, little brother."

"Robert," Norman said, "did you . . . did you *make* them go away?"

"Norman," Robert said, shaking his head. "Norman, Norman, Norman. How could *I* make people fall in love and run off together? I run a diner. I *could* make them a great plate of ham and eggs, though." He laughed and slapped Norman on the shoulder. "Gone is gone, right? No matter how it gets done. Look,

Myron Gunn and his friend are probably sunning themselves on a beach in Jamaica right now. What's important is that they aren't here. So enjoy their absence and stop worrying. Now. Let me tell you about this crazy thing that Susie said when she was sick the other day. She threw up, okay? And Mindy comes in to clean it up, and . . ."

Norman started smiling as Robert continued the story, and when it was finished, he laughed. He loved his brother, and he hoped that someday, somehow, he might be able to meet Robert's family.

Once the initial talk of Myron Gunn and Nurse Lindstrom was finished, they had a wonderful visit, but it was over surprisingly fast. It seemed as though Dr. Reed knocked on the door only minutes after Robert had entered. His brother promised to come back in a few days, and, for the first time, kissed Norman on the cheek when he left. Norman was happy, and read himself to sleep. He had no dreams.

Several days later, Norman was surprised to find Dr. Reed visiting his room in the morning after breakfast. Usually Norman used those few hours to read privately. He sat up quickly, since Dr. Reed looked concerned. Still, the doctor smiled and nodded to the book Norman was holding. "What are you reading today?" he asked.

"*Silvertip's Chase* by Max Brand," Norman replied. "There's a whole series of books about this Silvertip . . . they call him that because he's got these gray hairs at his . . ." Something was wrong, and Norman looked pointedly at Dr. Reed. "What is it?"

Dr. Reed sighed and sat next to Norman. "Oh, Norman, you're so full of conversation with me and with your brother. And even sometimes with Nurse Marie. But in all your time here, have you ever spoken—really spoken—to anyone other than the three of us? *And* Ronald Miller, when you had to?"

Norman, reverting in the face of what he considered Dr. Reed's criticism, didn't speak, only shook his head no.

"I know. I know you haven't. But you're going to have to start, and soon. You remember Dr. Goldberg?" Norman nodded again. "He thinks your socialization skills should be improving. Of course, I agree with him. But I had hoped that through therapy we might be able to improve that aspect of your personality. And you've been . . . reticent, Norman. While you've shown enough improvement for me to continue as we've been doing in the past, Dr. Goldberg would like to see faster progress."

"But . . . but why? I mean, what does it matter if I like to stay by myself? And just talk to you and Robert? I'm not hurting anybody."

Dr. Reed sighed. "I hate to say it, Norman, but it's a question of efficiency. At least where Dr. Goldberg is concerned. The doctor likes to see results. His goal isn't to see that you walk out of here, but it *is* to return you to as close to normalcy as you can get. That way you can become a part of the general population here instead of the special designation that you now have. For example, we still don't think that you can take your meals in the dining hall, since that's a prime socialization environment. With people sitting on either side of you and across from you, you *have* to relate in some way to them, which you *don't* have to do in the less structured area of the social hall. There you can just sit and read a magazine or watch television without interacting, you understand?"

Norman nodded.

"You can answer me aloud. I'd prefer that you did."

"Yes . . . I understand."

"You see, the way Dr. Goldberg looks at it, if you can comfortably join the other patients in the dining hall, then three times a day that frees up Nurse Marie or other nurses and attendants to work with patients who need their help more than you might."

"I see," Norman said.

"But as your doctor, those concerns are secondary to me. What's most important is moving you forward, and I don't care how fast or slow as long as you're making progress, which you've been doing steadily. Unfortunately, Dr. Goldberg doesn't feel the same way." Dr. Reed took a deep breath.

"The doctor is going to visit you again, Norman. Just him and me. No Dr. Steiner or Dr. Berkowitz. But like the last time, he's going to want to engage in conversation, just the way I do with you. There's nothing to be scared of. And you don't have to say much, just enough so that he knows you're responding verbally to him. Just pretend that he's me, if that helps. Or Robert. Though I wouldn't mention your brother to him, since he doesn't yet know about the visits, and I wouldn't want him to prohibit them. I think your meetings with Robert have had a good effect on you." Dr. Reed put a hand on Norman's shoulder and looked intently into his eyes. "He's going to come here, Norman, to your room. He wanted me to bring you to his office, but I thought you'd be more comfortable here. Is that true?"

"Yes."

"Please try, Norman. Talk to Dr. Goldberg. That's all he wants, to see some progress. Will you try?"

"Yes," Norman said. "I will. I really will."

Dr. Goldberg visited Norman that afternoon. He and Dr. Reed came into Norman's room together. This time, Norman set down his book, stood up, and smiled, trying to see only Dr. Reed and not the big man with the steel-gray hair and beard, who hulked in front of him like a bear. In fact, after a first brief glance at Dr. Goldberg, Norman kept his gaze fixed on Dr. Reed.

"Norman, you remember Dr. Goldberg?" Dr. Reed asked. Norman looked quickly at Dr. Goldberg, then away again. The smile felt fixed and rigid on Norman's face. He knew what he needed to do. He needed to look directly at Goldberg, smile even more, extend his hand for the man to shake, say, *Why, of course. Hello, Dr. Goldberg, and how are you today?*

But when he looked at Goldberg, he remembered the man's first visit with the other doctors, and how crowded his little room had seemed, to the point of Norman's not being able to breathe. He remembered being terrified to speak, remembered the way the man had loomed over him, as if daring him to talk. Oh yes, he remembered Dr. Goldberg, all right.

"How are you, Norman?" Goldberg said, and Norman thought he must be smiling, his *voice* sounded like he was smiling, but Norman didn't look at him. Instead he looked at Dr. Reed, and when he saw the vast disappointment in Reed's face, Norman looked down at the floor again. "Are you going to talk to me today?"

Norman didn't say anything. He just looked at the floor.

"Dr. Reed has been telling me that you've gotten very verbal in the past several weeks. So I thought I'd come and see for myself." From the corner of his eye, Norman could see Dr. Goldberg cock his head as though he was waiting for Norman to answer. Still, Norman said nothing. "Dr. Reed," Goldberg said, "would you mind leaving me alone with Norman?"

"Doctor, is that wise?" Reed said. "Norman has never been violent here in the hospital, but—"

"I'm sure that will not change if I talk to him in private," Goldberg said. "Please." It was not a plea, it was a command.

Dr. Reed left the room, and Norman heard the door squeaking

closed. It stopped just before the lock mechanism would take effect. Dr. Goldberg came closer to Norman so he could speak softly to him. He was several inches taller than Norman, and bent his head so that he could talk directly into Norman's ear.

"Norman," he said, "are you going to speak to me?" He paused. "You speak to Dr. Reed, yes? I don't think it's asking too much for you to talk to me as well. It's *important* that you speak to other people, you know. Now, Norman, I don't mean you any harm. You don't have to be afraid of me. I'm just trying to discover what's best for you, the method of treatment that will serve to return you to normalcy. You understand?"

Norman gave his head a quick, short nod.

"Good, good," Dr. Goldberg said. "I've allowed Dr. Reed to treat you with psychoanalytic therapy these past few months, nothing else, and he's assured me that you've been making progress. But as the superintendent of this institution, Norman, I have responsibilities, and I take them seriously. I have to see firsthand that you're improving. And you can show that to me by simply carrying on a conversation. Now will you do that?"

Norman wanted to, but he felt afraid, and he didn't know why. He opened his mouth, but no words came out.

"Norman?"

He tried again, and a little whine escaped his throat. He shook his head in frustration, quick little jerks, and kept looking down. He could feel tears edging into his eyes.

"I know you're trying," Dr. Goldberg said, "but you have to do more than try. I know you can do it. Speak to me, Norman. It's that simple."

Norman felt his heart beating faster. His stomach roiled, and he was short of breath.

"I can't stress too strongly the importance of this, Norman. If you won't speak, I have no choice but to conclude that your therapy will have to be changed. Now let me explain what happens during the therapy that I believe we'll have to adapt to. The name is unfortunate, since the various 'shock' therapies are, in one sense, not shocking at all, but . . ."

Norman scarcely heard what Dr. Goldberg said after that. He'd heard some of the men discussing shock therapy in the social hall, both electroshock and the insulin shock that they used to use. Norman had heard of them before he had entered the state hospital, but he'd never really known much about them, and from what the men said, the procedure sounded like something out of a nightmare, as bad or worse than that terrible force feeding he had witnessed.

Being strapped down while jolts of electricity were poured through your brain, or receiving such high-dosage injections of insulin that you would go into a coma . . . it was horrible, and this was how Dr. Goldberg was proposing that Norman should be treated.

". . . So you see, Norman, these therapies have been highly successful in the past, and I see no reason that they might not be equally beneficial in your case. You need have no fear, despite what you might have heard about electroconvulsive therapy. These are merely horror stories to frighten people." Dr. Goldberg paused, then said, "Of course, if you were to talk to me today, or, shall we say, in the next few days, you could continue your traditional psychotherapy sessions with Dr. Reed. So Norman, it's really up to you. It's your decision, isn't it? Now . . . is there anything you'd like to say to me before I leave you today?"

With all his heart Norman wanted to speak, but he couldn't. A lump of fear the size of a fist clogged his throat, and he found himself gasping like a beached fish.

"All right, then," Dr. Goldberg said. "I'll leave you for now." He walked to the door, opened it fully, and left the room.

Norman sat down, trembling all over. He heard Dr. Goldberg talking in a low voice to Dr. Reed, and he heard Dr. Reed reply in a somewhat animated, even angry tone, though Norman couldn't understand the words. Dr. Goldberg spoke again, much in the same tone as before, but for a longer time, and Dr. Reed, when he responded, spoke in a softer tone.

Then Norman heard footsteps fade away down the hall, and Dr. Reed appeared in the doorway. He looked sad, and didn't come into Norman's room. He said, "Dr. Goldberg wants to speak to you again in three days. If you don't respond to him . . . you'll no longer be in my care, Norman. I'm sorry. We'll discuss this later, but now I just . . ." He shook his head. "We'll talk later. But we'll resolve this, Norman. We will." He gave a forced smile and left the room, locking the door behind him.

Norman sat trembling for a long time. He didn't want to cry, but felt tears push through. For a moment, he wished his mother were there to tell him what to do. He wished that she would have spoken to Dr. Goldberg, pretending to be him, but then he realized that he couldn't have trusted her to do that, that even if she had been willing to come back once he allowed her to, she probably would have been herself, and that would have been far worse than not talking at all. After Mother opened up on Dr. Goldberg, he would probably have had Norman shocked, drowned, and force-fed whether or not Norman was willing to eat. No, he was better off without Mother, no matter how frightened he was.

And then he thought about Robert. Whenever Norman had a problem, every time that Robert came to visit, that problem seemed to go away. And Robert was coming to visit tonight.

"And I'm frightened," Norman told Robert as he concluded his story about Dr. Goldberg's visit earlier that day.

Robert glumly pursed his lips and nodded slowly. "What does Dr. Reed think?" he asked Norman.

"Well, we had our therapy later, and he's convinced that I can . . . break through this fear of mine and talk to Dr. Goldberg. That's what we worked on today and what we'll do tomorrow. We're trying to identify the roots of my fear, and once we've defined it, we can find a way to conquer it . . . at least that's what Dr. Reed says."

Robert shook his head. "Little brother, I think it's terrible that you're put in this position. I mean, that you should have to perform for this old headshrinker like a trained monkey. What he's really saying is do what I want you to do or I'll torture you. He doesn't have the right to do that. Even if you'd gone to *prison,* they couldn't do that."

"Yes, but . . . I can't very well tell him that. Dr. Reed is in charge of my treatment now, but Dr. Goldberg can change that anytime. I'm a patient, Robert, not really a prisoner. Well, I *am* a prisoner, but . . . oh, you know what I mean."

Robert chuckled. "I do. And I know something else. Nobody is going to torture my brother, not while I'm around, got me?"

"Robert," Norman said carefully, "I don't want you to . . . I'm concerned that you might—"

"Hold it," Robert said, holding up a hand. "I know what you're thinking—that I had something to do with getting rid of your other . . . problems. But I didn't. It was an escape and an elopement, nothing more. So maybe Dr. Goldmine will have a change of heart. But believe me, Norman, nobody is going to give you shock treatments. Dr. Reed doesn't want that to happen . . . and *I* don't want that to happen. So it won't."

"But . . . please don't—"

"We've been lucky about things so far, little brother. No reason our luck can't continue, right? Like that lucky piece of yours you showed me, that petrified wood."

Norman dug into his pocket and brought out the small stone. Its smooth, polished surface gleamed warmly. "Maybe . . . maybe *you* should have this," Norman said. "You've given me so much. This is the only thing I have to give you."

Robert laughed. "What have I given you?" he asked, a sly look on his face.

"You gave me . . . a brother. A friend. Someone who understands. Who cares about me. Here. Take it," he said, holding out the piece of petrified wood.

Robert looked at it, then took it, felt its smoothness, turned it in his fingers, and slipped it into his pocket. "Okay, little brother. Thanks. Better than a rabbit's foot—and healthier for the rabbit, huh?" He grunted, reached down, grabbed his ankle, and made a mock grimace. "That sure would smart," he said, and laughed.

Norman laughed too, but, as they continued to talk, he couldn't banish from his mind the image of a cleaver coming down onto the leg of a soft, brown rabbit, splitting fur, flesh, and bone. Even after Robert was gone, it lingered, finally vanishing when he slept.

12

The following evening, a man sat in a black car at the edge of the parking lot of the State Hospital for the Criminally Insane, and thought that it was a good night to be hunting. The weather wasn't as intense as the storm that had hidden him on his previous visit. There was neither thunder nor lightning, but there were dark clouds from which fell a drenching rain. It made people run quickly to their cars, and not bother to notice strange vehicles with strange men inside them.

He had parked where he could see the large 1958 peach-colored Lincoln Premiere coupe that was licensed to Dr. Isaac Goldberg. He didn't have to recognize the man when he appeared in the parking lot, and that was good, since nearly everyone's face was once again covered by umbrellas. All he had to do was watch for the man who got into that Lincoln. He knew what to do when that happened.

A man came out of the building, a black umbrella making him anonymous. He walked to a car that the man recognized as belonging to Dr. Felix Reed, and he recognized Reed as well when the door opened and the dome light went on. Go in peace, Felix Reed, the man thought. I have no war with you.

Dr. Isaac Goldberg, the man he wanted to take, was still inside the building. It would be easiest if he just came out, but, if he didn't, maybe the man would have to go in after him. It would be difficult, but not impossible. He had done it before. He wondered if he had enough patience to wait.

However he chose to do it, it was a job that had to be done. He owed it to that victim with whom he shared his blood and his heritage, that unseen, forgotten victim who had suffered so much. But not forgotten by him.

Justice would be served tonight.

The man had done his homework. He started thinking about what would be the easiest way into the facility.

Dr. Elliot Berkowitz and Nurse Marie Radcliffe paused outside Dr. Goldberg's office door, and Berkowitz knocked. "Come in," Dr. Goldberg called, and they entered the office. Goldberg was sitting behind his desk, a pile of papers in front of him, and a pen in his right hand. He looked, Marie thought, a bit annoyed at being disturbed.

"Ah, yes," Goldberg said, setting down the pen. "The Tillson case. Please, both of you, sit, sit . . ."

Dr. Berkowitz then proceeded to give Dr. Goldberg the most recent report on Jacob Tillson, a fifty-three-year-old schizophrenic who had lived with his father until Tillson beat him to death with a lug wrench for whispering inside his head while he slept. Tillson had calmed down considerably in the four years he had been in the hospital, but was starting to have some violent outbursts, one of which Berkowitz had witnessed, and two others which Marie had seen.

"Mmm-hmm," Goldberg said, nodding. "And what course, Dr. Berkowitz, would you recommend?"

"I think he should be removed from the general population until we're able to get these outbursts under control."

"And how do you hope to do that?"

"An intense round of psychotherapy—he's been significantly cut back—and I think we should change his meds. He's been on chlorpromazine for several years now, and I'm thinking that one of the newer antipsychotics might be more effective."

"The newer drugs are in development," Goldberg said. "but I'm not sure that there's anything as effective as Thorazine, at this point. And to take the patient out of the general population and isolate him, well, that's a step backward, is it not? I wonder if electroconvulsive therapy might make him more tractable."

Shock therapy. Of course, Marie thought. Goldberg's solution for everything. She looked at Berkowitz to gauge his response.

The younger doctor stretched out his first word for a long time. "I'd . . . like to consider that as a last resort."

"Why?" Goldberg asked. "We've discussed this before, and I thought you were in agreement that these therapies are highly effective, yes?"

"Yes," Berkowitz said. "But I'm just thinking that if the same results can be achieved by less . . ." He paused.

"Less . . . *inhumane* methods?" Goldberg said. "Is that what you are thinking, Doctor?" Berkowitz paused just a bit too long. "I believe you are. So you think that I, after what I have gone through in my life, after the inhumanity I have seen, you think that *I* would suggest treatments that you consider harsh if I did not think the results would be superior to other, less invasive therapies?"

Marie suddenly felt that she should not be there, that this should be between mentor and pupil, but Goldberg's flash of anger faded, and he sat back and smiled benevolently. "I can understand how the younger generation might be hesitant to use such therapies, but you must believe me, Dr. Berkowitz, I have seen their effectiveness over many decades. And their superiority to more 'modern' methods. Tell me, do you know German?"

"Just a smattering. From my mother."

"Ah, unfortunate. Otherwise I would lend you my copy of Meggendorfer's *Allgemeine und spezielle Therapie,* which is filled with successful case studies. As an alternative, let me find some journal articles that may prove instructive to you. And, since you *are* in a learning situation, try the newer drugs on Tillson if you like, and let us see what happens. If you prefer to keep other therapies as a 'last resort,' as you put it, so be it. But remember, we deal in results. Now, is there anything else?"

Berkowitz seemed properly chastened. "No, sir, thank you."

"Very well," Goldberg said. A small smile cracked the corners of his mouth as he opened his central desk drawer. "But before you go, would you like a cookie?"

Berkowitz smiled shyly and took an Oreo from the proffered package. "Thank you, sir."

Goldberg held out the package to Marie, but she murmured a "No, thank you," and he put the cookies back in the desk.

"Nurse Radcliffe, would you remain a moment, please," he said. "Thank you, Dr. Berkowitz."

Berkowitz stood, smiling sheepishly, and left the office, closing the door behind him. Marie smiled as well, wondering what Dr. Goldberg had in mind.

"Nurse," Goldberg said, "you deal with our patient, Norman Bates, on a regular basis, do you not?"

"I do."

"How does he communicate with you?"

"Well, now it's verbally. He's far from chatty, but he relates to me, gives brief answers to questions. The only one he really talks to at length is Dr. Reed."

"You know this for certain?"

"I'm . . . pretty sure. Dr. Reed has told me that Norman talks quite freely during their sessions."

"But you have not witnessed this?" Goldberg asked.

"Well . . . no, not really."

"Regrettable." Goldberg sighed.

"But I've seen some great advances in Norman since he arrived here. He's much more open, aware of things around him—"

"*Ja,* I'm sure he is," Goldberg interrupted as he got to his feet, and walked to his record player. "Thank you, Nurse. Now, if you'll excuse me, I have a pile of paperwork and a lengthy opera to get through this evening." He gingerly lowered the tone arm onto the record, and Marie heard a blare of familiar music.

"*Die Meistersinger,*" she said as she stood.

"Ah, an aficionado!" said Goldberg, grinning with delight.

"Not really," she said. "We played it in high school orchestra."

"And what was your instrument?"

"The flute."

"Very nice," Goldberg said. "Do you know the opera or just the overture?"

"Just the overture, I'm afraid."

"Well, I envy you your discovery. That dour anti-Semite produced one of the jolliest operas ever written in *Die Meistersinger von Nürnberg.*" Goldberg held up a boxed set of recordings. "This is Kempe conducting the Berlin Philharmonic. Ferdinand Frantz plays the delightful Hans Sachs. This is my first time hearing this version. It just arrived in the post from New York."

"You certainly have a lot of operas," Marie said, gesturing to the rows of boxed sets.

"Being otherwise childless, these are my children. I play them carefully, and just as carefully replace them in their liners and boxes when done. Dust is the enemy of records, Nurse Radcliffe."

"Well, I'll remember that. I'll leave you to your opera then," Marie said, moving toward the door.

"Believe me, I shall have my fill tonight! Five long-playing records, ten sides. I expect it to keep me company until midnight while I do my work. The switchboard has orders to never put through calls to me after seven." He chuckled. "It's blasphemous to have the masters interrupted by the cacophony of a telephone. Thank you for answering my questions about Mr. Bates, and I hope you have a quiet evening, Nurse."

"You're welcome, Doctor. Good night."

Marie closed the door behind her and stood in the silent hall for a moment, wondering what their brief conversation meant for Norman. Probably the same thing that it meant for Jacob Tillson. Shock treatment. She knew how timid and fearful Norman was, and how terrified he was of any therapy other than his sessions with Dr. Reed. If Dr. Goldberg had his way, Marie hoped that it wouldn't throw Norman back into his previous catatonia.

The tension of the meeting with Drs. Berkowitz and Goldberg had worn her out, but it was still a long time before she could go home. She was on evening shift starting today for two weeks, which meant in at five in the afternoon, out at two in the morning, and it was only eight o'clock now. Night staff was skeletal but necessary, and its duties were shared among the nurses with the least seniority, of whom Marie was one. At least it only occurred three times a year. Attendants would bring Norman his breakfast and lunch, while she would still see him at dinnertime.

The only good thing about her new schedule was that Ben Blake was on the same evening shift, so they could meet during their breaks. Their relationship had intensified during the last few weeks. When their days off were the same, they went out to dinner or a movie at the Fairvale Cinema, and some nights they stopped at Delsey's for burgers and a beer, but never more than one. They were intoxicated enough with each other's company.

Marie was, at least. She wasn't sure how Ben felt about her, but thought he seemed as *interested* (if that was the word) in her as she was in him. They hadn't yet slept together, but Marie wanted to. She hadn't actually been with a man in that way, though she'd come close. She hadn't wanted to get pregnant, and, to be honest with herself, she hadn't really felt about anyone the way she felt about Ben Blake.

Ben was the kind of guy with whom she could imagine settling down and even raising a family. He was good-looking, treated her well, was fun and interesting, and they had a lot in common since they worked at the same place. There was always something to talk about.

But, more than that, Ben made her feel like no one else ever had. She felt as though he *wanted* her, not just sexually (though that was a big part of their mutual attraction), but on a more complete level as well.

In short, she really liked this guy—maybe loved him, and she couldn't wait until her break when she could see him again.

As he put on the fifth side of *Die Meistersinger von Nürnberg,* he thought about Hans Sachs's final aria:

> *Habt Acht! Uns dräuen üble Streich':*
> *Zerfällt erst deutsches Volk und Reich . . .*

And in his head he translated the original German into the language of his host country, the land in which he now lived and which he loathed:

Beware! Bad times are nigh at hand:
And when fall German folk and land
In spurious foreign pomp ere long,
No prince will know his people's tongue,
And foreign thoughts and foreign ways
Upon our German soil they'll raise;
Our native art will fade from hence
If 'tis not held in reverence.
So heed my words! Honor your German Masters
If you would stay disasters . . .

But the disaster had come, hadn't it? And honoring their German Masters hadn't prevented it.

He turned the knob, puffed on his cigar, and sat back down as the tone arm dropped into the groove and the opera resumed. His attention drifted away from the papers on his desk, and he glanced around the office, his gaze falling on the various appurtenances of Judaism, what he thought of as his props.

There was that idiotic menorah, which he had bought in a Buenos Aires pawnshop all those years ago. And there that *verdammt* Star of David. If he only had a dollar for each time someone had said how beautiful it was, that piece of *Scheisse* made up of stones, bearing all the artistry of a brain-damaged ghetto urchin. He flicked his cigar at the symbol, lobbing a chunk of gray ash toward it.

Then he chuckled, let his eyes blur and go out of focus so that the single minor change he'd had made in the piece by a trusted craftsman became apparent. Ah, yes. If it hadn't been for that subtlety, there was no way he could have sat all these years beneath the symbol of the hated *Juden*.

How ironic that he, who held Jews in such contempt, had been forced to live as one for the past sixteen years. And how doubly ironic that in the field of psychiatry in the United States, most of the practitioners were Jews. At least here, far from the cities and their cesspools of racial filth, Jews were few and far between.

At least until that young Berkowitz kike came along, and he had not only to mentor him, but to treat him as a *Bruder* in Jewry. What a farce. He remembered giving Berkowitz a cookie, and took the package out of his drawer. He removed the Oreo at the end of the row, thinking that the Jew's fingers might have brushed it, and dropped it in the wastebasket.

Still, matters could always be worse. Out here, he was respected and treated well. His stolen reputation had done much of the work, and his native German efficiency and craft, that *heil'ge deutsche Kunst* of which Wagner had written and Sachs had sung, had done the rest. After all, he was a psychiatrist, and a good one in his native land. And when those whom he had to fool expected brilliance, that was what they got.

He was paid very well, drove a nice car, smoked dollar cigars, drank good liquor, listened to and collected his fill of the operas, which made his life a joy, and was *safe,* buried as he was in the persona of a victimized Jew, and not in the South American jungles, as were so many of his erstwhile colleagues and friends, friends with whom he had not been in contact since the end of the war.

He had just started to think about some of them when the sound of the Nightwatchman's horn interrupted his reveries as well as Walther's song. In another moment he heard the *Nachtwächter* sing:

> *Hear, good people, what I say,*
> *The clock has rung the day away,*
> *So tend your fire and tend your light*

That no one shall be harmed tonight.
Praise God, the Lord . . .

He put his cigar safely in the ashtray, sat back in his comfortable chair, closed his eyes, and thanked the *deutsche Gott* for his
good circumstances. The papers on his desk could wait for several minutes. Perhaps he would give his mind a break and simply
appreciate the music for a time, fade into that half-sleeping, half-
waking state in which musical notes seemed to take on physical
shapes, and in which the singers seemed to possess him as he pos-
sessed them, so that singer and listener were one.

The business of running a hospital left little time for such unal-
loyed pleasures, but he felt that he was deserving of a self-granted
boon every once in a while, as the euphemism went. Americans
had so many absurd sayings like that. *Once in a while* meant occasionally, while *once* meant one time only, the opposite of occasionally. Adding *in a while* did nothing to clarify it, so that it now
meant "one time only in a period of time." Idiotic.

Idiotic like so many other Americanisms. Take *make a killing*
and *bump off,* he thought. *Make a killing* didn't mean to kill, it
meant to make money, while *bump off* meant to kill. So he himself had *bumped off* many in his day, but had never *made a killing.*
Just silly.

Enough, he cautioned himself. His eyes were closed in order
to enjoy the music more, not to fulminate on the foolishness of
the English language. The notes, the magnificent notes and words,
those were what he needed to pay attention to, not American
Dummheit.

He made himself relax and listen more attentively, and in a
short time Richard Wagner had borne him away. He felt himself
retreating from cares and memories until he fell fully into the
music, down and down a sweet black velvet well of sound.

He awoke to silence and darkness. The darkness was strange. Surely his desk lamp had been on when he had fallen asleep. Why then was it now off?

Truth be told, he had never liked the dark. The fear had begun when he was a child, and it still remained. It was a ridiculous thought, but he always had the feeling that the Jews could creep up on you in the dark.

His hand trembled as he reached out for the desk lamp. He found the base, then slid his hand upward until he reached the switch. He turned it, and light flared into his eyes, making him close them again. In that self-imposed darkness, he thought once again about his aversion. He had psychoanalyzed himself many times to find the roots of his fear, and had long ago discovered that it was due to the old Jewish crone who had sold dried fish on *Friedrichstrasse*.

She had terrified him when he was a child. His mother was partly to blame for that, with her stories of Jews stealing Christian children for a number of horrible reasons. One time as they passed the old woman's stand, his mother whispered to him, *Aber ist, das, Fisch?* The thought chilled him. *But is that fish?* Was it? he had wondered. Or did the old woman sell something unthinkable instead?

Her beak of a nose, the hairy wart on her cheek, her near-toothless grinning mouth, gray hairs creeping out like spiderwebs from under her head covering, and her right eye, always weeping with yellow pus—all these haunted his dreams and made him wake screaming, calling for *Licht! Licht!* before the old woman came crawling over the foot of his bed, creeping onto his skinny body, bringing her hideous face up against his in the blackness, wrapping her skeletal fingers around his throat.

His mother, always one for economy, would leave a stub of a candle in his room, just enough to allow him to get back to sleep before it burned out. He always wished the candles were longer.

But the light was on now, and there was no reason to fear. He opened his eyes again, blinking against the bright lamplight. In a moment, he would rise and play the next side of *Die Meistersinger*. Still, he couldn't help but think about the old woman a moment longer, the bogeyman of his youth, and how he had gotten his revenge on her for frightening him so.

Ah, perhaps not on her specifically, but on the Jews, oh, yes. Revenge a thousand times over. Still, as many as he had put into their graves—or up chimneys, he corrected himself—she still haunted him. He still saw her at night in his dreams, in the darkness, creeping up on him, her mouth grinning, her bony fingers reaching out . . .

And then the lamp went off again. He hadn't touched it.

He froze, and for the first time he felt that someone else was in the room, someone who had first turned off the light, and then, after he had awakened, pulled the plug from the socket. The socket in the wall behind him.

He hadn't looked behind him.

Fingers wrapped around his throat from behind. He tried to hitch in a breath to scream, but the grip on his neck was implacable, fingers that clutched and bit into his throat like fangs, stifling him.

Then he felt something long and cold and sharp drift into the flesh beneath his breastbone, drift like smoke, like music, and a rushing sound filled his head, as of millions of dissonant voices singing at once, and he knew that the old woman and her entire tribe had found him at last.

"*Licht . . . Licht . . .* ," he whispered, just before he sank into the deepest darkness of all, and his light was gone forever.

13

Ben Blake stood at the window of the break room looking out at the rain. He sipped his coffee and thought about Marie Radcliffe. He had been looking forward to seeing her on his current break, but she hadn't shown. Probably got hung up with a patient somewhere. The nursing staff was minimal at night, and when something happened, it was all hands on deck.

Ben was disappointed. He was starting to think that he might be in love with Marie. She had an effect on him like no other woman he'd known. It had started when she'd opened up to him about her father on their first date, and their relationship had grown more intimate ever since. Not in a sexual way, but he thought that might not be far off. He wanted it, of course, but he wanted more. She might, he thought, really be *the one*. Kind and caring, she'd make one hell of a mom, that was for sure, and a great wife too.

Slow down, boy, he thought. Let's not get ahead of ourselves.

He was alone in the break room, so he switched off the light in order to see outside, through the windows. Ben loved wild nights like this, with the rain and wind blowing, moon and stars blotted out by heavy clouds. He looked at the horizon, the ridge-line of trees, scarcely visible in the darkness and the storm.

But a sudden motion of gray against black caught his attention. Something near, almost directly below him, glided across the lawn of the exercise yard, and, as his eyes adjusted, he saw it was a person, moving stealthily but quickly. It was either someone in a black hooded windbreaker or a ghost, he thought, but, in spite of all the stories he'd heard about the hospital, he didn't believe in ghosts.

Now, who the hell? Who'd be outside on a night like this?

Then he thought of Ronald Miller. It was a nutty idea, but what if Miller had never left the hospital grounds? What if he'd hung around, as some of the nurses had feared, stealing food, hiding out, waiting for a moment to strike? Even if it *wasn't* Miller, it was suspicious as hell.

Ben considered the direction in which the dark shape was moving, and could think of only one entrance to the hospital there. Behind the building near the right side was a short ramp that led down to a basement door behind which lawn equipment was stored. Once in the relative shelter of those steps, a person could work as long as he wanted on the door lock. No one was getting out from the inside, but from the outside it wouldn't be impossible to jimmy the padlock and break in.

But who the hell would want to break *in* to the crazy house? Maybe, he thought wryly, somebody crazy? Like Ronald Miller?

Ben ran out of the break room and over to the ward where Dick O'Brien was on shift. "Come on—emergency!" he said to Dick, and explained as they ran through the halls and down the basement stairs.

"You really think it could be Miller?" Dick asked, panting as he ran.

"Don't know, but it's *somebody*."

As they neared the room with the outside door, they stopped running. Ben led the way in, walking slowly and listening. The light from the corridor illuminated the interior of the room just enough so that he could see the shapes of the lawn equipment—mowers and a small lawn tractor. On hooks and racks against the wall was an assortment of hand tools.

They stopped walking and listened intently. At the door, Ben could hear what sounded like someone rubbing metal on metal. There was a sudden snap, as of a hasp breaking, and a rattling sound.

Dick moved to the wall of tools and grabbed a small shovel. Ben thought that seemed like a good idea and took what he thought was an edger, and gestured to Dick to move against the wall at the side of the door. The noise continued outside. There was a scraping sound, then a climactic *click*. The inset lock had been forced.

Ben licked his lips, held the edger like a baseball bat, and watched as the door slowly opened. In the doorway, he saw the shadowy shape of a man moving into the room. "Easy, partner," Ben said. "Let's get those hands high in the air, huh?"

But instead of raising his hands, the man reached behind him and his right hand came back holding something. Ben squinted to make out what it was and felt the hair on his neck prickle as the dull light glinted off the metal of a pistol.

"Okay," he said, slowly lowering the edger. "Okay, no need for that, just—"

But he didn't have to finish his sentence. Dick swung the shovel at the man's head, there was the sound of steel against skull, and the pistol fired with a dull *pop*. Fire sparked from the muzzle, but the shooter had already started to fall, and the bullet harmlessly ricocheted off the cement floor. The body hit the floor face-first with a crack that made Ben think the nose had broken for sure.

Dick dropped the shovel and they both knelt by the man's

side. Ben turned him over, but didn't recognize the face with the bleeding nose. "Who the hell . . . ," Dick said.

"Never saw him before," Ben answered. He took the gun and set it on the floor where the man couldn't reach it, then felt his wrist for a pulse. It was there, good and strong. "You didn't kill him, anyway," he told Dick. "Let's tie him up."

They turned on the light and found a roll of baling wire hanging on the wall. A hedge trimmer cut the pieces easily. They bound the unconscious man's wrists behind him, then wrapped more wire around his ankles. By the time they were finished and had firmly shut the outside door, the man had started to moan and move slightly.

"Go upstairs and call the cops," Ben told Dick. He picked up the pistol, which he now saw was an automatic. "I'll watch him. Send some guys down and we'll take him upstairs."

Dick ran out of the storage room, and Ben heard his footfalls echoing down the corridor. When he looked back at the man tied up on the floor, the man was looking at him with dark eyes. "Head hurt?" Ben asked as he picked up the man's pistol. When there was no answer, he said, "Who are you, anyway?"

The man didn't speak. He only looked at Ben with deep anger in his gray eyes.

"The police are on their way here now. You gonna clam up for them too?" Nothing.

"Okay, suit yourself. You don't have to talk to me. They'll get it out of you."

It wasn't the dream that woke Norman Bates in his room. It was the dampness of his scalp against the pillow. The cotton pillowcase was saturated with his perspiration. He noticed that first, then remembered the dream, and sat up in the darkness.

It was patchy, and he could recall only fragmentary glimpses of it, like a remembrance of when he was a very young child, before the machinery of memory had assembled itself in his mind. A dark room, a figure before him, narrow walls, dragging something heavy, then a large room, the smell of dampness thick in the air, and beneath it a weightier smell, a smell of rot and corruption. And death.

Norman whined deep in his throat and stood up, trying to banish the bits and pieces that remained of the dream. He felt his way to the door, slid back the slot, and looked into the hall. He could see nothing but the wall on the opposite side, but at least there was light, and a slight breeze that came through the slot, chilling but drying the sweat on his neck. What, he wondered, had he seen? Had it been only a dream? Or had he once again seen through Robert's eyes, seen what Robert may have done, or, Norman hoped, what Robert had only imagined, desires and fantasies so strong that they spanned the gap between brothers, between twins?

Norman closed his eyes and breathed in the fresher air from the hallway until he felt better. Then he went back to his bed and turned over his pillow so the dry side was facing up. He lay down and tried not to think about the dream. Because, after all, that's what it was. Only a dream.

Just before he drifted back to sleep, he wondered vaguely why, if it was just a dream, he could still smell, very faintly, that odor of corruption.

Marie Radcliffe was at the nurses' station of Ward D when Dick O'Brien came running down the hall toward her, followed by three other attendants. "Marie!" he yelled. "Go get Dr. Goldberg! Me and Ben caught a guy trying to break in down in the cellar."

"Is Ben okay?" she asked as the men ran by.

"He's fine, yeah," Dick called over his shoulder. "Get the doc, okay?"

Marie dashed down the corridor, turning toward the row of offices. Dr. Goldberg's door was closed, and she knocked loudly, but there was no answer. It was after midnight, and he might have gone home, but most of the time when he worked late, he slept on the daybed in his office. She knocked again, even more forcefully, but there was no response.

Marie turned the door handle and found it was unlocked. She pushed it open and called, "Dr. Goldberg?" There was no answer, so she entered the office.

The desk lamp was on, but Goldberg wasn't seated at his desk, nor was he lying on the daybed. The room seemed to be empty. The papers on the desk were stacked neatly, and the chair was pushed up flush to the desk. Had Dr. Goldberg changed his mind and left early? If he had, he would have had to walk past the nurses' station at which Marie had been sitting most of the evening.

She walked over to the door to the doctor's private bathroom and knocked lightly. Hearing no answer, she opened the door and turned on the light. The room was empty, the shower stall dry.

Then Marie went over to the record player. A red light at the bottom of the console indicated that the power was still on. She opened the lid and looked down at the turntable. A black-and-white angel sitting on a record looked up at her from an otherwise red label. She leaned farther over and read, WAGNER "DIE MEISTERSINGER VON NüRNBERG" ACT II (PART 2), and saw the number 5 at both the nine and three o'clock positions on the label.

Side 5? But Dr. Goldberg had said there were ten sides and he had intended to listen to them all. If he had changed his mind, why hadn't he put the record away, since he was so meticulous about caring for his "children," and turned off the machine?

Maybe he'd gone to the break room to get some food or coffee from the machines, though that seemed unlikely. Whatever the answers, Dr. Goldberg wasn't in his office.

Marie was crossing to the door to search for him elsewhere when her peripheral vision caught a glimpse of something glinting on the floor, a small object on the carpet just beneath the desk. She knelt, and when she saw what it was, a little shock passed through her. It was the polished piece of petrified wood that she had given as a good luck charm to Norman Bates.

She picked it up and looked at it more closely. There was no mistaking something she had carried in her pockets and her purse for years. But how did it get here? Marie knew that Dr. Goldberg had recently talked to Norman, but that had been in Norman's room, not Goldberg's office. Perhaps she would ask Norman about it, then thought that it might be wiser to talk to Dr. Reed about it first.

She dropped it into the pocket of her uniform and went to look for Dr. Goldberg.

Even with the strong wind blowing the fresh rain through the air so that it drenched his face and clothing, the man still thought the swamp smelled rank and corrupt, like a cemetery in a nightmare, with open graves and coffins whose lids had rotted away, exposing their residents to the elements. It was a fitting simile, he thought, since a graveyard was precisely what it had been and was again.

True, he was using it as a graveyard for automobiles, but Norman Bates had been faithful to the original meaning of *graveyard*.

He had sunk Mary Crane in it, along with her car, not all that long ago. And now the man was only following in Norman's footsteps.

Collar up against the wind and rain, he watched as the Lincoln slipped slowly into the muck. In the darkness, its peach color had turned black against the dark of the swamp. Odd that Goldberg had chosen such a color, he thought, almost feminine. Perhaps the psychiatrist might have benefited from some treatment himself.

Be that as it may, the car was sinking more quickly than Myron Gunn's. He had chosen a different place, a dozen yards or so to the right of where he had sunk the previous one. It wouldn't do to have Goldberg's Lincoln slip into the muck, hit the other one, then stop dead. He could imagine the sign such an occurrence would cause:

To ensure a tidy swamp,
please dump all victims' cars next to rather than behind each other.
Thank you.
The Management

He chuckled to himself as he watched the car slowly sink. He'd had to be more patient tonight. The black car was there, the one he saw earlier, the one that obviously didn't belong. And, as before, there had been someone in it. So he'd waited to take Goldberg's car, waited until the stranger had gotten out of his own car and melted into the stormy night, moving around to the back of the building.

Once the stranger had gone, the man moved fast, under cover of night and rain, jumped in the car, and drove it away unseen. It was a long shot that people would think Goldberg had followed Myron Gunn and Eleanor Lindstrom's lead and hit the highway, but it had worked out nicely before, and maybe Goldberg had his own secrets that he wanted to hide. At least it would confuse the police more to have Goldberg disappear rather than have his body found. In this case, his death wasn't a given.

Over the sound of the rain, he heard that nauseating, sucking sound that told him the swamp was fully claiming the car. He watched with deep satisfaction as the trunk and finally the tips of the tailfins went under the surface. Thick, viscous bubbles of muck and mire belched their way upward, and then the car was gone.

He pressed his hat down more tightly on his head and turned away from the swamp, beginning his long, wet walk back to his own car.

An hour later, in one of the patient interview rooms of the state hospital, Captain Banning and Sheriff Jud Chambers sat across a table from the man who had been discovered in the cellar. The man was now handcuffed, and behind him stood two highway patrol officers. A leather wallet lay on the table, with an assortment of cards spread out on the table's wooden surface.

"All right, Mr. Dov Bergmann, if that's your name," Captain Banning said, "you've got some interesting ID here. Seems you're from Israel, huh?"

"I'm not answering any questions," Bergmann said. "I want you to call the nearest Israeli consulate and inform them of my detainment."

"Oh, you do, do you? Well, I'll tell you something, Dov, my friend. You haven't been detained, you've been *arrested*. And I don't care where you're from. You're not gonna see the backside of any consul or even a lawyer until we get some questions answered here."

"I have the right to counsel," Bergmann said.

"I told you, Dov," Banning said, as if explaining to a child, "no consul, no lawyer."

"I said *counsel*. An attorney. Do you not have that right in the United States?"

"Well, I couldn't tell the difference, with your accent. And you're a foreigner, so you got no U.S. rights," Banning said.

Jud Chambers leaned toward Banning and whispered, "I'm not sure that's right."

"Don't worry about it," Banning whispered back. "I'm not having this guy walk out of here on some diplomatic-immunity bullshit."

"Well, I don't think he's really a diplomat," Chambers whispered.

"Just let me handle it . . ." Banning raised his voice, "Now, look, Dov. You're in my jurisdiction. You, a foreigner, break into a state institution with a loaded handgun, which you then fire at people who are authorized to detain you until an official arrest takes place. Which has been done. And I want to know what you were doing here with a gun. You're not gonna see daylight again until I get answers."

Bergmann looked down at the tabletop, his mouth a thin line, and did not reply.

The silence was broken by the sound of the door opening. Another officer came into the room. He was holding a portfolio made of thin cardboard with an attached elastic band around it. "Found the car his keys fit," the officer said. "This was under the seat, along with some other weapons and stuff."

Banning motioned the officer out, then opened the portfolio and looked at the paper files and photographs inside. Some of the documents were in Hebrew, but others were in English, German, and French. For several minutes, Banning browsed and read what he could, passing the papers to Jud Chambers, who was the first to speak. "I'll be damned," he said softly.

"Holy hell," Banning breathed in response. He looked up at Bergmann. "Who are you with? That Jewish secret service? The one that got Adolf Eichmann last year down in Argentina?"

"Mossad," Jud Chambers said.

"I prefer to speak to an Israeli consul," Bergmann said.

"You broke in here to *kill* somebody, didn't you?" Banning said. "What these papers say . . . you came in here to kill Dr. Goldberg?"

Dov Bergmann looked at Captain Banning for a long time. "All right, then," he finally said. "It's all there in front of you. Maybe . . . maybe if I tell you *nearly* everything, it can end here."

"Maybe," Banning said. "But what do you mean, *nearly*?"

"I cannot tell you who I work for. That I cannot do."

Banning nodded. "We'll see. Depends on what else you say."

"All right, then," Bergmann repeated. He looked over his shoulder at the two officers behind him, then back at Banning. "I prefer to have as few people as possible hear this. Unless you're afraid I can overcome you both with handcuffs on."

Banning looked at the two men and gestured them out of the room with a jerk of his head. When they were gone, Bergmann continued, "First, I didn't come in here to kill Isaac Goldberg. I came in here to *execute* Kurt Gephardt."

"The guy in here," Banning said, holding up the papers.

Bergmann nodded. "Dr. Isaac Goldberg died in 1944 in the Mauthausen-Gusen concentration camp in his own country of Austria. He was worked to death. They called it 'extermination through labor.' The following year, when the Third Reich went up in flames, his identity was taken over by Kurt Gephardt, who, to all intents and purposes, *became* Isaac Goldberg, only, *this* Isaac Goldberg had survived the camps. This happened frequently, and it was easy to accomplish, as nearly all family members and friends of the dead man whose identity was stolen were dead as well. Gephardt—now Goldberg—traveled to America and continued his . . . career."

"You mean as a psychologist?" Banning said.

"A psychiatrist," Bergmann answered. "Gephardt was a psychiatrist as well as Goldberg. With stolen identities, the Nazis tried to make the matches as close as possible."

Banning shook his head. "So you're saying this Gephardt lived all these years as Goldberg? And nobody ever found out?"

Bergmann nodded. "There was a physical resemblance between them, but it mattered little, since all of Goldberg's documentation had been destroyed by the Nazis, so there were no photographs, at least none that would readily surface. But as you see"—he nodded at the sheaf of papers Banning was holding— "we found one. Enough for our team to determine that the prewar and postwar Goldbergs were not the same man."

"So then this Gephardt," Banning said, "is a war criminal? I take it he did something pretty bad for you guys to come after him like this."

Bergmann took a deep breath. "Have either of you ever heard of Aktion T4?" He gave it the German pronunciation, then said, "Action T4." Both Banning and Chambers shook their heads. "It has a long history, but I'll keep it concise. It was a program of forced euthanasia for the Nazis to get rid of undesirables."

"Jews?" Jud Chambers asked.

"There were Jews among the victims." He smiled bitterly. "There always were, and the Jewish patients were the first to go. But the victims in this case were *anyone* who didn't conform to Hitler's idea of what German genes should contain—people with chronic illnesses, physical disabilities, the mentally ill. Since the best young men of Germany were dying at the front, the weak and sick and insane shouldn't be left to procreate freely at home. A balance had to be reached. That required *Gnadentod*—'merciful death.'"

"Euthanasia?" Banning said.

"Yes. From 1939 to 1941, seventy thousand people labeled undesirables were put to death under the program. And do you know where these extermination centers were located? In mental hospitals. So psychiatrists ended up sentencing their own patients to death. Dr. Kurt Gephardt was there from the beginning."

Jud Chambers shook his head. "How were they killed? Gas?"

"Now that," Dov Bergmann said, "is an interesting story. Children with birth defects were killed by chemical injections, but that wasn't efficient enough for the vast numbers of adults who were to be killed. So they tried carbon monoxide gas, and it worked so well on these 'mental defectives' that deadly gas quickly became the death of choice for the Third Reich. Aktion T4, in short, was the birthplace of the Holocaust. And Kurt Gephardt was one of its godfathers."

Banning leaned forward as he spoke. "But you said that it only went until 1941, this Action T4 thing."

"The policies established in Aktion T4 continued unofficially until the end of the war. Two hundred thousand more people, many of them children, died. And Kurt Gephardt was there all the time, sending them to their deaths with a brief examination and a signature."

Bergmann had gone pale, and he squeezed his eyes shut for a moment before opening them again. "Do you suppose I could have a cigarette?"

Banning took a Camel from his pack and handed it to Bergmann, who took it with handcuffed hands and put it in his mouth. Banning lit it for him. "So Dr. Goldberg is really Gephardt," he said.

"We have undeniable proof."

"And you were coming in here to, what, assassinate him?"

Bergmann inhaled smoke and blew it out. "I think it best not to discuss our plans in that regard."

There was silence in the room for a moment, then Jud Chambers whispered, "Goddamn . . ."

The word seemed to bring Banning to life. "The first thing we need to do is confront Dr. . . . whoever he is with this. You've made a serious accusation, Mr. Bergmann, one that you were ready to kill him over. He's got to be allowed to respond to it."

"Oh, by all means," Bergmann said lightly. "Perhaps you should call him on the telephone and inform him . . ." He paused and his face grew stern, his words icy, ". . . so that he can *escape*. Honestly, do you believe that Gephardt is going to just come in here to answer these accusations? He'll *run*. As soon as they get a whiff that something isn't right, they're gone. Gephardt's been lucky. We had no idea of the truth until information recently came into our hands. We don't want to lose him."

Banning nodded. "Okay. He's not in the building now, we know that, but—"

"*What?*" Bergmann cried, trying to leap to his feet. "He was here when I broke in—his *car* was here! Are you saying he left between the time I came in here and now? When all the . . ." He seemed to be searching for the English word. ". . . *fuss* was going on?"

"Well," Chambers said, "now I think on it, I might've seen his car heading out the road when I was coming in. Big light-colored Lincoln, isn't it?"

Dov Bergmann spat out some foreign words that the other two thought might have been curses. "He's *gone!*" he said. Then more softly, he added, "Why was I so impatient?" He shook his head and answered his own question. "I suppose I just didn't want to waste another night. And now . . . see what I've wasted now . . ."

Banning and Chambers saw tears in his eyes. Banning turned and barked toward the closed door, "Keene! Harris!" The two troopers came back in. "I want you to go to Dr. Goldberg's house and see if he and his car are there. If he is, tell him he's needed out here right away and bring him back—in your car. Don't let him out of your sight for a second, got it?"

Keene and Harris nodded and left. "If he's there, they'll bring him back," Banning said.

"He won't be there." Bergmann took a final drag on his cigarette and crushed the butt in the ashtray. "Honestly, I don't think any of you will ever see your Dr. Goldberg again."

14

When the police arrived at the home of the man known as Dr. Isaac Goldberg, they found neither the man nor his car. After receiving this news, Captain Banning allowed Dov Bergmann to call the nearest Israeli consulate, with the caveat that he should speak only in English.

After several minutes of conversation, Bergmann told Banning that the consul-general was connecting him with the Israeli embassy in Washington, DC, and then, after he further explained the situation, Bergmann looked at Banning again. "They're getting in touch with the U.S. Department of State. They'll want to speak to you."

Several minutes passed during which, Banning assumed, the embassy was speaking with the State Department. Finally someone came on the line identifying himself as Under Secretary of State Chester Bowles, who told Banning that the State Department would send several agents to bring Dov Bergmann to Washington. He also told Banning that Bergmann was to be isolated, and that absolutely no one was to speak to him further.

"The State Department would prefer," said the officious voice on the phone, "that as few people know of this occurrence as possible. These events must *not* be made public in any way. May we count on your cooperation in this regard, Captain Banning?"

"Yes, sir. Absolutely."

"Excellent. Our agents will be coming from the nearest field office. They should arrive before noon. Again, thank you for your efficiency. And your silence. Let me give you our number. In the event that the person known as Isaac Goldberg should return to the hospital, you are authorized to hold him, and you will notify us immediately."

Banning wrote down the number and hung up. He followed the orders, seeing to it that the Israeli was given food and a comfortable room with reading material. Then he and Sheriff Chambers waited for the agents, whatever agency they might be from. Banning guessed the CIA, while Chambers hazarded the FBI as his choice.

"So who's in charge of this place now that Goldberg, or whoever he is, is gone?" Banning asked Chambers.

"Guess it's Nick Steiner. He's been here longest."

"Let's get him on the horn," Banning said, picking up the phone. "Somebody's gotta take charge around here, even if we can't tell him why."

Dr. Nicholas Steiner arrived shortly after Bergmann had been isolated, just after 8:00 a.m. Banning and Chambers took him into the same room in which they'd interrogated Dov Bergmann and told him what they could, which was that a man they had in custody had broken in last night, that some "law enforcement officials" were picking him up later, and that Dr. Goldberg had disappeared along with his car and would probably not be back.

"That's it?" Steiner asked after waiting for more information.

Banning nodded. "That's it. Sorry we can't tell you more."

"And *why* can't you tell me more?"

"It's, uh . . . government policy."

"Government. You mean like *you?* The highway patrol?" He turned to Chambers. "Or the sheriff's office, Jud? You have important state secrets I'm not aware of?"

"State secrets is pretty much it, Nick," Chambers said. "Captain Banning's being straight with you. This goes . . . kinda deep. Or pretty high. Both, I guess."

"Where's Dr. Goldberg?" Steiner asked.

"Pardon?" Banning said.

"Where . . . is . . . *Goldberg?*" Steiner repeated, as if to a child. "The superintendent of this hospital? My immediate superior? What in God's name do you mean, he's 'disappeared?' To where?"

"If we knew that," Chambers said, "he wouldn't have disappeared."

Steiner sighed and flopped back in his chair. "Maybe this place really *is* a madhouse." He sat up again. "I'm just trying to determine where Dr. Goldberg is. Has he been kidnapped? Has he too succumbed to temptation like Mr. Gunn and eloped with a nurse? Or has he run off to become a basso profundo in a traveling opera company?"

"A *what?*" Jud Chambers asked.

Steiner gave a grunt of frustration. "Gentlemen, *please.* Surely you can tell me *something.*"

"Look," Banning said, giving the sheriff a sidelong glance, "we can tell you this much and no more. It seems he's gone off on his own. Of his own free will. And he won't be back. And that's it, okay? Case closed."

"You're not looking for him?" Steiner asked.

"*We're* not looking for him, no." Banning paused. "But if somebody . . . if anybody saw him again, we'd want to know."

Steiner frowned and looked intently at Banning. "He's *done* something, then."

"I didn't say that."

Steiner nodded. "He's done something . . ." He sat back again and gazed at the wall and beyond it, into the middle distance. "How little we really know each other . . ."

Before the car came to take away Dov Bergmann, Drs. Reed and Berkowitz had arrived at the hospital, as had Head Nurse Wyndham and Head Attendant Wiseman. Dr. Steiner called them all into a small meeting room and explained as much of the situation as he knew.

"I wish I could answer the questions you must have," he told them, "but I don't know the answers myself. I can only assume that Dr. Goldberg had secrets of his own, and they were enough to . . . drive him away. I don't necessarily subscribe to the scenario that he won't return—this place was his life, as far as we all know, and for that reason I think we should keep his office the way it is indefinitely. As far as I know, it's not a crime scene, so if we need any files that the doctor had there, feel free to go in and get them. I've already contacted the state board and informed them of Dr. Goldberg's . . . disappearance, and they've appointed me acting superintendent and promise to appoint a new one within three months." Steiner paused. "Any questions . . . that I *can* answer?"

Dr. Reed raised an index finger. "Was there any suggestion of, what, foul play? I mean, I heard from an attendant that there was actually a shot fired in the basement."

"I heard that too," Steiner said. "I've talked to the attendants involved, and apparently this intruder is somehow involved with Dr. Goldberg's absence, though I don't know how, and no one seems ready to tell us. There is the rather unlikely possibility that this has something to do with . . . national security, perhaps? But this is only speculation on my part, I really have no idea."

Elliot Berkowitz raised his hand, and his voice sounded shaky. "Did Dr. Goldberg leave a note or anything? He just disappeared without a word?"

"That seems to be what happened," Steiner said. "I'm sorry. As I've said, I wish I could tell you more, but I simply don't know. Rest assured that if any information comes out, I'll share it with you. Feel free to tell the nurses and attendants as much as you know, including the likelihood that Dr. Goldberg will *not* return."

The agents who were to take away Dov Bergmann arrived shortly before noon. There were four of them, including the driver, and Captain Banning and Sheriff Chambers watched as they got out of the new black Ford sedan that parked imperiously in front of the main entrance. All of the men were wearing similar black suits and dark glasses against the sun, which had reappeared with the passing of the storm.

A sandy-haired man, the tallest of the four, identified himself to Banning and Chambers as Agent Shepard and showed an FBI ID. Chambers glanced at Banning and smiled. He had guessed right.

Banning led the men into the hospital, where they went directly to the room where Dov Bergmann was being held. Two of the agents got on either side of Bergmann, handcuffed him, and accompanied him to the car, while the tall agent took out a sheaf of papers, one of which he handed to Banning to sign.

"Prisoner transfer form," the man said. "Cut and dried." Banning gave it a quick once-over and signed it, then handed it back.

"Thanks for your cooperation, Captain," the agent said. "The papers you found?"

"Right here," Banning said, handing over the portfolio found in Bergmann's car.

"And the prisoner's handgun?"

Banning had wrapped it in a handkerchief to preserve any fingerprints, and he gave it to the agent, who slipped it into his suit jacket pocket and handed the handkerchief back to Banning.

"We got a pair of heavy wire cutters that must've been his too. He used them to cut through the chain-link fence and get to the cellar door he came in. You want them?"

The agent nodded. "Definitely. If it's evidence, we want it. We'll also want the car he used." Banning handed the agent the car keys they had taken from Bergmann, and had a deputy retrieve the wire cutters.

Together they all walked out to the black Ford. Bergmann, still cuffed, was seated in the middle of the backseat between two of the agents. The man called Shepard got in the driver's seat and started the Ford, while the original driver walked out to the parking lot to get Bergmann's car. The agent behind the wheel gave a two-finger salute to Banning as they pulled away.

"FBI," Jud Chambers said as they watched the car disappear down the lane, Bergmann's car in its wake. "I win."

"I don't recall making a bet," said Banning, turning back toward the building.

When the state hospital was no longer visible in the rearview mirror of the black Ford, one of the dark-suited men took a key out of his pocket and unlocked Dov Bergmann's handcuffs. Bergmann stretched his arms and rubbed his wrists. "Sorry, Asher" he said, looking down at the back of the seat.

The man next to him gave a great sigh and shook his head. "What in *hell* were you thinking, Dov?"

"I got anxious," Dov Bergmann said. "It was foolish. I thought I could get in and eliminate him on my own. Save us all the trouble of taking him back home."

"You were to act as a *scout,* not an assassin," said Asher. "Record his movements, nothing more. Instead, you not only get caught, but you spook Gephardt. He'll go underground so far, we might never find him. Director Harel is *not* going to be pleased with you. Nor with the team." He paused and looked out the window. "The only good thing," he finally said, "is that this was the easiest extraction of an agent we've ever made. You didn't tell them too much?"

"Well, you already realize that they know who their Dr. Goldberg really is. But they don't know who I am. They . . . suspect. But I never told them."

"Let's hope," Asher said with a smirk, "that the orders from their government preserve their silence. And, with luck, if Gephardt *should* reappear, they'll call the number I gave them." Asher lit a cigarette and offered one to Dov Bergmann, who took it. "Now. I think we should go to Gephardt's house and search it. Such a good Nazi is bound to keep some of his treasures."

The man on the other side of Bergmann said, "Do you think that's wise?"

"It's always wise to gather more evidence, Yitzhak," Asher said, "and if anyone should question us, after all"—he took out the fake FBI ID he had shown Captain Banning—"we do work for *their* government."

The agents easily broke into Kurt Gephardt's suburban split-level house. No one came out of nearby houses to question or challenge them. In a bedroom closet was an entrance to the attic. When they pushed aside the plywood panel, they immediately found a shoe box filled with memorabilia of Gephardt's Nazi years, including civilian citations in Gephardt's name, and a photograph of Gephardt posing with Dr. Karl Brandt, Hitler's personal physician and the overseer of Aktion T4.

They took the box, locked up the house, and drove away, never to be seen near Fairvale again.

15

The reactions that greeted the disappearances of Ronald Miller, Myron Gunn, and Eleanor Lindstrom were only dust devils compared to the hurricane that blew into the State Hospital for the Criminally Insane when the news of Dr. Isaac Goldberg's vanishing was announced. Nurses, attendants, cooks, janitors, the entire staff, felt rudderless as the news—and the rumors—spread.

Even though the evening shift, including Ben Blake and Dick O'Brien, had gone home, word had spread about the man in the basement with the gun. With no one knowing *anything* about Goldberg's disappearance, it was only logical to assume that the two events were connected. And conversations throughout the day produced scenarios even more exotic than the reality of what had occurred.

The more anti-Semitic staff members thought that Dr. Goldberg was a Communist, and that the arrested man was a CIA assassin. Others thought that the intruder was a jealous husband of an as-yet-unidentified nurse with whom Goldberg was carrying on an affair. Still others suggested that the shooter was a vengeful

Nazi who came to finish what the concentration camps had not been able to accomplish.

Only a very few subscribed to the theory that Dr. Isaac Goldberg was not whom he seemed to be. One of those was Tom Downing, the attendant who'd discovered that Ronald Miller was missing. He was the first, in a conversation in the break room, to link it to the Eichmann case, which he had followed closely. It was mere imagination rather than any evidence that had brought him close to the truth.

"What if," he said to Eddie Abbott, another attendant, "Goldberg wasn't Goldberg at all, but somebody like Eichmann? He just *pretended* to be Goldberg. For years, you know?"

"That's screwy," Eddie said.

"Nah nah, stay with me—the guy who broke in, he was one of those Jewish agents, and he came to kill him. Goldberg knows the jig is up, and he takes a powder."

"So Goldberg's like a Nazi or something? But why pretend to be a Jew?"

"Who's gonna suspect a Jewish guy of being a Nazi, right? It's the perfect disguise . . ."

Dr. Elliot Berkowitz, getting a hot chocolate at the coffee machine, overheard the conversation, and the idea, absurd as it was, gave his stomach a twinge. When Dr. Steiner had told them about Dr. Goldberg's disappearance, Elliot had felt lost and displaced. He knew why. He had come to look upon Goldberg as a father figure, and had grown dependent upon him. The older man's approval had been nurturing for Elliot.

He had looked for other father figures once he was old enough to learn of his natural father's death, but every single one had betrayed him in some way, had fallen short of the image he had of his own ideal father, who had been taken from him by the Nazis.

And to think now that the man whom he had trusted and respected, his brother in faith, could be one of the monsters who had slain his father and much of the population of Europe was more than his spirit could bear. He uncomfortably recalled Goldberg's defense of Wagner, and wondered if it was due to more than aesthetic appreciation.

What could make Dr. Goldberg run away? Knowing that he had been found out made perfect sense, but only in the event that the threat was ongoing. If the man who meant him harm had been captured, the threat was over—*unless* there were others who would continue to carry out the threat. What if those others were Mossad? And wouldn't that tie into what Dr. Steiner had said about *national security, perhaps,* as he had so delicately put it?

A wave of nausea passed over Elliot, and he sipped slowly at the watery hot chocolate. Then he remembered Dr. Steiner telling them that they were to feel free to enter Goldberg's office should they need any papers that he had.

Elliot had given Dr. Goldberg two of his case files to evaluate, and he thought that he could make a good argument that he needed them to record additional data, should he be found in Goldberg's office. He threw what was left of his hot chocolate in the trash can, and left the two attendants arguing quietly over Downing's Mossad theory.

There was no one outside Dr. Goldberg's office, and Elliot knocked gently on the door. When there was no answer, he looked up and down the hall, then went in, closing the door behind him.

The lights were off, and only a small amount of sunlight came through the curtained windows. Elliot turned on the desk lamp and looked around the room. The polished stones that made up the Star of David on the wall drew his attention, reflecting back the lamplight in muted tones. He'd often admired the simplicity of the work, with its different colored stones creating the patterns that made up the symbol of his nearly forgotten faith.

But there was no time now to admire it.

First, Elliot found the case files that Dr. Goldberg had been reviewing. They were on top of a pile of papers on the desk. Holding them in his left hand, to immediately show to anyone who might disturb him, he began to open and look inside the seven desk drawers, one above the central knee space, and three on either side.

The center drawer held pretty much what one would expect— pens, pencils, rubber bands, a stapler, and paper clips. But there was also a cellophane package of Oreo cookies right in the middle, half of them gone, and Elliot smiled as he remembered Dr. Goldberg saying, *Would you like a cookie?* in that droll Teutonic dialect as he held out the package to him. Why the hell not? he thought, and put an Oreo whole into his mouth, chewing as he proceeded to search the other drawers.

He went in order from up to down on the left side, then the right, so it wasn't until he opened the final drawer on the bottom right that he found that for which he had been searching, and praying not to find. It was inside a small white box of shiny cardboard that might have once housed a cheap pair of cuff links or tie clip. But when he took off the lid, he found a watch chain.

Elliot thought the metal was brass, and it was heavily tarnished. The chain was made up of four swastikas, three small ones joined by two single links each, and, at the end opposite the clasp, a larger one dangling from only one link.

A memento. A keepsake that must have had deep meaning for this sudden stranger who was not, *could* not, be Dr. Isaac Goldberg.

Elliot set the chain on the desk, put the lid back on the box and replaced it, then shut the drawer. He walked around the desk, looking at the chain as if it were a snake poised to strike. Then he reached out and picked it up again, weighing it in his hand. He would keep it, keep it to remind himself never again to seek a father, never again offer a child's heart to any man.

He slipped the chain into his pocket, and felt tears blur his eyes and cloud his vision, so that when he looked up at the gleaming stones in the Star of David, he saw for the first time another pattern in the overall design. It was made up of paler stones set in rows. The effect was subtle, but looking at it with tear-filled eyes made it much easier to see the symbol the pale stones created from the X crossing the central hexagon of the six-pointed star, and from the lines on the northeast and southwest sides of the hexagon, and the left side of the top point and right side of the bottom point.

What was revealed was what had been there all along: a large swastika centered in and superimposed perfectly over the Star of David.

The social hall opened late, so Norman Bates didn't hear of Dr. Goldberg's disappearance until midafternoon. Patients were engaged in conversations with attendants, and there was a constant hubbub of talk in the large room. Even those patients who were usually mute were expressing themselves orally if not actually verbally, howling or moaning, sensing that something was very wrong.

Finally Norman heard one of the annoyed attendants tell several curious and yammering patients, "All right, I'll tell you what I know—Doc Goldberg has left. He may be back, he may not, I don't know. Nobody else knows either. Doc Steiner's in charge for the time being, and that's about it."

Norman walked slowly to the nearest empty chair and, ignoring the voices all around him, sat down and thought about the way he was feeling, just the way Dr. Reed had told him to. He had to confess to himself that his first emotion was relief. If Dr. Goldberg really was gone, there would be no confrontation with him, no demands to engage in a conversation, and, he hoped, no further threats of those terrible shock treatments.

But the other emotion that nearly overwhelmed his relief was fear. It seemed too coincidental that right after his brother Robert told him that he didn't have to worry about Dr. Goldberg, the man would disappear. Had Robert gotten rid of Dr. Goldberg the way Norman imagined he had gotten rid of Ronald Miller and Myron Gunn and Nurse Lindstrom? With Goldberg's death, Norman was safe, but at what cost? Had he turned Robert into a murderer?

If he had, he knew that Robert would be caught eventually, and he didn't want to lose the brother that he had only just found. At the same time, how could he let Robert keep killing? He knew all too well how one murder could lead to another.

He had to talk to Dr. Reed again. What the doctor had said about it being impossible for Robert to be responsible for these disappearances made sense, and Norman had told himself a hundred times that it was only his imagination working overtime. Still, he couldn't shake the feeling. There were too many coincidences. Yes. He'd talk to Dr. Reed. At his session today. He'd tell him everything, about his dream last night, and how Robert had told him that no one would give him shock treatments, and how Robert would protect him, and how every time Robert had said that, someone who could hurt Norman had died, and . . .

Norman.

Oh, no, Norman thought. I didn't hear that. It was just imagination, my stupid imagination . . .

You're a fool, boy.

Norman tried to ignore the voice in his head, tried to stay on his previous train of thought: he would tell Dr. Reed about his fears, and Dr. Reed would say, *Yes, but how could Robert have done these things?* and he would explain that Robert—

He's lying to you, boy.

He would explain that Robert *couldn't* have done anything, that he couldn't have gotten into the building—

You never could tell when people are lying to you, could you, Norman? You believe anything . . .

Dr. Reed would prove to Norman that it wasn't his brother, that it *couldn't* be, not Robert—

You believe what you want to, no matter what your eyes and ears tell you. You never could put two and two together, Norman.

Shut up! Shut up, Mother! I'm not listening to you!

Don't you want to hear the truth, boy?

Not from you! I don't want to hear anything from you!

Norman, I—

NO! You already got me into enough trouble, didn't you? You killed Mary Crane! You killed the detective! You're not lying to me again!

Norman, you know good and well that it wasn't me who killed that girl, it was you and your dirty thoughts, your—

"Shut *up*, Mother! Just shut the hell *up!*"

He shouted so loudly that it made his throat rasp with pain, so loudly that all the talking in the social hall died away as everyone turned to look at Norman Bates sitting alone in a chair, his head down, looking at the floor, shrieking at someone who had died years earlier, murdered by her own son's hand.

Norman realized what he had done and looked up to see all the faces, the dozens of pairs of eyes, staring at him, the madmen embracing him as one of their own, and the sane eyeing him with concern and a touch of fear. He tried to say, *I'm sorry,* but it came

out as only a harsh croak. Then he tried to smile, to show everyone he wasn't insane, he wasn't talking to voices in his head.

But it was too late, and two attendants came over to him, their
attitudes officious though not menacing. Norman kept smiling,
though as they got closer he couldn't meet their gaze and looked
down at the floor, still smiling. He wanted to appear friendly, but
was afraid that the tense grin made him look cacklingly insane.
Still, he maintained it as his only defense.

"You okay, Bates?" the larger of the two attendants asked.

Norman, still looking down, tried to nod, but felt as though
he were wearing a neck brace. Still, he managed a slight up-down
jerk of his head and an audible grunt that he hoped signaled an
affirmative response.

*Do you know what you look like, Norman? You look like a grinning
idiot.*

Be quiet, Mother. Please be quiet.

*You look like a madman, boy, with your toothy grin and your rolling
eyes. These men will think you're insane. And they'll be right.*

Norman pressed his eyes shut and clenched his fists. He had
made her go away in the past and he could do it again. He just had
to believe in himself, the way Dr. Reed had taught him. Mother
wasn't there, not really. *Norman* was there. He was the only one.
And he would *be* Norman. He would be what he was when he
talked to Dr. Reed . . . and what he was when he talked to Robert. *Yes. That was it. Think of Robert. Think of talking to him.*

Norman felt himself relax. The tension left his neck and shoulders. His fists unclenched. He opened his eyes and turned and
looked at the two attendants. "I'm fine," he said in clear and distinct tones. "I'm sorry for causing a disturbance. I just had . . . an
unpleasant memory. I'll try and keep myself under control in the
future."

The two attendants looked at each other as though Norman

had just spoken to them in ancient Greek, and Norman himself was amazed by his own fluency. These were more words than he had spoken in months to anyone other than Dr. Reed and Robert.

"Well, okay," said the larger attendant. "See that you do."

They walked away and Norman saw that nearly everyone had stopped looking at him. They were all talking again. That was good. He had learned something today. Maybe he had even made a breakthrough, as Dr. Reed hoped he would. He would tell Dr. Reed about this during his session today.

Norman felt proud of himself. He considered asking his mother who the crazy one was now, but chose not to, not so much fearing the venom of her reply as dreading any reply at all.

Marie Radcliffe hadn't told anyone about what she had found in Dr. Goldberg's office. After her shift ended, she'd driven away with Ben Blake, who dropped her at home. Despite warnings to the contrary, he'd told her as much as he knew about what had occurred with the intruder in the basement.

When she was finally alone in her apartment, it was three-thirty in the morning and she was exhausted. Still, there was no way she could sleep after what had happened at the hospital.

Slowly, she tried to put it all together. When she remembered Dr. Goldberg's demeanor earlier in the evening, she couldn't conceive of his being alarmed in any way. On the contrary, he had been relaxed, a bit piqued over Dr. Berkowitz's desire to avoid shock therapy, but that was all. He'd seemed joyfully anxious to delve into his opera and the evening's work, not at all apprehensive.

It was possible that he'd gotten a phone call, but unlikely, since he'd told Marie that he had the switchboard shut off calls to his office after seven o'clock. So what else could have warned him that someone was after him and caused him to flee—*before* he had listened to more than five sides of *Die Meistersinger?*

What bothered her most was the presence in Dr. Goldberg's office of the piece of petrified wood she'd given to Norman Bates. Try as she might, she could come up with no scenario to explain its presence there on the floor. As far as she knew, Norman had never set foot in that office. When Goldberg had talked to him, it had been in Norman's room. Could Norman for some reason have given the stone to Goldberg?

That made no sense to Marie. She was aware of the way that Goldberg's visit and demands had upset Norman, and the idea of his turning over a symbol of his own strength and self-assurance to the man who threatened him was unthinkable from a psychological viewpoint. Could Goldberg have been aware of the stone and Norman's attachment to it, and confiscated it? Though Goldberg's techniques could be cruel, taking away Norman's good luck piece would have simply been unnecessary cruelty, if Norman had even been foolish enough to reveal the stone to Goldberg in the first place.

Another alternative was that somehow Norman had gotten into Dr. Goldberg's office, as utterly impossible as that sounded. She remembered cautioning Norman about not letting the stone fall out of the shallow pockets of the patients' uniform pants he wore. It *might* have done just that, particularly if Norman had been doing something . . . *active* in the room.

She tried to separate her personal feelings of warmth, even affection, from the situation. Regardless of what horrors Norman had perpetrated, he was sick, not evil. He reminded her of a big, awkward child who had been used by the occupying spirit of his mother, even though it had been his hands that had done the killing. But still, she had to think of him as a past and prospective killer, no matter how much she liked him.

Supposing Norman *had* been in Dr. Goldberg's office? What had he done there?

What would he have *wanted* to do?

He feared Dr. Goldberg because Goldberg was anxious to begin shock treatments on him. But would he have feared him to the point of killing him?

Marie thought about the other people who had disappeared. Ronald Miller, Myron Gunn, Nurse Lindstrom—all people who had posed threats to Norman Bates. And now Dr. Goldberg, who posed still another.

But even if Norman had the motive, how could he have had the means? This wasn't just a hospital, it was a maximum-security prison as well. He would have had to get out of his locked room, get past the attendants, perform the killings, and get rid of the bodies while not leaving any evidence, then somehow get back to his room. It was impossible.

Still, every one of the four people who had vanished was a person whom Norman Bates would have wanted to disappear. And a possession of his had been in Goldberg's office the night *he* disappeared.

Marie knew she had to talk to someone about this, and the only person she thought she'd feel comfortable telling it to was the one person who felt about Norman the way she did, and that was Dr. Reed. She'd been tempted to tell Ben, but she was hesitant to place Norman in a delicate position, and it really wouldn't be professional. Dr. Reed was Norman's doctor, and she was Norman's nurse, and this was a patient-oriented issue. Best to talk to Reed first and see if there was an explanation before she started telling others about it.

Marie got undressed, grabbed a quick shower, and climbed into bed. She held the piece of petrified oak in her hand, looking at it in the light of her bedside lamp. Finally she turned off the light, but held the stone for a long time before she fell asleep, its round smoothness warm against her hand.

April 14, 1918

Disaster has struck. Utter and complete disaster. The state board of inspection has withdrawn the license of the Ollinger Sanitarium. My life's work, my greatest dream, crushed by the loose words of one who found here a cure for his malady, a thankless, ungrateful creature whom I released and proclaimed returned to vibrant mental health, one of the most successful recipients of Spiritual Repulsion Therapy, that J.R.

Oh, why should I hide names anymore, especially his? This Judas, this traitor. Joseph Ridgway is his name, a near–charity case whose father put him here for the act of unnatural sex with his own sister, who then drowned herself. The youth refused to admit his guilt, rather blaming his father for all that had occurred, but after his therapy he was quickly cured of all his illness and subterfuge, admitted his guilt, and was eventually released.

Somehow he gained the help of one of my most trusted aides, Clarence Brewer, a man who knew all the mechanical workings that abetted my therapy, and together they went to the state board and convinced them that what I was doing here was not only quackery but criminal fraud. My former assistant even told them of the secret ward in which are kept the pitiful sacrifices that had to be made for what I hoped to be the ultimate success of my therapy.

But now, alas, thanks to the thankless, the success of that ther-

apy shall have to come in the lifetime of another more fortunate than myself. Board inspectors came only a week ago, in the company of both Ridgway and Brewer, who first revealed to them all the physical secrets of my therapy, and finally took them to the formerly hidden ward in the basement.

That they were shocked would be an understatement. I admit, conditions in that ward had deteriorated significantly, but these were special cases, why couldn't they understand that? I tried to explain that these patients were beyond caring whether or not they were smeared with their own filth, that the constant screaming of patients in the next cage had nothing to do with whether they slept or not, that they were completely indifferent to the quality of food they ate. Could they not see that?

I was forced to turn over my records, and the board contacted the families of every patient, informing them that the sanitarium was being shut down and that they would have to move their relatives to another facility within seven days. They came, but I could not bear to face them. I had enough funds left to pay part of my staff for that final week, and they were the ones who took the patients to their families when they arrived. I remained in my quarters.

There was only one man who breached my privacy, the husband of a patient. He broke in my door, struck me across the cheek so that I fell to the floor, swore that he would see me hanged, and, if that did not occur, that he would whip me to death. He kicked me in the ribs before he left. Barbarian.

By the end of the seventh day, all the patients except four had been removed. These were all in the basement ward. There had been no responses from their families, who may have thought that the board would move them to a state facility, thus sparing them the expense and trauma of finding a private sanitarium. The board was not so merciful—or merciless, as one might think of it.

For the greatest mercy that could be shown to these unfortunates would be to end their dreadful existence. Such lives are not lives at all, but mere existence in an earthly hell, tortured by the demons of one's own mind. I regret the conditions of these poor creatures, but I begin to think that their condition has become my own as well.

Abandoned, misunderstood, martyred, on the brink of the Great Abyss with no hopes of rescue. What lies ahead for me is shame, dishonor, arrest, imprisonment in a place even worse than what houses these dregs of society, even death itself at the hands of such as my recent attacker.

I cannot face such a future. That I, who wished only for the betterment of mankind, should be driven to this end makes me question the existence of the Deity. I see only one way out of this situation.

The last of my staff has just left the building. I have paid everyone what they were owed. My debts, at least the financial ones, are settled. The only living souls within the walls of the Ollinger Sanitarium are myself and the four caged denizens of the basement ward.

When I finish writing this final entry in my journal, I shall place it with my books, there to perhaps be read in years to come by some new pioneer in the field of mental health. If it inspires him to revisit and refine my therapy for the uses of a new generation of patients, then I shall not have lived in vain. I do not wish to leave it as a suicide note, however. In that case I fear it might be used only in the courts that investigate this final action, and then be forever buried in some legal storehouse. Far better to place it among my reference volumes and trust to an unforeseen future.

As for my final act, there is an underground gas pipe to the kitchen, a short section of which runs through a corner of the basement ward near the ceiling in the northwest corner. I intend to enter the ward, seal up the door (there are no windows to be concerned about), and then use a crowbar and a hacksaw, if necessary, to break that gas pipe and let the gas rush into the ward. In a short time, I suspect that the residents and I will drift off into a sleep from which we will never awaken. This will be a blessing for those souls that have known no rest for so long, and the final palliative for my own torments.

I have no idea if anyone shall find us or not, or if the state board, now that the patients are released, will simply ignore this facility and allow it to sink into ruin. If so, I could not have a more appropriate tomb. Yet I suspect that those who invested their money to have the sanitarium built will find some use for it, in which case the dead will eventually be discovered. I will be discovered, with my poor patients, who trusted me to heal them.

I now write the final sentences in this journal and place it among my books. May he who someday finds it be wiser than I. And may whatever God exists have mercy on whatever part of my spirit may survive my death.

Adolph Ollinger

16

When Marie Radcliffe arrived at work the next afternoon, the first thing she did was go to Dr. Reed's office. He was seated at his desk with the door open, working on some case files, but looked up when she knocked.

"Marie," he said. "Come in, please. Have a seat." She entered and closed the door behind her, earning a curious look from Dr. Reed. "Strange times indeed, aren't they?" he asked, shaking his head.

"They are," she said, sitting in the chair on the other side of the desk. "I take it there's been no news about Dr. Goldberg?"

"Not a word. But a lot of rumors. The most popular one seems to be that he was actually another Adolf Eichmann."

"What?"

"Yes, it sounds crazy," Dr. Reed said, "but it's really caught fire. The idea is that the man who broke in was an Israeli, and that Goldberg wasn't really Goldberg. When he knew they were on to him, he took off."

"I . . . don't see how that could have happened," Marie said. "There was no way for the doctor to know about the man. And I would have seen Dr. Goldberg leave. I went to his office as soon as they caught the man in the cellar."

She went on to tell Dr. Reed about how she had found the office empty, and how the opera recording had been stopped after side five. "I found something else there," she said quietly, then paused. "Dr. Reed, do you know if Norman Bates was ever inside Dr. Goldberg's office?"

Dr. Reed rubbed his chin for a moment, then said, "No, not that I know of. And I think I would know."

"Has Norman ever had . . . I don't know how to put this . . . Have you ever given him free rein inside the building?"

"Free rein? Do you mean have I ever let him wander about? On his own?"

"Yes."

"Of course not, Marie. You know he's always in the company of at least one attendant when he goes from one place to another, or on his walks for exercise."

"Is there any way he could have gotten into Dr. Goldberg's office?"

"Absolutely not." Dr. Reed gave a short shake of his head. "That would be impossible."

"As impossible as his getting out of his cell at night?"

Dr. Reed leaned back in his chair and crossed his arms. "Nurse, exactly what are you getting at?"

"Last night," she said, "when I went in to look for Dr. Goldberg, I found something in his office. Something of Norman's."

"Something of Norman's?" Dr. Reed repeated, as if trying to fathom it.

"This," she said, reaching into her pocket and coming out with the piece of polished petrified wood. "I gave this to Norman as a good luck piece. It was on the floor under Dr. Goldberg's desk."

Dr. Reed took the stone and turned it over carefully in his hand. "And you say you gave this to Norman."

"Yes. I'm sorry, I should have told you."

"No, that's all right. This is well within the limits of what patients may have. No sharp edges, too small to use as a weapon. A good luck piece, you say?"

"Yes. It's a long story."

"Well," Dr. Reed said with a reassuring smile, "maybe you'd better tell me anyway."

So Marie told him about her father giving her the stone, and about how she had given it to Norman to help him feel braver. "I should have let you know," she concluded.

"Well, you probably should have, but no harm done." He frowned. "And you found this in Dr. Goldberg's office?"

She nodded. "Dr. Berkowitz and I met with him at the end of the day. I don't recall seeing it on the floor then, but I might not have noticed it."

He looked up at her. "So what are you thinking about all this?"

Mouth still closed, she bit her lower lip before she spoke. "I'm thinking that there's a possibility that Dr. Goldberg never ran away. That something might have happened to him, here, in the building." She took a deep breath. "And that maybe Norman somehow had something to do with it."

Dr. Reed was silent for a long moment. "Wow," he finally said. "That's something that I'd rather not have heard."

"And that's something that I'd rather not have had to say," Marie said. "I think we both have a lot invested in Norman. Professionally and—"

"And emotionally, yes," Dr. Reed said. "I've bent over backwards to try and keep him from harm, and I know you have too . . . that day with Myron Gunn. That's why the mere *thought* of Norman reverting to what he was before . . ." He shook his head, and his mouth became a hard line. "Have you mentioned this to anyone else?"

"No. I thought I should discuss it with you first before I . . . before *we* let anyone else know about it. If that's necessary."

"I'm glad you did. As for it being necessary," Dr. Reed said, "I just don't know."

Marie held out her hand for the stone. Dr. Reed took one last look at it, then handed it over to her. "There's something else that concerns me," she said. "And that's the fact that everyone who's disappeared has posed a threat in some way to Norman."

Dr. Reed thought for a moment. "I see what you mean. Norman was certainly relieved when Ronald Miller escaped."

"If he *did* escape."

Dr. Reed nodded slowly. "Yes. And Myron Gunn and Nurse Lindstrom—he wasn't sorry to see them go either. As for Dr. Goldberg—"

"He was anxious to try shock treatments on Norman," Marie said. "And Norman was very upset about that."

"Exactly," Dr. Reed intoned, then jerked up as though coming out of a trance. "But it's just so . . . *impossible*, Marie. I mean, think about it—how in God's name could Norman Bates get out of his locked room, dispatch people, then hide their bodies where no one could find them, and get *back* to his room, all without being seen?"

"I have no idea. But then I wonder about *this* . . ." She held up the stone. "How did it get into Dr. Goldberg's office? How did Dr. Goldberg leave his office without me seeing him? And how likely is it that *four* people, all of whom posed a threat to Norman Bates in some way, would simply disappear over a period of several weeks?"

Dr. Reed seemed to consider what Marie had implied, then said, "That's not beyond the realm of the possible. There are reasons: escape, elopement, and flight. But that Norman Bates could have . . . killed them all *is* impossible." He sighed. "Look, let's keep this between ourselves for now. I'll talk to Norman— today. I'll ask him about the stone. Maybe Dr. Goldberg took it away from him, or maybe there's another way it got into that office, I don't know. But I'll find out. In the meantime, I don't want any crazy rumors flying around. Norman has enough to deal with inside his head as it is, okay?"

"I won't say a word," Marie said, slipping the stone into her uniform pocket. Dr. Reed thanked her for sharing her thoughts, and she left the office.

When she was gone, Dr. Reed slumped back in his chair and rubbed his temples hard with the heels of his hands. "Oh, Jesus Christ. Norman, Norman . . . ," he whispered. "What have you done?"

Dr. Reed visited Norman Bates in his room shortly before dinnertime. Norman smiled when he saw him. "Dr. Reed," he said, "I'm so glad to see you. Something happened today, something really good, I think."

Norman was surprised to see Dr. Reed frown. "Are you talking about Dr. Goldberg, Norman? About what happened to Dr. Goldberg?"

"Oh!" Norman said. The thought made him feel guilty. "Oh, no, not that! I mean, I don't really know what happened, but I hope it was nothing bad, honestly."

"You're not at all *relieved* about what happened? So you won't have to undergo shock therapy?"

"Well, I guess that part of it, yes, that's . . . that's a good thing for me. But I don't want anything bad to have happened to Dr. Goldberg. You believe that, don't you?"

Dr. Reed sat on the stool. "Yes, Norman. I believe that. Now. Tell me what happened today that you thought was so good. I'd like to hear it."

Norman excitedly told him about getting upset because he thought he had heard Mother, and about his outburst. He was almost pleased to see Dr. Reed's look of concern. But then he told him about how he had talked to the two attendants. "I talked to them just like I talk to you," he said, "or to Robert, and they looked surprised—it was great! So that's why I said I didn't feel happy about Dr. Goldberg, because I think I could have talked to him too."

"That's fine, Norman, fine," Dr. Reed said. "I'm very glad that happened and that you discovered that you were strong enough to engage with those men. That's excellent, and I hope it continues. However, there's something else I'd like to talk to you about."

Dr. Reed didn't seem as happy as Norman had hoped he'd be. He looked almost sad, and Norman wondered why. "Okay," he said. "Do you want me to lie down?"

"No, not yet. I have a question for you." He paused. "Nurse Marie gave you a good luck piece, didn't she?"

"Y . . . yes. How did you know that?"

"She told me. Do you still have it?"

"No. I don't."

Dr. Reed's face got very serious then, and Norman felt almost scared. "Where is it, then, Norman?"

"I . . . I gave it to Robert." Dr. Reed raised his eyebrows as if he were surprised. "Last time I saw him."

"You gave the stone to *Robert?*" It seemed to Norman that Dr. Reed was having trouble understanding something that seemed quite simple to Norman.

"Yes. For luck. You see, we were talking about luck, and he was telling me that he thought he needed some, so I gave it to him. Why? Did I do wrong?"

"No, Norman. At least . . . I don't think so."

"Did Robert . . . *do* something?" Norman felt his heart beating faster. "I told you before . . . I was worried about Robert, that he might be . . . oh, God. Did you, did you find the stone somewhere?"

"I didn't. Nurse Marie did. In Dr. Goldberg's office last night. After he . . . disappeared." Dr. Reed pursed his lips. "Norman, do you have any idea how it might have gotten there?"

Norman swallowed hard. "No. I don't. I really don't. It's like you said before when I . . . I brought this up, Dr. Reed: there's no way Robert could have gotten into the building, no way he could have done what . . . what I was afraid he was maybe doing."

"Then how did that stone get into Dr. Goldberg's office, Norman?"

Norman had no answer.

"Robert is going to be visiting this evening, Norman. Perhaps you could ask him."

Norman thought it through. "I could. But . . . well, what if *you* asked him, Dr. Reed?"

"I think he'd open up to you more readily than he would to me, Norman. There's probably a simple explanation—maybe he dropped it and Dr. Goldberg picked it up, something that simple. But we won't know until you ask him. Tell me," he went on, "have you mentioned anything about Robert to Nurse Marie?"

Norman shook his head. "No. Not to anyone."

"All right. Well, depending on certain things, we may have to tell her about him. But I'd like you to leave that to me. She's very curious, very concerned about having found this stone, as am I. I wouldn't like to see your relationship with Robert endangered.

I think it's been quite good for you. But we have to know certain things so we can be confident that nothing bad has happened, you understand?"

"Yes. Yes, I do." Norman paused. "Dr. Reed, has Nurse Marie told anyone else about this?"

"No, don't worry, she hasn't. And she won't, at least until you and Robert and I figure out exactly how that stone got in that office. But we will, and I'm sure there will be a logical explanation, all right?" Norman nodded, though he didn't feel at all confident. "Good. Well then, now that we've got that out of the way, let's have you lie back and relax, and we'll begin our session . . ."

That evening Nurse Marie brought Norman his dinner. Norman thought she seemed less friendly and more cautious in his presence, and she glanced back frequently at Ben the attendant, who was standing in the doorway.

She didn't say much beyond what was necessary while Norman ate his dinner. He thought she might talk about Dr. Goldberg's disappearance, or even about finding the stone in his office, but she didn't mention it at all. She smiled down at him several times when he looked up at her, but her smiles looked strange and forced to Norman. Once she asked him if he'd had a good day, and he said he did, but he didn't elaborate, and she didn't ask him to.

The longer the silence grew, the more annoyed Norman got. Nurse Marie was acting as if he, Norman, were somehow responsible for what had happened. Didn't she know him better than that? He wondered what she might have told Ben, who stood so close to her.

Dr. Reed had said she hadn't told anyone else, but Norman wondered. Over the last few weeks, Norman could tell that

Nurse Marie and Ben had been a lot friendlier to each other than they had been before. He wondered how far it had gone, if they had slept together.

He chewed his meat loaf and pictured the scene in spite of himself. It excited him, thinking of Nurse Marie and Ben in bed together naked, and him doing . . . *what* to her?

But he knew what. Doing what Norman had wanted to do to that girl, to Mary Crane, before Mother had—

"Norman?"

He tensed, thinking at first that the voice was Mother's, but it was only Nurse Marie's. Norman realized that his thoughts had made him stop eating, and that he had turned the spoon in his hand, and was holding it in his fist like a weapon.

He turned it back between his fingers, dipped it into the peas and carrots, and quickly brought it to his mouth so he wouldn't have to say anything. He looked at Nurse Marie, chewed with his mouth closed, and grinned. She smiled back, but he thought she looked scared.

Scared of him? Could she actually believe that he would want to hurt *her?* She, along with Dr. Reed and Robert, were his only friends. She had even stood up for him against Myron Gunn. But now . . . now she seemed to think that he was dangerous, all because of finding that damn piece of petrified wood. And that stupid little rock had made her think that *he* was a murderer or kidnapper or both.

But it wasn't him, he knew that—if it was anybody, it was Robert, but Norman couldn't say that, could he? He couldn't betray Robert, that was something he would *never* do, not his brother, who had made him feel human again, who had only wanted to protect him, had told him not to worry, had said he'd never let anyone hurt Norman, even if he had to . . .

No. No no no. He couldn't go there, he couldn't think that.

There had to be an answer, an explanation. If only Nurse Marie hadn't poked around in there and found that stone . . . no one else would have known what it was, or would have given it a second thought, but she had to be so *nosy*. And now he was in trouble for something he'd never done, and *Robert* was in trouble for something that he maybe did or didn't do, Norman wasn't sure, couldn't tell, didn't *want* to know, all because Nurse Marie couldn't keep her goddamned snooping nose out of what really wasn't her business—

There was a sharp *crack,* and Norman realized that he had snapped the plastic spoon in two in his hands. Dazed, he looked up at Nurse Marie, who was looking at him with wide eyes. She moved toward Ben, who stepped toward her and put his arm around her. He had lost his smile.

"I'm . . . sorry," Norman said softly. He looked down and saw that the broken piece of plastic had dug into the base of his left index finger, making it bleed. Ben reached out and Norman let him take the two broken pieces of the spoon.

"I'll get a bandage," Nurse Marie said. He heard her footsteps moving down the hall, and Ben stood, arms crossed, in the doorway looking down at him. Within a minute, Nurse Marie was back with a first-aid kit. She took Norman's hand in hers, first cleaning his small wound with alcohol, then putting an adhesive bandage on it. She didn't look at his face while she worked, though he looked at hers. It seemed pale and tense.

"There now," she said when she finished. "You should be fine." She forced a smile, but again he saw how artificial it was. He felt sad and angry at the same time. "Would you like to finish your dinner?" she asked.

He shook his head. "No, thanks," he said softly. She took his tray, and then she and Ben were gone, the door locked behind them.

In spite of his concerns and fears, Norman wanted to see Robert again desperately. He needed to see someone who wasn't afraid of him, and who wouldn't treat him as if he might, just *might,* be a monster.

He sat there trembling in the silence, and then, very softly, he heard it . . .

Norman.

Oh, God, no. Please . . .

Norman, listen to me.

No! Go away, Mother! You're not there—you were never there!

I was and I am. You listen to me, boy. A mother cares about her son, no matter how badly he treats her. And you've treated me very badly, Norman.

Mother . . .

You pushed me way down inside you, Norman. Why, I could hardly even breathe down there. But I could hear. And see. I could see what a fool you've been. And I wanted to help you, but you wouldn't let me. I wanted to show you the mistakes you've made.

Stop it, Mother!

I just want to help you, Norman.

I don't want your help! Just go away, Mother! You say you can hear me? Then hear that! Go away! Go away!

"Go *away!*" Before he realized it, he had shouted it aloud, and slapped his hand over his mouth, praying no one had heard in the hall.

It would be all right. People shouted all the time, quick, sharp outbursts that made you jump, and then nothing.

Norman tensed, listening, but he heard no more. Mother was quiet.

No. Mother wasn't there. She had never been there. He had to remember that. It was all in his mind. He had created her, but he could also drive her away, push her way down inside, like she had said.

No! Like *he* had said. In his mind was where she lived, and he had decided she was dead and silent. He just had to *remember* that. Mother was dead. She couldn't help him. And he didn't want her help. He didn't need it.

All he needed was his brother. All he needed was Robert.

17

Robert came to visit that evening, and Dr. Reed opened the door for him as usual. When Norman and Robert were alone together and the door was closed, Norman told him about Nurse Marie finding the stone on the floor of Dr. Goldberg's office the night he vanished.

"It worried her, Robert," Norman went on. "She thinks *I* dropped it there or something, and she doesn't know about you. I didn't want to tell her that I gave you the stone, because then she might think that *you* . . . well, you know."

"What?" Robert said. "That I dropped it there when I was making Dr. Goldberg disappear?"

"Maybe. I think she believes I had something to do with it."

"And we know that's not possible."

"Well . . . no, it's not."

Robert nodded. "And who has the lovely Nurse Marie told about this?"

"Just Dr. Reed so far."

"He didn't mention it to me."

"No. We decided that I would." Norman tried to smile. "So I did."

"So much fuss over nothing. You know what probably happened, little brother? I didn't have it far down enough in my pocket, and when I was leaving, it slipped out, fell on the floor, and I didn't notice. This Dr. Goldberg came by shortly after, saw it, thought, *oh, what a pretty rock,* and picked it up. Maybe put it on his desk, and it got knocked off and landed on the floor." Robert shrugged dramatically. "And now Nurse Marie wants to make a federal case out of it. Ah, women." He sighed. "You can't live with 'em, and you can't kill 'em, know what I mean?" Then he chuckled to show he was joking, Norman thought. Or at least he hoped.

"Now this Nurse Marie," Robert said, "she's the one you like, right? The one who's nice to you?"

"Well . . . she *was.*"

"Hmm. That's too bad. You don't have all that many friends here."

Norman felt a chill prickle the back of his neck. "What do you mean, Robert?"

"Oh, just that you never know about people. You think you can trust them and then they turn around and stab you in the back. People like that . . . sometimes they're actually worse than the ones who come right out and admit they hate you. Because they don't only break your body, they break your heart."

Norman didn't know what to say. Robert had just told him what he'd been thinking, but didn't want to admit to himself.

"Now, as for Dr. Reed," Robert went on. "I have a feeling that he might be trusted to keep a secret. What do you think?"

"Yes!" Norman said quickly. Though Nurse Marie might have

disappointed him, Dr. Reed continued to be his champion. He
knew he could have no better friend in the state hospital. "You
wouldn't ever hurt him, would you, Robert?"

"Norman," Robert said, widening his eyes in mock surprise.
"I'd never hurt *anybody,* but especially not Doc Reed."

"What about . . . Nurse Marie?"

"Little brother, like I just said, I'd never hurt anybody. But if
people choose to get wanderlust and decide to hit the road, well,
that's hardly my fault."

"Robert . . ." He picked his words like he was feeling his
way through a minefield. "I wouldn't want anything to happen to
her. I wouldn't want her . . . to disappear. Like the others."

Robert looked at him for a long time without smiling. Then a
grin snapped into place. "Whatever you want, Norman. But
things usually have a way of working out. You're a lucky guy, good
luck charm or not."

"But you . . . you didn't do anything to Dr. Goldberg, did you?"

Robert gave an exasperated sigh and shook his head. "Didn't
you hear the story? Goldberg ran off because the Nazi hunters
were after him. He was a *Nazi,* Norman. See? It just proves what
I said about not being able to trust people. A lot of times they're
not what they seem. That's why we've got to stick together. Stand
up for each other. I look out for you . . . you look out for me,
right?" He held out his hand. "Like brothers do."

Norman took his hand. It was dry and cool and squeezed his
own hand firmly. "Like brothers do," he repeated.

Deep down, he thought he heard a single word:

Fool.

Norman was alone in the dark, waiting for Mother to return. He
had been expecting her, fearing her, and despite what he had told

himself about her being a creation of his own mind, he was sure she would come back.

He was also afraid for Nurse Marie. Despite her change in attitude toward him, she had done nothing wrong. Anyone in her position would have done the same, and in fact might have gone straight to the police. What Robert had said about her frightened him.

He hadn't prayed since he was a little boy, but now in the darkness he closed his eyes and thought, Oh, please . . . please, if you're there, don't let Robert hurt Nurse Marie. Keep her safe.

He repeated that prayer over and over, until he finally received an answer.

I will if you let me.

Norman clenched his teeth. He knew the voice. Mother.

Don't shout at me, Norman. Don't tell me to go away, because I won't. Not this time.

You have to, Mother. You're not there.

I am, Norman, and you know it, boy. A mother is always there when her son needs her.

I don't need you, Mother.

Oh, yes, you do. Because you've been a fool. You believe anything. You believe you have a brother, even though I told you that you didn't. But you didn't believe me.

No. No—you said yourself that maybe he was your son after all. You said that!

Even mothers can be fooled. But not forever. I watched and I listened, Norman. And eventually I knew. I knew what was going on, all right, even if you didn't. I tried to tell you, but you wouldn't listen. You wanted a brother so much you lied to yourself over and over. And you thought this Robert Newman was your brother. Oh, yes. "New-man," indeed—new and made-up.

No! He's my brother! He'd do anything for me!

There was silence for a time, then . . .

Would he?

In the silence that followed, a silence that pounded inside Norman's head, he became aware of a new sound. An ever so subtle rumbling, as of a great weight moving. Then there was a change in the air, and it became cool and dank. Though his eyes were still closed, the black inside of his eyelids seemed to brighten ever so slightly.

The rumbling stopped. Someone spoke a word that hung like dust in the air. And Norman Bates was no longer himself.

Marie Radcliffe wasn't at all happy about her assignment, but she understood the reasons for it. When Dr. Steiner had taken the place of Dr. Goldberg, caseloads were shuffled around like cards on a riverboat. Two doctors and a resident now had a workload that had been augmented by a missing and very productive doctor.

Most of the current case files were in filing cabinets on the first floor, but some older files related to long-term patients were kept in the storage room in the basement, the same room in which Judy Pearson had her upsetting experience. And since those particular older patients were being treated by doctors who hadn't worked with them before, those older files had to be taken out of storage and correlated with the newer ones, for a full picture of each patient's case and conditions.

It was Marie who had been asked to descend into the depths and retrieve the needed files. She had a list of names on her clipboard, but many of the files had been misplaced over the years. Some weren't in alphabetical order, but those were usually easy enough to locate. The greater problem was with files that held completely different records than those of the names typed on the tabs of the manila folders.

Usually it was the result of a long-ago doctor having put the wrong contents into the wrong folder, so Marie had to find the folder with the name of the patient and the actual file, and hope that it was a simple switch. What took even more time was the fact that the file cabinets were stuffed to bursting, and couldn't be easily riffled through. Instead, Marie had to lift out sections and put them on the worktable, keeping them in order while she sought to find the file that *might* contain the records of the patient she was searching for.

It was a tedious job, made even worse by its subterranean location and solitude. Marie had heard about Judy's adventure while retrieving files, but Judy was easily alarmed and was also a repository of every ghost story ever told about the facility. Marie doubted that Judy had seen anyone outside of her imagination. Her theory of Ronald Miller still lurking in the building was ridiculous.

It wasn't the thought of Ronald Miller that disturbed her. Rather it was the thought of Norman Bates. The more Marie considered her *own* pet theory, the more concerned she grew. That Norman could have done the things she suspected him of doing was incredibly unlikely, but still, when you eliminate the impossible, whatever's left, no matter how improbable, is the truth. Or something like that. She thought she'd once heard it from Dr. Goldberg, or whoever Dr. Goldberg really was.

She hadn't had a chance to talk to Dr. Reed to see what Norman had said about the stone, and she couldn't ask him herself at dinner with Ben there, even if she'd had the courage to. Maybe it *was* as simple as it falling out of Norman's pocket in the hall and Goldberg finding it. Maybe her imagination was just as wild as Judy Pearson's.

Whatever the answer, everything would be fine tonight. She had locked the door to the storage room from the inside, and

Ben had promised to come down and check on her when he had a break. With luck, she'd be done by then and could go back upstairs, away from this oppressive silence, and be among real, live people again, instead of these absurd ghosts of her own mind.

She laughed aloud and redoubled the intensity of her search.

Fight him, Norman. Fight him, boy.

"Robert. Are you there?"

"Yes, Doc. I'm here."

No! You hear me, Norman, I know you hear me!

"You have something to do tonight, don't you?"

"I . . . yes, Doc. I do. I have to protect Norman."

Norman! Don't be an idiot all your life. You're a bad boy and a bad man. For God's sake, face the truth. You killed the girl and the detective. You killed those other people too—the crazy one and that mean man and woman, and that doctor too. You killed them all. But you were lucky, boy. You didn't get caught, not yet. But you have to stop, don't you understand?

"And how are you going to protect Norman, Robert?"

Norman . . . I'm warning you . . .

"I . . ."

"Yes, Robert?"

"I have to . . . to make that nurse disappear."

No, you don't, Norman. Look at him! LOOK at the man who's been LYING to you!

Robert Newman raised his head, but it was Norman Bates who looked into the face of Dr. Felix Reed.

18

From the personal notes of Dr. Felix Reed:

. . . I'm not sure what to do at this point. The one thing I'm certain of is that Norman Bates has become the linchpin on which I hang my future. Only by bringing him out of his cocoon can I demonstrate to Dr. Goldberg how antiquated his therapies are.

Since the day I came here, I have been thoroughly disgusted by the nearly medieval treatment given to many of the patients. Cruelty is the modus operandi here, and Goldberg is its most devout practitioner. The heavy dependence on electroshock treatments is appalling if not criminal in itself. While it is true that some of these patients have done monstrous things, that does not give us as physicians and caregivers the right to do such things in return. This is intended to be a place of healing as much as a place of punishment.

If I can only prove to Goldberg that my less invasive and far kinder treatment works, I believe it could be the cause of massive changes here. Admittedly, it has taken time, but I have been able to reach Norman through nearly daily meetings in which I help him to relax and then simply talk softly with him. It almost approaches hypnotherapy, in which he enters a state of near-sleep. When his defenses are down, the true Norman Bates surfaces, essentially a moral and gentle man. Still, I have found something deeper as well, an anger that threatens to surface, but has not.

Perhaps my deep interest in him comes from the fact that I can identify with him. I feel that anger myself. What I do not have within me is the power to do something about it. Sometimes, when I'm completely honest with myself, I think that, if I could get away with it, I would simply eliminate some of the people who are the living embodiment of these deeply entrenched and torturous treatments. Progress often comes at a price . . .

. . . Last evening I made quite a discovery when I finally took it upon myself to explore the upper reaches of the closet in my office. The ceiling is high, and so are the shelves. I'd never even thought to look above the shelf provided, I imagine, for storing one's hat or gloves, and there is no light in the closet itself, but I heard a soft scuttling in the closet and used some matches to see if I could find its source.

I did find a small hole in the baseboard that might have given entry to a mouse, so I'll have a janitor set a trap. But far more interesting was my finding a shelf above the hat shelf, which contained several dozen books, magazines, and other items.

The printed materials, once I managed to get them down by standing on a chair, proved uninteresting, most of the magazines battered issues of Psychological Review, *and the books standard texts of the early part of this century. What proved far more rewarding, however, was a journal kept by the original head of* the Ollinger Sanitarium, Adolph Ollinger himself, and folded into it were floor plans of the building.

I stayed up most of the night reading the journal and was amazed to find that the building is honeycombed with passages, now forgotten as far as I know, created in order to aid in one of the most bizarre therapies I've ever heard of—terrifying patients into a feeling of guilt that was in turn supposed to cure them. The journal indicates how all too unsuccessful it was.

The locations of these passages are all clearly indicated on the floor plans, and one of the entrances is actually in what is now my office. From what I read in the details of the journal, I think the room was used as a costume room for the attendants, who played various ghosts that "haunted" the patients.

I found the entrance hidden by a three-foot-wide bookcase against the inner wall at the end of the room. There is a catch at the back of the top of the bookcase which, when pressed, allows it to slide to the side, revealing a narrow passage leading into darkness. As much as I'd love to explore it, it will have to wait until I bring a flashlight from home tomorrow. In the meantime, I'll place Ollinger's plans and journal, as well as my own, among the old books on the top closet shelf. I assume they'll be safe there, as I seem to be the first to have found them in over four decades . . .

. . . Tonight I found that the passage parallels the halls of Wards C and D. While the wall to the right, the Ward D side, is solid brick, there are seemingly entrances to every room in Ward C. That must have been where Ollinger put the cases on whom he wanted to use his "therapy." A patient room near the end of the corridor is currently empty, so I pressed what looked to be a metal plate on the wall, and was amazed to see a door appear and actually move slowly back into the passage, so that I had to get out of its way or possibly be crushed. They must operate by *hydraulics—I don't know much about the mechanics of such things, but they're very quiet. A low grinding sound of some sort, and that's all.*

The door was perfectly made, joined so well to the brick walls that I suspect you can only see the lines in the mortar if you look very closely. I'll check on this tomorrow. There's no control from inside the room, so patients couldn't escape. You could reach into the passage and push the panel so that it would lock you in the room, but there'd be no reason to do that.

I explored further, and found some narrow spiral staircases to get from one floor to another. There's one that leads to a passage that opens into two rooms in the cellar. The first is the small storage room, not too far from the laundry, where we keep old records, while the other opens into a room that I had no idea even existed. I don't know what it was used for, but it's quite large, with stone walls dripping with moisture, so that it's damp and almost tomb-like. There are pieces of rusted iron scattered about that look as though they may have been parts of cages. I'd rather not think about that. Its main entrance appears to have been sealed off.

Up above I discovered another passage that I believe opens into Goldberg's office, which makes sense. Goldberg's large office was probably Ollinger's back then, and the man had to have a way to observe his therapy in action . . .

. . . Several days have passed, and I haven't told anyone about my discovery. I have, however, begun to consider how I might use my information to my advantage regarding the changes that should be made in this facility. What I have in mind is most definitely a radical procedure, and one that I hardly dare think about, let alone write down. Still, it could prove to be invaluable.

I have seen in this facility some of the most barbaric, callous, and cruel treatment of patients that it has ever been my misfortune to come across. Often I wish that certain people, people whom I cannot personally dismiss, would simply disappear. What I've found gives me the power to do that.

Unfortunately, I don't believe that I could ever bring myself to kill, and, even if I could, I haven't the nerve to risk the consequences. But then I realize that I am surrounded by killers, and one in particular who might be useful.

Could Norman Bates be persuaded to kill again? He overcame the taboo against murder, at least in the killings of his mother and her lover. But it was "Mother" who killed Mary Crane and Arbogast and would have killed Lila Crane as well. If he allowed Mother to take over and use him to kill, might he not allow that again?

Still, Mother has proven too difficult to deal with. While Norman loved her in his way, he also hated her enough to kill her. There was no way to rehabilitate Mother—it was easier to banish her, and I've helped him do that, reach the point where he doesn't want her back.

But what about someone else? What if another personality could inhabit Norman? What if I could create another character within him? One he always wanted? He grew up a lonely little boy. What would have made a difference?

A sibling. Something that every smothered, lonely child wants.

Norman felt a shudder go through his body, a pulse of reclamation as he saw Dr. Reed smiling at him, just a glint of white teeth in the near-darkness.

"That's right, Robert. You *do* have to make Marie disappear. And I'll show you how."

Let Robert back in, Norman. You know what he is now.

But I'm afraid, Mother. Afraid of what he'll make me do!

You don't have to be afraid anymore, boy. I'm back now, and I'll take care of you. He won't hurt your friend, even if she is *a little chippie. Now show some gumption and let him in!*

"All right, Doc," Norman said, and was relieved to find that it was himself talking and not Robert, either inside or outside him.

That's a good boy.

He had made Mother proud, and it made him feel better, braver, stronger. He didn't understand what was happening, but he would find out. Mother was right. Dr. Reed had lied to him, and he had to find out about what. He had to find out everything.

. . . My treatment so far has approached hypnotherapy. It would be only a small step to go the whole way. Norman trusts me and has proven malleable. If I were to undertake true hypnotherapy, I could have him accept a brother figure, suggest it as a separate personality, have him carry on conversations with it only when I announce its visits, have that personality act as I direct, and have Norman forget those directives once they've been carried out. He did the same under the influence of alcohol and his own panic— all the easier to do under hypnosis.

If I can plant in Norman's mind the idea that he has a brother, one who was lost and has now returned and wants to form the bond that Norman never experienced, perhaps he could act as that brother, do things that the brother wanted done, the same way he acted as Mother. Of course, it's essential that what he wants done and what I want done are the same. So the reasons should be to protect Norman. Both the brother and I want to protect and help him, have him reenter society as best he can without further trauma or shock.

Another essential benefit of Brother is that once I indicate through hypnotic suggestion what needs to be done, I can be absent while it's occurring. I dislike thinking of it as an alibi, but that is of course what it is. The logistics, the actual physical planning, will be the most difficult thing to accomplish. Since I'll have to be conspicuously absent when Brother is doing his work, I'll have to place him in the passage ahead of time and have him wait, then go to his destination, do what needs to be done, and—

Then what? Leave the victim at the scene? Hardly. It would be ideal if the victims would simply vanish. After all, people can have reasons for disappearing. Those reasons can even be feeble and people will accept them. I can think of one conceivable reason for two of my malefactors already.

But. What if Brother should be caught in the act? Then Norman Bates somehow escaped from his room. And in the event he's captured, I'll plant a command that he'll remember nothing of how he got there. As uncommunicative as he already is, that should work well. Depending on whether Brother has already accomplished his mission, Norman will be considered more dangerous if he hasn't, or far more dangerous if he has.

Speaking of danger, I must consider that Norman may speak of Brother to someone else. That seems doubtful, since the only other person he barely speaks to is Marie Radcliffe. Still, I could tell him that he's not permitted to have visitors and that I'm making an exception, since I believe the relationship will do him good, so it would be best not to mention the visits to anyone else. I have no doubt he'll remain silent.

Another matter of concern is Norman's absence from his cell when Brother is active. I've already given orders that after dinner, no one is to disturb Norman but me. Attendants occasionally glance through the door slot, but . . .

———

"Here," Dr. Reed said. He handed Norman a long construction made of what felt like rolled blankets and beddings, bound together with cord. At first Norman didn't know what to do with it, but Mother did.

Put it under your blanket. You've done it before. Then take off your shirt.

Norman did as she said, and arranged the roll of beddings to look as much as possible like a sleeping person under his own blanket. He put his shirt on the bed.

"All right," Dr. Reed said. "Let's go."

Norman saw Dr. Reed draw back the quilted padding that covered the brick walls of his room. In the dim glow of the flashlight that Dr. Reed held, it seemed to Norman that the wall had actually moved back, creating an entrance. Dr. Reed passed through it and he followed, letting the padding fall back into place, after which Dr. Reed put his hand on some device on the wall, and the wall closed up again with the low rumbling Norman had heard earlier.

Follow him. Don't speak.

Norman obeyed Mother and trailed Dr. Reed down a dark tunnel that took several turns. They finally came to a set of stairs that wound down into deeper darkness. "Be careful," Dr. Reed said.

At the bottom of the stairs Dr. Reed opened another section of wall, and they stepped into a large damp room. "Equipment time," Dr. Reed said, and, leaning down, came back up with what looked like a folded sheet of plastic and . . .

A knife.

. . . A major question is what tool Brother should use. It can't be bare hands, since Norman isn't in the best condition. He's already proven himself proficient with a knife, so that may be best. A single

stab wound, then perhaps wrapping the victim in a plastic sheet, cleaning up the blood, and taking the victim to the hiding place.

In order for Brother's incursions to be successful and undiscovered, there should be little distance between the hidden entrances and the locations of the victims. This will necessitate patience, but that's a small price to pay to diminish risk.

I believe I've decided on my first subject. His absence will not improve the situation regarding treatment here, but, on the other hand, I loathe him for his treatment of Norman, as will Brother, who would certainly consider him worthy of elimination. It's a very low risk maiden voyage as well, since the passage opens both into Norman's room and the subject's. As for the subject's disappearance, with luck it may be thought a successful escape attempt . . .

. . . Everything went perfectly. I opened the door, spoke the key word to Norman, and told him to follow me. I was amazed to see the change that had come over what had been Norman. I gave him—or shall I say, Robert—the knife and led him to the secret entrance to Miller's room. Then I told him to count to 4,000 then follow my instructions, and I left.

Though I was extremely apprehensive, the next morning it appeared that Miller had vanished with no sign of a struggle. How he had escaped (since the entrance was not found) was a mystery, but that he had escaped was a certainty. When I looked later, the body was in the hidden room in the cellar, wrapped perfectly, and the knife lay beside it, carefully cleansed of any blood . . .

Norman took the knife and looked at it for a long time. Finally Dr. Reed said, "Robert? Are you all right?"

Answer him, boy. Like Robert would.

Norman thought for a moment, then said, "You bet, Doc. I'm fine."

Do you see, Norman? Look at what you've done.

The flashlight in Dr. Reed's hand didn't throw much light in the big room, but when Norman looked around, he saw, lying on the floor ten yards away, what looked like four cocoons, tightly wrapped and crimped at the ends.

"Observing your handiwork again?" Dr. Reed said. "Robert, sometimes I think you take too much pride in your work. What's our goal here?"

Mother prompted him. *To keep my brother . . .*

". . . keep my brother safe."

"And how are you doing that tonight?"

By making Nurse Marie . . .

". . . making Nurse Marie disappear."

Dr. Reed smiled. "You *can* be proud, Robert." He gestured to the four bodies wrapped in plastic. "Perfect crimes. And tonight you wait and count while I get far away from here, and we'll have one *last* perfect crime. And then everything will be fine."

. . . If the truth should ever come to light, some may wonder why I went to such lengths, why I could have not done these deeds on my own, rather than go through the extremely difficult process of having Robert be my proxy. The fact is that I never could have done the deeds. For me to plunge a knife into a human body would be impossible. That is why I have had to resort to this subterfuge to remove those who seek to treat psychiatry as a medieval practice.

Then how, they might wonder, do I justify using Norman Bates in this way? First, Norman has nothing to lose. He is already where I might be imprisoned if I were caught performing these actions myself, and he has no chance of ever walking free. Second, I have enabled him to fight for a great cause—indeed, his own cause, the cause of all who suffer from mental illness. Third, he is unaware of what his other persona is doing. Thus he feels neither guilt nor trauma from his deeds.

If what Norman commits are crimes—though I see them more as sacrifices made to bring about a more modern and compassionate age—then they are as close to perfect as crimes can get, with no victims, and the perpetrator not even aware of what he does.

But do I personally feel no guilt over people dying? Certainly not regarding Miller. He was mentally ill, but not to the extent that he should have been housed here. Recidivism among his kind is certain. And in only a few contacts with Norman, he set back my work by weeks. Society is far better off without him.

As for the others, they used our science to satisfy their own sadism. Gunn, Lindstrom, even Goldberg. Remarkable that a man who experienced what he did in the camps could be so unfeeling to the sufferings of others. And if he was what rumor suggests he was, I should feel overjoyed that he is dead.

But regarding Marie Radcliffe, I do feel guilt. She holds a piece of evidence that could be damning, and even if I told her that Norman told me that he dropped that evidence and Goldberg picked it up, I doubt she'd believe me. She knows something's wrong, and that Norman has something to do with it all, and sooner or later she'll reveal that to someone other than me. As great as the risk of one final disappearance may be, the risk of letting her live is greater. And so I sent her that list of patient file names that I needed pulled as soon as possible from the cellar storage room.

Mea culpa, mea maxima culpa.

As for Nick Steiner, I think he was uncomfortable with

Goldberg's policies, but always went along to get along. Now that he's superintendent—and I expect him to remain in that post—I think we'll see a positive change. It's not for my own advancement that I've done these things, but for the advancement of the field and of this hospital in particular.

"First, do no harm." Yes. But sometimes harm must be done so that greater harm to many more can be avoided. If there is a God, I pray that he'll forgive me for what I've done and must do tonight. I believe that the God of the Mind already has.

19

"Now you remember, Robert. You remember everything you were told, don't you?"

Yes, Doc.

"Yes, Doc."

I count to . . .

"count to four thousand . . ."

And while Robert mechanically repeated back to him the commands he'd been given, Felix Reed thought that at least this time he wouldn't have to go through the risky activities of stealing car keys and driving unobserved out of the parking lot and sinking still *another* car in the swamp. More people than ever would wonder where the hell Marie Radcliffe had gone to, but he'd told Robert to unlock the file storage room door afterward, so that it wouldn't be one of those goddamned locked room mysteries, in which they might stumble across the secret entrance. There'd been a chance of that with Ronald Miller, but Reed had been able to unlock Miller's cell door after Robert finished his job, and get away from the facility before Miller's absence was discovered.

This one was going to be dicey, but everyone had secrets. Reed himself was a prime example of that, wasn't he? He smiled as Robert continued reciting the litany of acts that would mark the final disappearance. Then he and Norman could both rest, and Robert could himself vanish, move to a different part of the country. There would be a tearful farewell, and Robert would be only a memory, never to return. And then this facility, finally swept clean of sadism and cruelty, would have a fresh start, and Norman Bates could heal slowly and without trauma.

At last Robert's recitation was complete. He had it all.

Everything would be all right now.

Mother . . . how did you know . . . all that?

I told you, Norman. I listen and I see. I heard what that doctor told you to do. I tried to tell you, but you wouldn't listen. You pushed me back. So I had to show you, so you can see what he really is. And what this Robert really isn't. *And now you know.*

Oh, God, Mother . . .

That's all right, boy. Mother will handle it. Everything will be all right now.

"Then we're ready to go, Robert. Follow me and I'll get you settled, and then I'll leave you."

Felix Reed turned to walk back to the entrance that led out of the large room, but when he heard no footsteps behind him, he stopped. Norman Bates was just standing there, the plastic sheeting in his left hand, the knife in his right.

"Robert? Didn't you hear me? It's time to do your work."

Reed was relieved when Norman started walking toward him. But then he noticed there was something peculiar about Norman's gait. It was almost effeminate, the hands held slightly up rather than at his sides, and the steps were closer together than normal. He was walking like a woman.

An older woman.

He stopped only a foot away from Reed, and he was smiling. It was a smile Reed hadn't seen before, neither Robert's confident grin nor Norman's sheepish half-smile, but a close-lipped smile with the corners of the mouth turned up high like a doll's. It seemed a cruel smile.

And when Norman spoke, it was in a voice Reed had never heard. It was higher and verged on cracking, an aural sheet of ice melting in sunshine. And it said, "Robert isn't going to do that."

Felix Reed felt as though the ground had dropped from under him. He was alone in the dark with a pet tiger that had done his bidding, and around which he had never felt anything but safe and secure. But the tiger had changed, gone feral again.

"Now, *Robert*," Reed said, hating the way his voice trembled, "let's not forget why we're here. We're here to help Norman, aren't we?"

"You're here to *use* Norman," the strange voice said.

"No, no . . . listen to me. You are *Robert*, and you are going to do what we agreed upon." Reed was shining the flashlight right into Norman's eyes, but they barely responded, fixed as they were on Reed's face.

"Robert isn't going to do *anything*," Norman said. "He can't. He's dead."

"No," Reed said, "Robert isn't dead. He's *here*."

"He never really existed," Norman said. "It's only ever been me and Norman. Why did you trick him? Why did you try and fool my *only* son?"

If he'd had the slightest doubt before, Reed was certain now. It wasn't Robert standing there with the knife in his hand. And it wasn't Norman Bates, either. It was *Mother*.

"I didn't try to fool him. I was trying to *help* him. I've only ever wanted to help Norman—to help *you*."

"You're a *liar*." The voice became even more bitter and harsh. "You wanted those people dead, and you wanted Norman to kill them for you. You tricked him into it, didn't you? Tricked my boy into killing for *you*."

"No, it was *Robert* who killed them, not Nor—"

"Liar!" Mother shouted, and Reed cringed, trying to think of a way out. "There *is* no Robert!"

"No, no!" Reed pleaded. "There *is!*"

Mother dropped the plastic sheeting, and her now free hand shot out and grabbed the flashlight from the doctor's sweating grip. She shined it full into his face, this man who had helped banish her, and had then used her boy as his assassin. His eyes were wild, and tears were in them. His crying made snot run from his nose, and the sight disgusted her.

"There *is!* There *is* a Robert!" he shouted again, and to her surprise, Mother saw the doctor's face change, melt, transform into the very image of Robert Newman that she had seen through Norman's eyes when she was chained deep down inside of him.

She could not accept even the *imagined* reality of Robert Newman.

Mother slashed up and across with the knife, and the blade ripped through the doctor's neck. He fell back, down onto the damp stones, and Mother dropped the flashlight, turned the hilt in her hand, sank to both knees, and stabbed down at that lying, false face, over and over again until its features were drowned in a red pool that appeared black in the flashlight's residual gleam.

Norman watched it all, unable to move, unable to stop Mother from doing what she did. Only when she finally released the knife, whose blade remained wedged in Dr. Reed's cheek, and stood up did Norman reclaim his own flesh.

He felt unmoored and lost, as though life itself were nothing but confusion. His brother was gone as though he had never existed. The only doctor who had cared for him was dead. And he had become a murderer again. Whether it had been Robert or Mother who used it, it had been *his* body that had lurked and killed and hidden away what had been done.

And now Mother, who had been dead and buried, had returned to save him, to claim him, to take over his life once more.

I know, Norman, I know, things didn't go the way you'd hoped, but life is full of disappointments. What matters is that I protected you from that doctor. Norman felt a sigh shiver his entire body. *You got into trouble again because your mother wasn't there, didn't you? Because you believed that doctor's lies and you sent me away. Well, I'm back now. And I'm going to stay.*

All right, Mother.

All right, Norman. Now, stop moping, boy, there's work to be done! You do as I tell you, and then go back to your room like a good boy.

He could remember nearly all of it now. Mother helped him to remember, just as she told him what to do every step of the way. As Norman wrapped Dr. Reed and the knife that had killed him in the plastic sheet and put him next to the others, he thought back to each one of those times, remembering the realities that had appeared disguised in his dreams.

When he was finished with Dr. Reed, he took the flashlight from the floor and went into the passage, up the spiral staircase, through the narrow turns until he came to the entrance to his room. He pressed the plate on the wall and moved to the side as the door opened. Then he pushed aside the padding, went in, took the rolled bedding from under his blanket, and set it, along with the flashlight, on the floor of the passageway. He stepped back into his room, reached around and pressed the plate again, drew back his arm and replaced the padding as the heavy door slowly closed.

Still obeying Mother, Norman went to his sink. In the dim light coming through the open slot in the door, he looked down at his bare chest and arms. Dried blood was all over his hands, some on his arms, and a bit on his chest and belly, but fortunately none had gotten on his uniform pants. He washed all the blood away with soap and warm water, and watched as the pink liquid went down the drain. Then he examined himself again. Mother noticed that he had some blood left around his fingernails and cuticles, and he scrubbed them until they were clean enough for her.

Then he dried himself thoroughly with a hand towel too small to hang oneself with, and put on his shirt.

Now lie down and rest, Norman. You've had a very busy day.

Thank you, Mother. Thank you . . . for helping me.

That's what a mother's for.

Norman lay there in the room, his eyes open. For a long time he thought about what Dr. Reed had done to him, and he remembered one evening, just a few years ago, when he and Mother had been watching television. There was an old silent movie on— German, he thought—about a doctor who hypnotized a sleepwalker and had him kill people. In a way, that was what Dr. Reed had done with him. That wasn't right.

It certainly wasn't, Norman. I won't let anyone fool you like that ever again. And I won't let anyone take me away from you, either. We'll always be together, just the way we both want it. We just won't listen to their lies. We won't listen to a single word they say.

That's good, Mother. That's good. I think I can sleep now.

We can both use some rest. Good night, Norman.

Good night, Mother.

20

TO: *Cosmo Danvers, MPH, MD, PhD*
FROM: *Peter Harrison, MD, PhD*
REGARDING: *The Ollinger Sanitarium*

DATE: *July 7, 1918*

My dear Dr. Danvers:
Attached is the report of what was found in the final inspection of the Adolph Ollinger Sanitarium. We have already
discussed this face-to-face, so the report will serve as a formality.
The members of the state board unanimously agree that the report should not be made public in order to save the families of
patients from even more pain than they have already incurred.
There is no point in revealing the more sensationalistic aspects of
this affair. On the contrary, the board has prepared a public
statement intended to quash many of the rumors which have cir-
culated.
We intend to state that the deaths of Ollinger and his remain-

ing patients were due to the Spanish influenza, and that the pa-tients' bodies were found in their rooms, Ollinger's in his bed. The remains will be returned to the families. Ollinger, having no family of which we know, will be buried in the local cemetery.

As for the building itself, I understand that plans are to close off the cellar room in which all the bodies were found. The stench which remains makes it uninhabitable, and there is no way to air it. As for the passageways which are said to exist, we have so far found no access to them.

That the building should have a commercial use at this time seems unlikely, since it is far from any major city. The consortium which financed and still owns it is planning to put it up for sale, though there seems no immediate plan to market it aggressively. I suspect that many of these investors, who had family members as patients there, might even prefer to see it go to wrack and ruin, and be forgotten. Indicative of this is the fact that they have done nothing with the building's contents.

Considering what has occurred there, I know of few con-cerned who would not be willing to see it crumble into rubble over the years . . .

When Dick O'Brien brought Norman Bates's breakfast, he knew something was wrong. Norman was sitting on his bed, looking down at the floor, just the way he had done when he had first come to the hospital.

When Dick put the tray of food on Norman's small table, Norman didn't sit down in his chair, look up, or acknowledge Dick's presence in any way. Uh-oh, Dick thought. That was bad. He called Norman's name several times, but there was no re-sponse. Dick left the tray and exited the room, locking the door firmly behind him.

He went to Dr. Reed's office, but Reed wasn't there. His overcoat was hanging in his closet, so Dick assumed he was somewhere in the building and went to look for him.

He didn't find him. Dick checked with Dr. Steiner, but Steiner hadn't seen Reed that morning. When Dick told Steiner about Norman Bates, Steiner went immediately to Norman's room, while Dick looked in the parking lot to see if Reed's car was there. It was.

Several attendants scoured the building looking for Dr. Reed, but no one found him. By that time, Dr. Steiner had finished his visit to Norman Bates. Norman had been completely uncommunicative, and Dr. Steiner couldn't help but wonder if there was a connection between Norman's condition and Dr. Reed's disappearance. Obviously Norman had suffered some overwhelming trauma, for him to return to his previous state.

Dr. Steiner too had come to the end of his tether. He sat alone at his desk and considered how four people had disappeared from the hospital. One could have been an escape, the double disappearance an elopement, the other a fleeing war criminal. Far-fetched, but not impossible.

But now Dr. Felix Reed had disappeared. His car was there, his office untouched, no evidence of foul play found. But he was gone.

Dr. Steiner looked at the telephone for a long time before he finally picked it up and called Captain Banning, then Sheriff Jud Chambers.

When the lawmen got there, they both reacted as if this was a scene they'd already played too many times. Captain Banning started organizing troopers and attendants for another thorough search of the facility, a search that was going on when Marie Radcliffe and Ben Blake arrived for their evening shift.

Once they learned what had happened and Marie had seen what Norman Bates had once again become, she went directly to Dr. Steiner, who was still with Captain Banning and Sheriff Chambers. In front of the others, she told him about finding in Dr. Goldberg's office the petrified wood she had given Norman.

"I told Dr. Reed," she said, "but no one else, and he was going to ask Norman about it, but he didn't tell me what Norman said."

"So what are you saying?" Banning asked. "You thinking this prisoner had something to do with Goldberg's disappearance? Or Reed's?"

"I . . . don't know. Maybe."

Dr. Steiner shook his head. "Even if he could have gotten out of his locked room, the ward attendant on duty would have seen him."

But Marie pleaded until they went with her to Norman's room. While Ben took Norman into the hall, the two policemen and Dr. Steiner went through his room, looking everywhere, including behind the padding that covered the walls. "Well," Banning chuckled when they had finished their examination, "unless he went through a brick wall, there's no way he could've gotten out of here."

That the now nearly catatonic Norman Bates was cleared of having anything to do with Felix Reed's disappearance did nothing to relieve the tension in the state hospital. No one could think of any reason whatsoever for Reed to have run off in the night without coat, automobile, or anything else one might deem necessary. The entire building was searched top to bottom, as were the grounds, in the event that Reed had gone for a walk and had an attack of some sort.

Reed's office was searched, as was his apartment, but nothing was found that shed any light on his absence. The searchers, highway patrolmen more accustomed to traffic stops than detective work, overlooked the top shelf of the closet.

Inquiries were made, and people were asked if he had been seen at Delsey's, where it had been his habit to get a meal and a beer between ending his workday and going home, but he had not been in that night. Still, there was no evidence of foul play.

Dr. Felix Reed remained missing, as did Ronald Miller, Myron Gunn, Eleanor Lindstrom, and the man the hospital staff had known as Dr. Isaac Goldberg. Though a number of people, including Dr. Steiner, Marie Radcliffe, and Captain Banning, questioned Norman Bates, he gave no answers, nor did he indicate in any way that he even heard the questions.

In the weeks and months to come, Dr. Nicholas Steiner was made permanent superintendent of the state hospital, and Ray Wiseman and Nurse Wyndham, respectively, became head attendant and head nurse. Dr. Elliot Berkowitz took over as Norman Bates's therapist, but by the time his residency ended, he had been unable to bring Norman out of the amnesic fugue state to which he had returned, passive to the point of catatonia.

Marie Radcliffe and other nurses fed him every meal as they had before. He would open his mouth and eat, but he would not pick up a utensil or a cup. Marie tried to return the piece of petrified wood to him, but he seemed to have no idea what it was, or who she was. Even though she told herself that Norman must have dropped it in the hall and Dr. Goldberg had picked it up, she only believed it half the time, and, in spite of Norman's passivity, was always on the alert for any unexpected movement on his part.

The entire hospital seemed to share Marie's state of tension for a long time afterward. Only when two more psychiatrists came on staff, and several months went by with no further incidents, did relative calm return to the facility. It was reinforced by Dr. Steiner's disapproval of any cruel or sadistic behavior on the part of the staff, and his reluctance to use shock therapies on any but the most otherwise hopeless cases, one of whom eventually proved to be Norman Bates.

Norman underwent two treatments, neither of which had any positive effect, and Dr. Steiner ordered that the therapy be abandoned in Norman's case.

Several months after Dr. Felix Reed's disappearance, two custodians cleaned out his office in preparation for the psychiatrist who was to replace him. The police had already searched the office, and Dr. Steiner had removed the patient case files and any other pertinent hospital business from Reed's papers. What was left was a small box of personal effects that was mailed to Reed's father, a widower in Topeka, who had declined the offer of his son's books.

The custodians were told to take them to the staff library, where they would be sorted and either retained or discarded. If the books were in poor condition, the custodians were to take them directly to the incinerator.

The two men took them by the armful off Reed's shelves and loaded them onto a cart. Most of the books seemed to be in good condition, and they threw only a few, beat-up paperbacks, or hardcovers whose bindings were detached, into the wheeled barrel they had brought for the junk.

There were some old newspapers and magazines on the shelf in the closet, and it was while they were removing them that one man noticed the upper shelf. He reached up and felt around with his fingers, made a sound of disgust, and looked at his hand.

What appeared to be a dark brown mold clung to his finger-tips. He wiped it on his uniform pants, then got a chair to more easily reach the top shelf. What he had first touched was Adolph Ollinger's deteriorating leather-bound journal, tucked inside of which were the old floor plans and the personal notes that Felix Reed had written about the case of Norman Bates.

"These must've been up here forever. The leather's rotting away, don't get it on ya," the custodian said as he gingerly handed a pile of books down to his colleague. "They're in lousy shape, and the old magazines too—just throw 'em in the barrel."

A half hour later, the contents of the barrel were dumped into the incinerator. Several minutes after that, they were nothing but ash.

EPILOGUE

While Norman Bates lay on his bed late one Friday night, locked in his room and in himself, a twelve-year-old boy named Adam was sitting on the davenport in his living room, watching a silent movie on *Horror Theater.* It was the first time he'd been allowed to stay up late alone, and he was huddled against the arm of the davenport, a knitted wool afghan tucked up around his shoulders. He was wearing both pajamas and a bathrobe, but the afghan made him feel safer, knowing that he could pull it up over his face if he had to. So far, he hadn't. Having his dad's reading lamp on helped too.

The movie was called *The Cabinet of Dr. Caligari,* and was about this doctor who was using a *somnambulist* (the word was new to Adam, but he figured it meant a sleepwalker) to murder people for him. When Cesare the Somnambulist opened his eyes for the first time, Adam thought he was going to have to go to the bathroom, but he didn't. That was the worst part. From then on he wasn't really scared, not even when Cesare grabbed the girl from her bed and looked like he was going to kill her before he just ran away with her.

The ending was kind of confusing, but the doctor at the asylum wasn't really the bad guy after all, and the guy who'd been telling the story was a patient himself, and he'd made it all up, and just *thought* the doctor was this evil Caligari.

When it was over, Adam turned off the TV and sat there thinking about the movie. It was amazing, he thought, that this crazy guy could have made up this whole story in his head and believed it. It was the first time in Adam's life that he fully realized that people could be sick in their minds as well as their bodies, and the idea kindled something inside him. In the days and months ahead, he would begin to consider becoming a doctor who studied and cured the illnesses of the mind.

But Norman Bates, free only in his dreams, would have to wait in darkness for another twenty years until Adam Claiborne grew up, became a psychiatrist, came to the State Hospital for the Criminally Insane, sat across from Norman, and helped to release him into the light once more.

ACKNOWLEDGMENTS

Thanks to Brendan Deneen, my editor, for so ably guiding this journey.

Thanks to Sally A. Francy, and Richard Henshaw for entrusting me with a fictional character that has grown beyond iconic.

Thanks to Nicole Sohl, and Bruce Kilstein for all their help.

Thanks to my wife, Laurie, and son, Colin, for their constant love and support.

Thanks to Mom and Dad, who, in 1960, let a little kid buy a very special paperback with a screaming woman and a rocking chair on the cover.

And thanks, most of all, to the author of that novel, the *primum mobile* himself, Robert Bloch, for creating not only Norman Bates, but an entire new genre of fiction as well.